# of Home

Karen Biery

Library of Congress Control Number: 2016953690

Hardcover ISBN: 978-1-943267-17-0

Tradepaperback ISBN: 978-1-943267-18-7

Cover: Karen Biery

Printed in the United States.

River Road Press

For those
without a voice....
past and present

Foreword

When I first heard about a fiction book being written about the Fairmount Children's Home, I thought, "How can that be? Fairmount was not a fictitious place, but actual buildings filled with thousands of real boys and girls that spanned nearly a century."

After reading Karen Biery's novel, I understand how fiction — derived from former resident's stories, elaborated, and changed — is created. I only ask the readers remember that this is a fictional tale about a non-fiction place.

Biery did a great job. Her novel will certainly make you think.

Enjoy.

Carolyn Becker Caskey

Author of *History of the Fairmount Children's Home*, published 2016

Author of *A History of Freeburg, Ohio*, 1842-1992

Preface

The idea to anchor this book to my second novel, pieces, came as an enticing thought and grew into a brainchild that will develop into an adventure series. Although each story will stand alone, a deeper insight into one of the main characters (Collin Sims) can be found by returning to my novel *pieces*. Look for many others in the future, with conceptual titles such as — *of bones, of others* — all of which are complete with its predecessor (pieces) as pieces *of Home*, pieces *of bones*, pieces *of others* continue to carry the reader through Collin's future adventures. Who knows, maybe Belle will join him on occasion.

For my readers who have traveled this literary journey with me through all five novels, you understand well how I love history and even more how I love to blend history with fiction to teach and enlighten many around us who close their eyes to the beauty of what once was. One reader said, "Biery gives us a history lesson without the realization that we are being taught." That comment made me smile.

I recall driving past Fairmount Children's Home after moving to Ohio. A nursery in the foreground covered much of the main house from the street's view. I turned to ask my husband a question when the sight of the Home became unobstructed.

"What is that?" I gasped.

"Fairmount Children's Home," he answered. It closed in the 70's."

Fairmount opened its doors to the disadvantaged children of Columbiana and Stark counties on October 20, 1876. The winning construction bid was $30,295.00. The 153-acre parcel sold for $90 per acre bringing the grand total to $44,065.00. Once the structures were complete, Fairmount Children's Home held an insurance value of $75,000.

Although I have not been able to find the exact number of children who lived in the Home, estimates claim over 5000 children called this group of buildings "Home." On July 1, 1976, four months shy of Fairmount's 100th birthday, the Home closed its doors.

Outside of my normal research, I conducted many interviews of people who lived, worked, or volunteered there — some by letter, in person, email and social media, and many via the telephone. A few families revealed their personal memoirs, and I am eternally grateful for their generosity in sharing this information with me.

In my general opinion, most viewed the Home as necessary. Many lived there due to deaths of one or both parents, others shared the lack of proper funding, housing, food, or general health as a reason they were brought to the home, while a few had no idea why their parents left them at Fairmount. Those children broke my heart.

I heard a multitude of funny, triumphant, sad, and unmentionable stories many of which you will find strung throughout the following pages. I have been given poetic license to bend the rules and stretch the imagination; after all, as a friend pointed out, it is fiction.

On December 8, 2002, The Fairmount Children's Home erupted into flames. Over 100 firefighters and 2.5 million gallons of water could not save the Home. It stood in a skeleton-state until it was pushed into a pile of rubble. Arson charges were never filed. No one accepted responsibility. After nearly 100 years of existence, only spirits and memories remained.

Today, the property is private and when I say private, I mean PRIVATE. The owners do not tolerate trespassers, although not much remains to view. My hope is to erect a historic marker on the site. I feel it will give much closure to those residents still with us and to those who have passed.

My hope, as always, is to open a window for the reader to see what life may have been like for the residents of Fairmount. Although the views of the children varied greatly depending on personal attitudes, time, and house rules, my intention is to entertain and pass on the belief that no matter what life throws at any individual, it is possible to rise above and move beyond.

Acknowledgments

My list of those to thank grows longer with each novel, but if I listed every name of those who aided in the assimilation process, it would cover several pages, so instead I will simply say...Thank you genuinely to all of you who helped in this process.

First and foremost, my sincere gratitude goes to the residents, visitors, employees, and family members of Fairmount for your comments, concerns, stories, open honesty, tears, laughter, memoirs, letters, emails, photographs, interviews, telephone calls...etc. I pray 'I did you proud' and you find enjoyment within the following pages.

To my parents, in-laws, step-children, sisters, aunts, family, and friends who supported, read, encouraged, suggested, criticized (lovingly), and helped me through this process, thank you...I love you. To my focus group readers/editors — Jeff, Evelyn, Laura, Anne, Jill, Carol, Sue, Sandy, Carolyn, Joyce, Pat, and Dwight — I could not have done it without you. To Sarah, who reminded me of this amazing story, thank you. To Carolyn Becker Caskey, thank you for your willingness to allow history to morph into fiction while building a valued friendship in the process. For David Shivers, president of the Salem Historical society, your thoughtfulness and help is always welcome. Finally, to my husband, Jeff, for his support, love, and encouragement, I cannot thank you enough. I love you dearly.

Time

for those who called Fairmount
"Home"

Brick by brick many men built
A safe place for children
To learn and to grow
And become better versions of people they know.

Year by year they came to this place
Awe-struck by size
Yet joy-filled for rest,
Clean clothing and food that helped them forget.

Thought by thought the walls became Home
Familiar, yet tough
And dependent on those
Whose fists fell like iron on many unknown.

Walk by walk their daily life moved
From childhood to commencement
Young to old
With or without cherishes to hold.

Off to start life as the best they knew how
By marriage, the service,
Or hunt for old homes,
Leaving many to live and die all alone.

Times were tough, not what we believed
From television shows,
Books, or family stories
But real struggles bent from misery.

Season after season the funding grew weak
Leaving a skeleton staff
With limits to spend
Crusting their attitudes like week-old bread.

But money would come and relief could be seen
Flowing from tables,
Through schools, and through rules
Loosening its grip, inviting their smiles to play fool.

The ebb and flow of all one once saw
Came only through gifts,
Man's money and heart
To aid the children with a push and a start.

The choices weren't theirs to come to the Home
Poor health, death, or drink,
Could perhaps be immune
But unloved, or unwanted was never excused.

So they came together with reasons untold
To create a bond
A family to hold
To help and encourage their lives to unfold.

But time permits elements to come and to stay
And break down the mortar,
Change the wood to decay,
And leave dreams piled in ruins at the end of the day.

For time can steal all that we hold dear,
Our health, beauty, and wealth
Our triumphs, our fears
Until we surrender to that we cannot change
For time is a thief that we wither away.

List of Characters

In order of appearance, not importance:
Belle Gates, sister of Henry and baby Willy
Henry Gates, Belle's oldest brother
Baby Willy, infant Gates boy
Daddy Gates
Miss Betsy, Belle's Matron
Craig, little boy in a coma
Louise and Silvia, two of many Matrons
Peter, James and John, Henry's roommates
Enoch Rumsted, the Headmaster
Sophie, Belle's friend
Janet Twill, the Headmaster's secretary
Jack, Henry's bedmate
Joey, Henry's friend and bedmate
Davis, band director and former inmate
Miss Adelade, the Home's schoolteacher
Madeline, Belle's bedmate
Gayle, the soap girl
Ben, Ray, Billy, Sam, Curt, Jane, Lucas, Tom,
Clarence — the Freshmen, & 4 unnamed.
Mr. Carl, Miss Adelade's replacement
Dorothy, Belle's friend
Amy, Anna, siblings on Easter
Charles, Director of the Board
Mae, Bucker chaperon
Abe, Jim, and one other, Bucker miners
Collin Sims, Treasure finder
Sharon Sims, Collin's mother
Bill Williams, Sharon's companion
Angie Wadeford, Daily View reporter
Tim Lorie, New York reporter
Jesse, Bill's deceased son
Helen, inmate sent to the nunnery

1

Belle watched a dragonfly cling to the exposed string of a window weight. He came to visit her often from the wetlands and begged her to follow him to a world beyond the distant tree row. The wind tossed his transparent wings daring him to let go and submit to their predetermined destination. Just as she began to whisper promises of safety, he lost his grip and disappeared from view.

"I'll see you again, my friend," Belle offered to the blank sky. "Until we meet again."

The latter phrase stuck in her throat. It was her mother's promise. One Belle clung to in vain.

She shook the thought from her head and crept toward the door. Placing her ear against it, she held her breath, and listened. The empty hall was silent. She turned the glass doorknob and jerked the thick walnut door toward her, knowing without the sudden motion the door would produce a loud clatter that would wake the household. Her experience seasoned her movements.

She counted the six doors to her left and five to her right as she stumbled over the crumpled hallway runner. When her bare toes touched the top stair tread, she lifted the hem of her faded cotton dress and ran as fast as her legs would allow. Without hesitation, she jumped from the bottom step, rounded the corner, and ran toward the door at the end of the hall.

With each silent stride, she moved closer to the white painted door. Apprehension grew until it became difficult to pull in air. Belle trembled as she reached toward the brass handle. Grimy from overuse, she withdrew her hand repeatedly while muttering reassurances aloud.

"You can do this. No one can hurt you. He's gone. He's..." A distant shriek silenced her thought. She grabbed the handle, opened the door, and slipped into the darkness.

Her heart thumped in her throat as she felt her way down the basement staircase. She bypassed the dangling string at the bottom. She wanted no light. She didn't want to see. She didn't want to remember.

Belle knew this path well. She walked ten steps and made a hard right. Her bare feet felt the transition between the hand-trowled cement floors and the cool well-laid brick. Even in total darkness, she sensed the narrowing of the walls. She sighed, not in disgust, anger or irritation, but in relief — to rush through her fears unnoticed, undetected and alone. She slowed her progress to a stroll.

The underground tunnel system of the Fairmount Children's Home connected all the buildings — five cottages, the main house, hospital, school, maintenance buildings and the gymnasium. Used mostly as a way to supply heat from the boiler room to the individual buildings, it also offered a way for some of the children to move about unseen by the staff, and mostly the Headmaster.

2

Belle stumbled upon the tunnel system one evening when she ducked into the opened door in the main house. One of the maintenance staff carelessly left the basement door unguarded and ajar. Being of curious nature, she took the opening as an invitation to explore. What she discovered amazed her.

A narrow tunnel led in a straight path to the boiler room located near the gymnasium. She noticed six separate channels each fitted with a large pipe suspended from the ceiling. The passageways of varied sizes led to each building and were over six feet in height allowing ample room for the maintenance man to stand erect to mend the heating system.

Over the next several months, the opportunity to explore the tunnels became an exciting pastime for Belle. Often, the entrance to the basement in the main house remained locked, so Belle simply walked outside and into each building until she found an unlocked entrance.

It was simple to identify the doors that led to the basement. Due to frequent use, the doors suffered much abuse. Dirt and grime covered the handles with remnants of black hand prints smeared across the jamb. Because of the constant dirt and grime build up, the children were required to scrub and paint the doors twice a year.

Belle painted the door in the center hall of the main building. Her steady hand and a job well done stood out among all others. The Headmaster took great pride in the appearance of the buildings and praised Belle highly for her attention to detail. Belle forced a smile with every compliment. Her talents behind the paintbrush became the main reason

Belle's responsibilities changed from the girls' cottage #5 to the main house. When Belle began to work in the large building, her life changed.

Children came to the Home from all over Columbiana and Stark counties usually accompanied by a disparaging parent. Whether the child's temporary stay lasted a few months or became permanent did not matter to the staff at Fairmount. The Home, built with pure intentions, aided families that could no longer care for their children financially, mentally or physically. The reputation ebbed and flowed as a direct reflection of the Headmaster, and the children prospered or suffered under his reigning rule.

For outside people visiting the Home, the main house served as the reception area. A new tenant entered the Home through the front foyer and was escorted into the parlor, sometimes referred to as the receiving room. Its ten-foot walls, covered in busy floral wallpaper, evoked a day spent in a lush summer garden meant to calm the waiting, yet the opposite occurred. By the time the Headmaster arrived to greet the guests, many had slipped away while others shook in fear of the days ahead.

Enoch Rumsted was the Headmaster when Belle arrived. He towered six-foot-four and intimidated the guests when he exaggerated his stoop through the six-foot double glass door frame. His plastic smile covered his gaunt face, cleanly-shaved and speckled with evidence of a poorly sharpened razor. His teeth, crooked and grossly discolored, drew attention to his large middle gap. It affected his speech slightly, although no one dared mention it, at least to his face. His long arms hung nearly to his knees and proved valuable when lunging to apprehend a child. Despite all his contemptuous features, he walked erect, proud of his assumed venerable position and reputation. His staff avoided him. The children hated him.

Belle quickly became the Home's greeter. She met the inmates, a common term used to describe the children that lived in orphanages, and settled them into the parlor. After cookies, milk, and the introduction to the Headmaster, she escorted the child to the infirmary for inspection and/or general hygiene if necessary. She hurried back to the main house to assume her welcoming position.

She wasted little time elsewhere unless the day seemed best frittered away by daydreaming. She spent the majority of her free time in the center hall running up and down the 125 steps of the circular staircase. Her long, thin fingers served as a polishing cloth for its railing. She dusted the spindles and kept the stair tread corners free of dust and crumbs. Occasionally, she slid down the banister, but only when alone for if caught, her punishment was certain.

The day Mr. Gates came to the Home he brought his three children — Henry, Belle, and baby Willy. The birth of Willy took the life of their mother and within three months of her death, their daddy brought them to live at the Home.

Belle recalled her daddy kneeling before her on the floor with tears streaming down his face. "I'll be back. I promise." He caressed her little hand.

Henry stood cross-armed with his back to his father. The calloused scowl on his ten-year-old face never left.

"I have to find some work, Belle. Steady work; the kind that will support our family."

Belle touched his unkempt face. "It's okay, Daddy. We will wait for you."

A white uniformed Matron took Belle's hand and pulled her from him. With the mention of freshly baked cookies, Belle happily followed. She tossed her final words to her father, "Until we meet again." The worn man stumbled out of the door without another word.

Baby Willy lay in a ragged blanket at Henry's feet. Henry knelt and gently picked up his pallid brother. He followed Belle and the woman into the kitchen.

Belle recalled passing that white painted door the day they arrived. A cold chill ran through her young body as she noticed the smudged message. The dark words — Help me — appeared clear from a distance yet with each step closer, the letters became fuzzy and smeared until she examined it up close. What appeared to be a cry for help from a distance was actually a cluster of grimy hand prints.

Henry grabbed her arm and stared at her with saucer eyes. "Did you see that?"

"See what?" She responded automatically.

"The door?"

The Matron's monotone answer hushed any thought of continued conversation. "Just the grubby hand prints from the maintenance man. He always leaves a mess." Without pause, she began to recite each house rule while Henry and Belle engulfed a multitude of sugar cookies.

Twice, Henry interrupted her presentation to ask for more information about the door. He wanted to know who wrote the words and why she pretended not to see them. She answered him by continuing to tick off the list of house rules. Interrupted by a sudden raspy cough followed by a loud scream, she knelt to pick up baby Willy. After inspecting his color, she quickly excused herself.

"This baby needs a doctor. Have another cookie or two. I'll only be a minute."

They followed her into the hall, each with a handful of cookies, and watched her disappear around the corner. They heard the opening and slamming shut of an unseen door. Immediately, Willy's voice fell silent.

Belle stood in disbelief of their whereabouts. Her empty eyes wide with fear begged the woman to return, while Henry inspected the hand prints masking the forbidden cry for help.

"Belle." He sounded desperate. "We can't stay here."

Spinning to face her whispering brother, she crinkled her nose and asked, "Why?" She looked down at the cookies in her hands and smiled. She could not remember the last time she ate one. "Henry, we have cookies."

Henry grabbed her arm and pulled her down the hall. His stride gained speed and Belle stumbled to keep up. He nervously repeated his command, "I'm tellin' you, we can't stay here."

As they neared the front foyer, Henry set his sights on the front door. The cookies he clenched in his fists disintegrated. Just a few more steps and they would be through the front door and running for their lives. He dared to take one last breath of the

Home's air and ran straight into an opened door with a thud.

The Matron gasped at their presence in the foyer. Her hands settled on Henry's shaking shoulders and turned him to face her.

"Good heaven's child. Now, you have a nice goose egg on your head." She shook a telling finger in the air, "I thought I told both of you to stay put. I needed to take your brother to the nursery. He has quite a fever." She put her arms around the two of them and ushered them toward the front door. "Now come along. Let's get you two checked by the doctor while I finish reciting the House Rules."

Henry hung his head in defeat and shuffled his feet, reluctant to advance. Belle, happy to gorge another cookie, followed the woman toward the hospital without resistance.

A large lump formed in Henry's throat as he stared back at the door. The letters appeared clearer, more desperate, at his distant glance. His sister bounced beside him oblivious to the warning, as the Matron led them out the door. Her continuous chatter bounced off Henry's ears. Only the words "Help me" held his attention.

2

The assault of ether inside the hospital gave Henry an instant headache. Heavy grey curtains separated each examination room. In the center, stood a single bed sheeted in white. On the back wall hung a lone shelf stacked with several open boxes. Its placement was far above the reach of a child.

Henry stumbled into the first room available. He thought his head would explode. The Matron told him to sit and wait for the doctor while she helped Belle settle in the examination room beside him.

The children listened to the click from an exposed nail on the heel of Matron's shoe as she walked through the curtained corridor. A faint moan came from the distance.

They could hear her mumbling, but were unable to discern her words. Within a few minutes, she reappeared with two paper gowns, first giving one to

Belle, and pulling the adjoining curtain open wide enough to pass through, she placed the second one on Henry's lap.

"Remove all of your clothes, including your underwear." She opened Henry's gown, and placed her head through the round opening at the top. She looked at Henry and then at Belle to be sure the little girl could see her around the partially drawn curtain and that both understood the command. Blank, wide eyes greeted her.

"Do you understand? I said take off your clothes and put this over your head." She repeated her display. The children's faces remained fixed, eyes wide and mouths agape. The Matron's attitude softened a bit. "The doctor needs to complete an examination. We need to be certain of your state of health." She placed her hand on Henry's shoulder. "If the doctor finds anything undesirable, you may stay here for quite a spell." She walked toward the opened curtain and smiled at Belle, while placing her hand on the curtain's edge. "Regardless, you will stay here for at least two days," she offered another thin smile, "Until you are given a clean bill of health." She yanked the curtain closed.

Belle watched the curtain move violently until each wave finally settled into the softness of their natural folds. Her jaw began to quiver.

"Henry?"

Fighting his own emotions, Henry hesitated before answering. "It will be okay, Belle. Just do as she says."

"But I'm not sick."

"Neither am I, but they have to check us out." He muttered and then added in a whisper, "Whatever that means."

Henry slipped off his shoes, pulled his t-shirt over his head, and shimmied out of his jeans. He stood in only his underwear with his head drooping and stared at his big toe peeking out of his over-worn socks. He walked over to the curtain divider and checked on his sister.

Belle sat on the edge of the bed, clothed in her bright yellow Easter dress. The only piece of clothing she had removed was her hair bow. She held it in her hands. Her unruly, curly hair hung in rings of banana curls covering her face. Her body trembled.

Henry whispered, "Belle, it will be okay. I promise. I will be right here beside you."

"I wanna go home."

Henry swallowed the immediate lump and wondered how they could ever get through this horrid experience. He choked on his lie. "There's nothing for us there, Belle. This is home now."

Belle's head snapped at her brother's words. Her flushed face and watery eyes glared at him. "Daddy is there."

Henry's head screamed his reply, although the words never formed. "Daddy left us here. Daddy didn't want us. Daddy is worthless. Daddy's never coming back. I don't care what he said; he's never coming to get us."

He hung his head and shuffled back to his bed. He pulled his socks from his feet by placing his heel on the opposite toe yanking his foot out of the fabric. He slid his underwear to his knees and kicked them across the room. He jumped on the edge of the bed fully naked and hung his head. He listened for any movement from his sister and heard none.

It seemed hours before they heard a door slam. Quickened steps, muffled at first became clearer and closer until finally stopping at Belle's curtain. The aged doctor dressed in a long white lab coat, echoing his hair color, opened Belle's curtain.

He sighed, "I see you are not quite ready for your exam." He waited for a reply. The little girl never moved. "The longer you sit there, the longer this will take. Remove your clothes and replace them with the gown." His words were automatic, void of emotion.

Belle used the back of her hand to wipe her nose and eyes and then pushed the curls from her face. She slid from the edge of the bed and began to undress.

The doctor opened Henry's curtain expecting to see the same. Surprised to find him fully naked, with his clothes thrown about the room, he grinned at the display of anger and confidence.

"I see you had a bit of fun with your clothing." His eyes moved to the resting place of each garment encouraging Henry's eyes to follow. They did not. The boy sat still, glaring at the doctor.

"No need to wear your gown?"

"Nope."

"Shall we get started then?"

Henry shrugged his shoulders.

The doctor and Henry became very well acquainted over the next few minutes. First, he checked Henry's hair for lice, his body for bed bug bites, and teeth for decay. Finding none the doctor moved through the balance of his checklist, finishing with a rectal exam. It was the longest twenty minutes of Henry's young life.

Belle watched wide-eyed from the crack in the curtain. Her paper robe flapped open as she jumped back on her bed. Her curls still swayed when the doctor entered her room. Being much younger and sheltered than Henry, she began to tear.

"There, there," the doctor patted her knee. "This will be over soon, especially if you are as healthy as your brother." He forced a caring smile.

Belle's exam lasted a few minutes longer than Henry's. Not because of any findings, but due to the fact he had to leave to find a nurse before he began her internal exam.

Belle whimpered. "Henry?"

"It's almost over."

"But..." Belle began to cry.

"You'll be okay. He won't hurt you. I'm right here, Belle."

She heard his words, but they gave no comfort. She did not understand why he went to get the nurse. That differed from her brother. She began to tremble.

Soon the soft patter of footfalls grew closer. The curtain opened. A tall, thin woman with tightly drawn brown hair twisted into a bun walked to Belle's bed.

"Put your head here," she patted the top of the bed, "and bend your knees. Put your feet on the bed."

Belle did as directed. The internal probing hurt. She whimpered once and immediately received a scolding. She lay with her head turned from the doctor and nurse and concentrated on the wetness of her tears as they slid off her face. It seemed an eternity until the nurse told Belle to turn over. The second exam seemed worse than the first. Belle yelped and whimpered until they were finished.

The doctor turned to the nurse. "Clean her up. Everything is fine."

Belle dared to open her eyes. The nurse wiped her with a few damp towels. Belle held her breath at the sight of a few blood smears.

The nurse noticed Belle's uneasiness. She patted her ankles. "It's perfectly normal to see a bit of blood during your first internal exam. Everything looks good. You shouldn't have to go through that again." She watched Belle's relief manifest into a flood of tears. "I just need to do one more thing, and then you can re-dress."

The nurse held up a pair of scissors and a brown cotton dress piped in white ribbon. The exaggerated sailor collar, crudely sewn, covered the top to nearly the waist. The panties were dingy white and air-dried stiff. She received one pair of socks but no shoes. Both Henry and Belle's original clothes were gathered and taken from the room. Belle crumpled her hair bow into a wad.

When the nurse left, Belle rushed into her brother's arms. He held her until her sobs subsided. Her long hair, newly trimmed to her jaw line, made her appear older. Henry sighed at the innocence lost.

Henry began to fidget. His stiff underwear made his privates itch, and it became difficult not to constantly scratch. Finally, Belle released her grip.

"What's wrong?"

Henry grabbed at his zipper and pulled the fabric away from his skin. He danced around the room,

14

grabbing, pulling, and itching. He pulled his pants off and yanked off his underwear. Belle giggled at her brother's antics until a large black carpenter ant crawled out of the fabric onto the floor. Both gasped and then burst into laughter. Immediately, Belle felt her tension release, although she was too young to understand the impact.

As the doctor explained, the pair should plan on a minimum two-day stay before they could go to their respective cottages. The medical staff sequestered all new children until they proved to be clean of any communicable disease. After reasonable time of supervised care, their age-appropriate cottages separated them.

Henry and Belle whispered to each other from their beds alienated by the heavy curtain. Henry fell asleep twice as Belle continued to chatter. He woke up to the calling of his name.

"Henry? Are you sleeping?"

"Huh?" He hesitated, "Nope,"

"Okay. Well, then, what do you think?"

Having no idea of her question, he shrugged his shoulders. "I dunno."

Knowing his sister well, he added, "What do you think?"

"I think he will."

"Really? Why?"

"Because I just do."

"Why?"

"Don't you?"

"I dunno."

"Henry!" she scolded. "He's our father. Of course he will come back."

Henry shook his head. He doubted they would ever see their father again. He wondered what kind of person dumps three children off in a strange place and expected strangers to take care of them? No, he knew they saw the last of their father, but he dared not say that to his baby sister.

He sighed and simply offered, "I hope you're right."

He heard no response. Belle had fallen asleep.

Henry listened to the sound of faint moans deep into the night. After a few hours of sleeplessness, he threw the sheet from his body and tiptoed toward the sound.

Settled in the far corner, behind a double curtain, a young boy lay on a hospital bed. Henry guessed the boy to be four or five years old. He lay on his side, his head bandaged on a blood-soaked pillow. His eyes were slightly open as was his mouth. His soft moans, nearly in consistent rhythm, came amid his deep sleep.

Henry watched with great interest. He wondered what ailed the boy. He noticed a single chair pulled close to the boy's bed. Although the chair sat empty, it appeared well used.

He crept back toward his bed. After one last check on his sister, he crawled into his own bed. He hated to admit it, but the bed was clean, soft and comfortable. Tonight he had no demands, no worries, no father, mother, or siblings. He was alone in a strange place, with strange people, with only his thoughts, without the need to be brave. He covered his face with his pillow and sobbed.

"Henry? Are you sleeping?"

Belle's face appeared less than an inch from his. "Not now," he yawned. Judging from the rancid taste in his mouth, he had slept for several hours.

"I can't sleep."

He slid over to the far edge of the narrow bed and lifted the top sheet. "Come here. Sleep with me."

Belle slipped into Henry's warm bed. It seemed more comfortable, warmer, and certainly safer. Within minutes, she drifted to sleep.

When they woke in the morning their covers lay on the floor, and Belle had the entire pillow. Henry's arm pulsated and tingled from lying on it. Belle woke in her normal sweet mood. Henry felt agitated, stiff and tired. Together they crawled out of Henry's bed.

"I wonder what time it is." Henry asked more as an outspoken thought than a question.

Belle answered with the innocence of a five-year-old, "How would we know?"

Henry looked around for a window, walked into Belle's curtain area and looked again, but found none. "We need to find a window."

They peered out the curtain. Hand in hand, they pattered down the corridor to the far end, near the only other patient. The door was locked.

Henry listened to the shallow, yet steady breaths of the little boy and prayed that Belle would not notice. That sight would be the last thing he wanted his sister to see.

"Come on." He tugged on her hand. "Let's go that way." He pointed to the room's opposing side.

Henry tried to recall the location of the entrance door. He became frustrated with himself because normally his sense of direction would carry him through, but much of yesterday's arrival remained a blank. After ten minutes of aimlessly wandering, as well as opening each curtained room looking for a window, he remembered the door's location. He pulled Belle to the first exam room and opened the left curtain. They walked down a narrow walkway toward the light from a window. It also was locked.

Unable to go outside, they peered up toward the window and watched the clouds roll by. They were dark, low, and ready to burst. A distant roll of thunder made Belle feel chilled.

"It's early," Henry whispered.

"Then, let's go back to bed." Belle yawned.

"Oh. I have a better idea," sarcasm laced his voice. "Let's go back to our own beds." He pretended to shove his little sister. "You're a bed hog. I almost fell out twice."

They both giggled as they tiptoed back, each to their own bed. Henry fell asleep immediately. Belle lay on her back and listened to the rain.

They spent most of that day in and out of bed, mostly due to boredom. The nurse came to check on them twice. Henry watched her walk past the little boy's exam room both times without stopping. He fell asleep wondering.

3

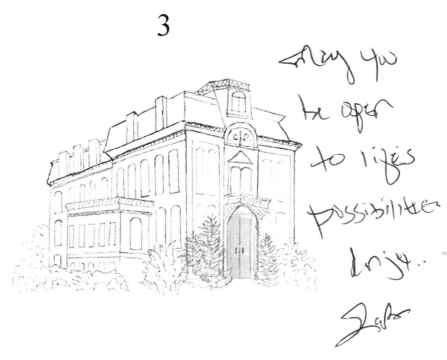

May you be open to life's possibilities.

Enjoy.

[signature]

The next morning, Henry woke before dawn. His body ached, despite the benefit of solitude throughout the night. He slid from his bed and opened Belle's curtain. Her bed was empty. Instinctively, he knew where she would be — in the only curtained area they had not explored. He ran toward the young boy's exam room.

Belle stood frozen just inside the curtain. The shadowed room seemed to warn of any noise; even the boy's shallow breaths seemed distant. A lone chair sat at the foot of the bed draped with a forgotten beige wrap.

"Belle!" Henry scolded.

Her head spun toward her brother. "You told me this was storage."

"I did?" He shrugged.

She turned and spoke in a normal volume. "You know you did. Why?"

The little boy stirred at her voice. Soft moans curled from his drawn mouth. His bloody pillow lay on the floor.

Henry looked back at his wide-eyed sister. "Let's get out of here."

They ran down the hall barely settling into their beds when they heard the loud opening snap of the door's lock. Soon the air drummed with the sound of many voices each struggling to speak over the next. The volume seemed deafening to both Henry and Belle after two days of near silence.

The nurse pulled open Belle's curtain first. Henry's came next. "Out you two go. We need every one of these beds."

The prospect of leaving the hospital was promising, yet terrifying. He sat in his bed unmoved.

The nurse motioned for him to come. Belle stood by her side. "Come now, Henry. I haven't all day." The trio walked out the front door.

"Who are all those people?" Belle asked looking over her shoulder.

"A large family just arrived."

"How many are there?" Henry pressed for an answer.

"Eleven." The nurse's tone was automatic.

"Eleven?" The children echoed with disbelief.

"I don't think I even know eleven people." Henry mused. "That's a huge family."

"There are three more."

"What?" Henry shouted immediately aware of his volume. Lowering his voice, he added. "Why aren't they here?"

"Too young," was all she offered.

They walked in silence from the hospital, past the school and into a large open gravel area, referred to as the 'Play Area'. Several children chased one another in circles while others gathered in groups. A few children remained isolated and stood along the edge of the grass, watching the others. Two stood off to one side with sheets draped over their heads.

One particular pair of girls caught Belle's eye. They each held a stick with a flat ring on the end. The ring had string woven throughout and they hit an object back and forth. The target, shaped in a narrow V, appeared to have a rounded nose and feathers attached to it somehow. She overheard one of the girls accuse the other of purposely missing the "birdie." She became so engrossed that when a Matron took over nurse's tour the switch went unnoticed until the new woman's voice startled her.

"It's called Badminton," the Matron said, rather cold and unattached.

Her white uniform was clean and neatly pressed. Her hair, drawn into a bun on the back of her head, appeared so tightly drawn that it smoothed the wrinkles from her face. Even her eyes seemed pulled toward the knot.

"Huh?" Belle was equally confused by the word and the woman.

"The game." She pointed to the pair of young girls. "They are playing Badminton with rackets and a shuttlecock, sometimes called a birdie."

21

"Doesn't look like a bird to me." Belle wrinkled her nose.

The young woman did not respond. Her goal, to give the Gates' children a guided tour, became clearer with every step.

"These are the cottages, where you will be staying. This one is cottage #4 and #5, together as a duplex. Number 4 is the young boy's cottage; #5 is the young girl's cottage." She touched Belle on the shoulder and pointed to cottage #5. "This is where you will be, Belle."

Belle stared at the large red brick building. It appeared in decent shape. Sporadic peeling paint made the trim appear dark and damp. Judging from the amount of white paint chips that littered the immediate ground it seemed as if the paint preparation had begun.

"Since we have an abundance of boys at this time, these three cottages are theirs. Number 1 is for the oldest boys — high school age. Many have just graduated and are preparing to join the service. For whatever reason," she shrugged, "most are joining the Navy." Her thoughts trailed off and then quickly returned. "I suppose it's because Ohio lacks an ocean." She chuckled at her own joke.

The children listened without comment. Both were awe-struck at the size of the 'Home.'

"Cottage #2 is where you will be, Henry. Cottage #3 is for the boys a few years younger." She pointed to the top floor of the main house. "On the third floor of the main house is cottage #7. That is for the high school girls. All think it is best to have the high school boys and girls separated," she winked, "for obvious reasons."

The children's gaze remained blank.

By the time she finished speaking, they had walked past cottages #4, 5, 3, and 2. They stood in front of cottage #1. She pointed to the right, "That little building is where they keep the band instruments." Henry opened his mouth to speak, but the Matron cut him off.

"All of the children are encouraged to explore their talents. The band is simply one avenue. If that is not your interest, I'm certain you will find another that suits you."

They continued past the front edge of cottage #1 and she pointed to a plot of soft dirt in the distance. "That is the ball field. It is also used for band practice and other activities on occasion."

Henry smiled at the idea of playing ball. He had quite a talent with the baseball bat. His mind wondered to his last home run.

It was at the opposing team's church field. It was the top of the fourth and Henry's team trailed by two runs. His teammates were on first and third. Henry swung at the first pitch. The bat's loud crack startled the crowd, but Henry knew from the resonating vibration that he connected perfectly with the ball. It sailed high over the pitcher's head. He made a futile attempt to glove the projectile, but the ball streamed ten feet out of his reach.

Henry rounded first base in what seemed to be five strides. His feet scuffed the bag at second, just in time to hear the rustle of the tree limbs as the ball continued through its branches. He floated past third and greeted the entire team jumping and slapping his back at home plate. He never cared that his team lost that game by one run. The sound of the bat and fluidity of his swing, coupled with the disgruntled opponent's faces, made his season. Each time Henry gripped the handle of a hickory bat that memory rushed over him like a warm shower.

The Matron and Belle called to him from a distance. The sound of their voices, united with their hand gestures, snapped Henry back to reality. He ran to meet them.

They rounded cottage #1 to the far edge of the gravel play area. Another large building stood before them — the gymnasium. The building was too small and the ceiling too low to play regulation basketball games, so only practice occurred within. The garage for the staff's vehicles sat next to the gym, and finally to the far left was the boiler and maintenance room — the birthplace of the tunnel heating system.

Behind that building, the main barn stood in the center. It was a large bank barn, with a steep slope to one side. A lush pasture behind the barn provided plenty of grazing opportunities for the cattle, although its use occurred only in the warmer months. It seemed that every living creature at the Fairmount Children's Home was subject to a list of strict rules.

They entered the main barn with the Matron. For a fleeting moment, the smell of fresh hay, grain, and dung seemed like home. The lower level housed the animals and milking facilities. The upper level accommodated the feed.

24

The barn's haymows were amid the upper beams. A Carrier hay trolley ran along a long metal track carrying the wood and rope sling for loose or baled hay. Once the trolley reached the mow, the children would pull a lever to release the hay from the sling and then stack the baled hay, or use a pitchfork to toss loose hay into the corner.

Soft fur brushed against Henry's leg, wound around his second, and fished its way back through to the other side. A short-haired gray cat stared up at him. Her white-tipped paws made her appear to wear booties. Henry knelt and picked her up.

"She's so cute," Belle squealed. "Does she have a name?"

The Matron laughed. "Oh my, no!" She waved her arms in the air. "Look around. There are twenty or more barn cats."

Henry looked toward the haymow. Eight little eyes stared down at them. The cat squirmed until Henry released her. She jumped from bale to object until her final leap landed her just beside the kittens. She greeted them with a few licks on the head and moved out of sight for their feeding.

Belle stood with both hands clasped tightly against her chin. Her feet danced with excitement. "Babies." She loved babies, especially the ones who were the runt of the litter. "I wonder how many there are?"

Without acknowledgment, the Matron placed her hands on both children and urged them to move forward. "We still have much more to see."

"More babies?"

The Matron wrinkled her nose, "Maybe."

Henry took in as much information about the barn as he could. His eyes bounced from corner to corner, up to the ceiling and back again. Some how, some day, this place would be useful. As they walked out the door, two long whips hung on an old square nail. He shuddered at the thought of their purpose. He would soon find out.

A silo, which stood between the main barn and the chicken coop, stored corn silage for cow feed. It stood tall and unaffected by time. Even the metal top defied nature. It had nine rectangular wooden doors that ran vertically to the top. Their metal handle had a peculiar mechanism to secure it from springing open from the interior weight. Their hinges, over a foot in length, appeared to be hand hammered and ancient.

Beside the silo, the chicken coop housed over 1400 white Leghorns. As long as the birds produced eggs, they were free to live, but once their productivity waned, they went to the slaughterhouse. The children referred to it as a place of "last rights." The Matron's obvious fear of the fowl kept them from an interior tour. The only word she used to describe the buildings and its inhabitants was "dirty." Since baked chicken was a Sunday occasional meal for the two-hundred plus hungry children, the building sat empty for the majority of the week outside of "Slaughter Saturday." On that day, it bustled with a flurry of activity, feathers, and blood.

A hog barn and equally sized penned area sat opposite of the chicken coop. Pigs of all sizes enjoyed the mud pit together. Henry counted at least thirty babies, nearly twenty half-grown, six sows, and only one boar. The families seemed to get along fairly well until feeding time.

Belle pinched her nose with her fingers, "Pee... yew. That stinks."

Henry nodded his head in agreement, but added no comment. He had never witnessed a hog slaughter before and by the size of the grown ups, it appeared the day may soon come.

"On occasion," the Matron offered, "one of the little ones gets trampled at feeding time. If that happens, we have a hog roast."

Belle's face illustrated her disdain. "Then what do you do with it?"

Henry chuckled, "Eat it, silly. That's what a hog roast is."

"Depending on the size of the pig, it may not be much more than a mouthful per child." The Matron shrugged her shoulders. "Regardless of the size, it is a welcome treat. If the weather is cool, we roast it in an open pit amid a bonfire." Licking her lips she added, "Then we can finish the night with roasted marshmallows."

Both children smiled at the thought of hot, melted marshmallows sticking to their fingers by the warmth of a fire. Henry could almost smell the wood smoke. Belle could nearly taste the toasted sweetness.

The tour finished with a view of the distant cow pasture, and vegetable gardens. A few of the older children, dressed in straw hats and shorts, knelt on the ground to weed the rows of root vegetables. Their mud-caked knees seemed nearly the same color as their backs and shoulders. Outside of no visible shirts on the boys, their attire seemed minimal and none of them wore shoes.

"Ow!" One of the girls hopped around on one foot. She sat on the ground and picked at the sole of her foot until she pulled out the prickle that caused her discomfort.

"Where are their shoes?" Henry questioned.

"Shoes?" The Matron stopped a bit before continuing, as if searching for the right words to answer his question. "Shoes are collected at the end of the school year and disbursed again in September when school starts." She coughed into her hand. "That way the shoes don't get ruined in the muddy fields."

"What about when they leave to go somewhere?" Henry asked, although he could not think of a single place the children would go.

"Well, there are exceptions. Everyone has a pair available to them if they attend church, play ball, or go to the movies."

"Movies?" Belle squealed.

The Matron laughed, "Yes, Belle, movies. There are two theaters in Alliance. Both have different features. The bus leaves one hour before the movie starts and waits until both shows are over to bring everyone Home.

"I've never seen a movie." Belle giggled.

"All you need to go is money."

Belle's smile slid to a frown. She muttered under her breath, "I don't have any money."

The Matron pretended not to hear her. "Well, this ends our tour. I'll walk you back to your cottages."

They walked in silence. Henry felt as if he was walking toward a death sentence, and Belle's despondent expression seemed permanent. They watched as their tour guide waved to another young Matron heading their way.

"Hi, Silvia," the newcomer said. "Are you ready for your vacation?"

"I truly am," she answered with the most emotion heard all morning. "Right after dinner."

"Do you want me to finish here?" The young woman twirled her finger over Henry and Belle's head.

"Oh Louise, that would be great. Then maybe I could get an early start."

"That's fine with me." She covered her mouth with her hand. "I won't say anything."

"Thank you. You're a dear."

Henry and Belle watched Silvia walk away. Louise shrugged her shoulders and said, "Well I guess you are stuck with me, at least until I get you two settled. I will be filling in for Silvia for the next two weeks, while she enjoys her vacation. I won't be in your cottage though. Silvia takes care of the older girls in cottage #7 in the main house."

Her voice, more pleasant and rapid, melted the angst in both children as they walked toward their respective cottages. She followed each to their beds and gave the instructions for sleeping.

"Henry this is your double bed."

Henry smiled. The bed was the same size as his mother's.

"I'm not sure who you sleep with, but two of you place your pillows here," she patted the top of the bed by the headboard. "And the third one's pillow is here." She tapped the pillow at the foot of the bed.

Henry's face echoed Belle's earlier frown. He wrinkled his nose.

"Three people sleep in this bed?"

"Yes." Her curt reply came as a slap with words. "Okay, Belle, your turn. Let us go to your cottage."

"Do I sleep with three people too?" Her voice was barely audible.

"No, there's only two in your bed. We have a lot more boys than girls."

Belle smiled, although she dared not glance at her brother.

After they found their beds, the substitute Matron took them to the laundry room. With the aid of an elderly woman, they sized up the children and gave them their clothes for the week — one pair of shorts, two shirts and four pair of underwear.

"Pay attention to the dirt. These must last one week. If you get them dirty, you will wear them dirty until Saturday night baths. That is when you will receive fresh clothes." She placed her hands on her hips and shook her finger at them. "Use it up. Wear it out. Make it do or do without."

Henry felt a pain deep in his stomach. He placed one hand over his abdomen and the other on Belle's trembling shoulders. He attempted to comfort her with a tight squeeze. He wondered how they could ever make it through.

Each carried their minute stash of clothing to their cottages as if walking the final paces of a duel. They walked to the basement, located their locker, and opened it. Belle placed her clothes neatly on the bottom of her locker while Henry shoved his on the top shelf. The sound of the slamming metal doors closed a permanent chapter in their books.

Henry ran up the stairs and out the front door until he stood in front of Belle's cottage. He waited for ten minutes without moving. Finally, she came to the door. They walked to the edge of the gravel and plopped down in the short grass. The play area was empty save three boys.

Henry, holding Belle in front of him, watched the boys toss a ball with little interest. His flood of unused emotions wore him down. He wondered how he could remain strong. He wondered why they were there. How his father could leave them and if he was ever coming back. Yet mostly, he wished this whole experience to be a bad dream.

In mid-thought, all the children came rushing out of the cottages. They rushed across the grounds like a swarm of bees. Within a few minutes, the hive pushed through the door into the main house. Just before vanishing from sight, one boy turned and motioned for Belle and Henry to come. He cupped his hands over his mouth and yelled, "Dinner!" They popped up like a piece of crisp bread from a warm toaster and joined the others in the main house.

Following the noise of the crowd, they entered the dining hall. A sea of long tables, placed in row after row, end to end, held the majority of the children. A few stood along the outside wall, without seats. Henry scanned every table for a chair or a stool and found none. They walked toward the children that stood.

All were given a bowl of soup, two pieces of bread, one floating in the reddish liquid, and an apple. The high school boys slid to the floor to eat. Belle and Henry followed. Using the dry bread, they dipped and ate, while others lapped the soup. Belle watched in horror. No one spoke. The multitude behaved like starved animals.

Henry ate all of his stewed tomatoes with out taking a breath between bites. Belle picked, tasted, winced, and shivered before surrendering her bowl to her brother.

"You better eat it, Belle," he whispered. "Looks like this is all we get."

"But I don't like it."

Henry looked around the room. Half of the children had finished and half still picked. The children with full bowls of stew bartered for their neighbor's apple in exchange for the soup. Some bargaining succeeded; others shook their heads.

Belle choked down half of the liquid and pushed the fleshy tomato chucks off to the side. After a few more bites and a multitude of shivers, she handed the bowl to Henry without looking up. She felt him take the bowl from her hands and replace it with his apple. A thread of tears streamed down her cheeks.

"It'll be okay, Belle." Henry wondered if he had a penny for every time he said that, he would have enough money to treat the whole Home to the movies. His thought made him smile, although the grin did not last.

After their meager dinner, they walked back to the lawn and sat together under the shade of a large maple tree until the shadows grew long and thin. As dusk approached, they surrendered to the house rules and followed their roommates to their cottages.

"Good night, Belle." Henry tried to sound cheerful.

Belle hugged him and sobbed.

"It'll be okay, Belle. I promise. It'll be okay."

4

"Henry?" Belle whispered to her brother.

Henry wrestled with the blankets wrapped around his body. He was lucky enough to have only one bed partner. The third boy was visiting his aunt for the summer.

"Henry?"

Still foggy from an abrupt awakening, it took a few minutes to focus on his sister's trembling voice. "Huh?" he managed.

"I can't sleep."

"What time is it?"

"I don't know. The moon is up."

Her five-year-old innocence brought tears to his eyes. Henry lifted the covers of his double bed. "Come here, Belle. Sleep with me."

A quiet whisper from the bed a few feet away startled them. "What's going on?"

"Huh?" Henry whispered, but before he could offer an explanation, a second voice joined the conversation.

"Is it time for breakfast?"

A third boy answered in haste, "Don't go without me."

Everyone labeled the three rambunctious boys as "the triplets." Placed on the front porch in the middle of the night, they arrived without identity, family origins, or identified ages. The Headmaster named them Peter, James, and John. It appeared they may be siblings, yet no resemblance presented itself. Their hair, body shape, and facial features drastically differed. The idea of triplets seemed unlikely, but not knowing from where they came, the staff listed them as brothers and noted their birthday as one year prior to their arrival date. No one to date had claimed them or refuted any of the Home's assumptions.

Henry, now fully awake, answered them abruptly. Annoyance laced his tone. "It's my sister. She can't sleep."

"How'd she get in here?"

In his stupor, Henry had not considered how Belle came to stand before him. Henry recalled the only house rule that he remembered:

Rule #1–No child is permitted outside after dark.

Peter interrupted his thought. "Do you know what will happen to her if the Headmaster finds out she broke Rule Number One?"

James and John simultaneously gasped, and whispered, "Yes. It's not good."

Henry glanced at the two boys who stood only one foot from his bed and wondered silently if they could be brothers. They certainly acted similar.

Henry, now more agitated than before, lashed out. "She's a scared kid dropped off in this miserable place just a few days ago by our useless father!" Each word escalated until he stopped just shy of full volume, awakening their entire cottage of thirty-seven boys.

Within minutes, heavy footfalls echoed through the hall. In a flurry of flying blankets and clothing, Henry shoved his baby sister in a corner and covered her with two blankets and as many pieces of clothing that he could gather. He ignored her muffled statement and warned her to be silent.

She whispered for the fourth time, "He's not useless."

Henry dove on top of his bed toppling his pillow onto the floor. He bent over the edge to retrieve it and hit the floor with a loud crash.

Bang! The door flew open and bounced off the foot of Peter's bed, while the man pushed the button to turn on the ceiling light. The brightness pierced the boys' eyes.

"What's going on in here?" His looming voice hung in the air like a heavy blanket.

To the boys' dismay, the voice was not that of their Matron, but of the Headmaster. He waited not for an answer before shouting his second question. "Who is responsible for this racket?"

Peter, James, and John lifted their fingers simultaneously and pointed to Henry. The Headmaster lunged at Henry with his lanky arms and pulled his ears upward forcing him to his feet.

Henry yelped from a hot, sharp pain that ran deep into his ear canal. His instincts forced his fists into the stomach of the Headmaster.

Immediately, the man's face burned red. He pulled harder on Henry's ear and forced him out the door. The Headmaster screamed his order to the rest of the boys cowering in their darkened room.

"Lights out! All to sleep! NOW!"

Peter turned off the light and slipped back into his warm covers. James and John mimicked their brother in silence.

No one offered any help to Belle. She sat alone, heaped with a musty blanket and a pile of discarded, soiled clothes. She shook in fear and wept for her brother. She only wanted his comfort in this strange place and instead she offered Henry up to Satan himself. She had lived in the Home for barely three full days and already caused a major issue. The words of her brother regarding their father rang in her ears. She fell asleep, propped up in a corner, praying for her daddy's return.

Henry's head swooned from the pain inflicted within his damaged ear. He stumbled multiple times as Enoch forced him across the lawn. They walked toward the main house and up two flights of stairs. Alone on the upper floor with the Headmaster, Henry finally opened his eyes. Enoch stood before him suspending two different straps. His face gleamed with delight.

"Well, Henry. Which one do you choose?"

Henry pointed to the flat, wide strip of leather. It was considerably shorter than the other thin, somewhat rounded one that simulated a horsewhip.

"Say it," the Headmaster taunted.

"Say what?"

Henry's disrespectful, sarcastic tone made the Headmaster clench his fists. The whips swung wildly manifesting his anger. His reply, barely above a whisper, sieved through his tightened jaw.

"Tell me with your mouth not your finger which punishment you prefer...," he moved his face to inches from Henry's, "... and then I will choose which to use."

"That one," again Henry pointed to the wide belt.

"Remove your shirt. Turn around against the wall."

He barely finished the last word before the first strike came. Henry, in mid-motion of removing his shirt, felt the searing pain across his ribcage. He struggled to free his arms before the second strike. He stood in the middle of the room, refusing to turn his back.

In thirty years as the Headmaster, Enoch never encountered such defiance in a child. Most children feared the idea of his heavy hand and submitted to his rule without force. In nearly every case, the child retreated with tales of terrific torture and undo cruelty when in fact they suffered a few lacerations with the promise of more if their behavior remained unchanged.

Enoch took pride in his reputation as a hard man without remorse. In his mind, it helped maintain control of the two-hundred-thirty children who lived on the property. He only recalled one time that his explosive temper overtook his actions and that child deserved his wrath, or so he justified with each glance at the boy's facial scars.

Asking the children, past and present, if Enoch held his temper, the answer would be a resounding no. The abuse took place behind closed doors in what the children referred to as the "dark room." No one outside of the perpetrator and the delinquent entered the room. The sentence mostly ended the same with the child spending hours strapped to a plank board table, bound, unable to move, until they surrendered. The process length depended on the child. Enoch remembered most as an hour, but the children recalled days. The truth lay closer to the children.

As Enoch stood before Henry, his body shook with contemptuous lust for control. His plan for swift, strong force proved erroneous. Henry's insubordinate stand swelled into a five-minute staring contest. In less than seventy-two hours, since Henry's arrival, Enoch branded him a difficult challenge and a troublemaker. Enoch's display of power seemed flawed.

"Turn from me and grab the handles!" Enoch finally shouted to Henry.

Henry refused. His skin burned. His eyes seeped, yet his feet did not move.

Enoch kicked Henry's feet from under him. He pulled him to his feet by his ear.

A loud pop followed by raging fire made Henry nauseated. He doubled over in pain and covered his ear with the palm of his hand. The riotous whine suddenly stopped. Henry stumbled at his hearing loss.

Enoch shoved him toward the wall fitted with the two handles and ordered. "Hold on!" Random authoritative words spewed from his mouth. Their rapid pace made them unrecognizable.

With both straps in motion, Henry suffered an assault unlike any before him. The narrow whip ripped at his flesh as it wrapped around to his rib cage. The flogging continued until Enoch's arms ached from overuse. When the Headmaster settled to his senses, he gasped at the horror.

Henry's body desperately hung to the handles on the wall. His knees barely touched the floor leaving his legs and feet in an awkward position. Blood speckled his bare feet.

Enoch lifted his body hoping for life, relieved when he found a pulse. He placed Henry's body, pants and all into a tub of cool water. Henry never flinched. After smearing his wounds with a home-made salve and wrapping them in fresh gauze, Enoch laid Henry on the wood table and fastened head, arm and leg restraints over the boy's body. He turned off the light and walked out the door. The sound as he turned the lock echoed emptiness.

Enoch walked across the dark lawn hoping his conscience would permit a few hours of sleep. For the first time since accepting the position as Headmaster of the Fairmount Children's Home south of Alliance, Ohio, he questioned the length of his service. His arms ached. His legs felt lead-filled and his head swooned with guilt. He pulled his tired body up the front steps and shuffled his feet toward the front door. He entered and gave no thought of relocking it. After stripping his blood-splattered clothes, he collapsed onto his soft bed without moving the covers. He stared at the ceiling. Sleep would not come.

5

When Belle opened her eyes, the light of the moon conceded to the pastel hues of early dawn. Her body, uncovered and damp with sweat, lay on the heap of her makeshift bed. The triplets respired in unison although none stirred from the night's drama. She pulled her wrinkled thumb from her mouth.

Quietly Belle crept from the corner toward the closed door. She placed her hand over her heart hoping to slow its rapid beat. She turned the knob and slipped into the empty hall. As she tiptoed down the stairs, she heard the room begin to stir. She ran toward the front door, turned the knob and jumped when it freely opened.

Belle ran like never before. With two cottages between hers and Henry's, the demanding sprint sapped her energy leaving her gasping for air as she approached the front porch of her duplex cottage.

"Please...please," she whispered between her labored breaths, "Don't be locked."

When she found the door ajar, a sigh of relief manifested as a loud moan. She pushed the door open and ran straight into the belly of her Matron. Without question, she wrapped her arms around the plump woman and began to sob.

Surprised at the uncommon shower of affection, her reaction to return the hug came slowly until her maternal instincts, no matter how corroded, responded with a warm embrace. She patted Belle's back softly.

"There, there, dear. It'll be okay."

She knelt to the floor in front of Belle. She knew she had only minutes before the Headmaster would arrive. She needed to prepare Belle for what lie ahead and knew her time was limited for an explanation.

"I know you love your brother." Her words were hurried and on point. "You can't run away in the night. Rule #1 clearly states that." She lifted Belle's tear-stained face. "Were you told of all the rules?"

Belle shook her head.

"Did you understand them?"

Again, Belle shook her head. A loud, gruff voice startled them.

"Then why did you deliberately disobey?" The Headmaster stood in the open doorway, with clenched fists ground into his hips.

He looked at the plump woman sternly. With only a look, she knew she would pay for her outward show of affection. He simply forbade all physical contact unless it came from him in the form of correction. He glared at the Matron until she removed her arms and they hung limply at her sides. He motioned for Belle to come toward him.

"I'll take this from here."

Belle wailed at the proposition and increased her grip around the Matron's hips. The woman pulled Belle's arms from her and squeezed her small shoulders.

"Let go of me!"

Belle dropped her arms immediately. The Matron's drastic attitude change confused her. She turned to face the Headmaster who appeared to morph into a monster before her.

He grabbed her wrist and pulled her to him. The strength of his hands felt like a crushing weight as he placed them on her shoulders and forced her out the door, down the steps, and across the lawn toward the main house.

"I want to go home."

Belle's plea barely audible brought a crooked grin to the Headmaster's face. He yanked on her arm again and mocked, "You are Home."

The morning light lit the sky in brilliant colors, but its beauty went unnoticed. The windows, filled with a multitude of children's faces, told the tale of coming events. Horror filled their eyes and Belle could not look away.

When they entered the main house, the older girls held their breath. No one moved. All listened to Enoch's deliberate footsteps as they pounded each stair tread covering all but a soft echo of Belle's whimpers. He pulled her to the top of the staircase and walked toward the dark room.

He turned on the light and tossed her body on the floor. He groaned as he took his position on the only chair in the center of the room. The light pull swung violently from his heavy tug. Exhausted from the evening's ordeal and the lack of sleep, Enoch spent much time sneering at Belle. Somewhere deep within, he struggled with his punishment routine and in his masked guilt, withheld his initial action against her.

He began by explaining his position and the rules, commencing with Rule #1. The fictitious consequential banter of bears and cougars dragging children off in the night came with absolute certainty. After years of spilling the same tale, it became gospel in everyone's mind, including his. At times, while pressured in the dark room, some of the children confessed sightings. After over an hour of a lengthy explanation of each rule and its consequences if broken, the Headmaster stopped. He grew weary of listening to the drumming of his own voice. The two sat in silent stares.

Tears welled in Belle's eyes. "I just wanted to be with my brother."

"Did you break a rule?"

"I was scared."

"Did you break a rule?"

"Where is my brother?"

"Did you break a rule?" his voice began to escalate.

"Is he okay?"

"Did you break a rule?"

"He was only protecting me."

Nearly shouting, he sneered, "Did you break a rule?"

Belle looked at him searching for any sign of softening and found none. Her tears flowed freely. She struggled to breathe and soon began to cough.

During her emotional outburst, Enoch repeatedly asked the same question until he reached the pinnacle of his volume. "DID YOU BREAK A RULE?"

Belle shook her head.

"Confess it with your mouth not your head."

"Yes, I did."

"Did what?" Again, he screeched.

She looked at him and wrinkled her nose. Finally understanding that he wanted her to repeat her offense, she hung her head and replied, "Yes, I broke a rule."

Finally satisfied, he lowered his voice. What he said next surprised Belle.

"How do you think you should be punished for breaking Rule #1?"

She wanted to shrug her shoulders as her only response, but decided to add a verbal response. She assumed he expected an audible reply. She whispered, "I don't know."

He rose from his chair. "Well I do."

Belle gulped when he displayed two belts — one long and thin, the other wide and a bit shorter. She did not attempt to hide her tears. Her parents never spanked her although she witnessed Henry's swat with a switch once.

"But...I..."

Enoch hushed her plea before it began. He did not want an excuse and truth be told the psychological torture pleased him immensely. "Pick your punishment."

Belle raised her trembling hand and pointed toward the thin belt. "That one." She covered her face in her hands.

The corners of Enoch's mouth curled slightly joyous of her inexperienced ill choice. "Remove your shirt," he demanded as he recoiled ready to strike.

Belle grabbed the bottom of her cotton pajama top and struggled to pull it over her head. She stumbled and fell face down on the floor, her arms wrapped in the binding cloth.

Enoch pulled her to her knees and tore the top from her body. Buttons flew from the neckline and bounced across the polished wooden floor. Belle watched them skirt, slide, bounce and wobble until each settled to a stop. He lifted her head to face her assailant. An odd grin covered his face. Belle remembered no more.

6

Rule #2–No back talk or disrespect will
be tolerated.

Henry spent the night and the greater part of the
morning unconscious, unaware that Belle rested a
few feet from him. He woke cognizant of his agony,
yet quickly succumbed to the bondage and slid into
the haze of grey in which he slept.

Belle woke in a silent, darkened room. She lay on
her back, her wrists and ankles restrained by wide
bands of rough fabric. Her skin raw, red, and chaffed
burned from their constant rub, aggravating her
abrasions. A makeshift vice held her head immobile.
Her torn pajama top hung loosely over her frame.

Tears fell from her eyes puddling on the bare table. Draining mucus slid from her sinuses down her

throat forcing a deep agitated cough. She felt she would drown.

"Belle," Henry whispered from the darkness. "Try to be calm. You will be okay."

"But...I can't breathe," she whimpered.

"Then stop crying."

After a brief moment, Belle's cry faded to a whimper and then wilted into a deep sigh. Henry waited a bit longer to ask the question that burned within.

"What did he do to you, Belle?"

Her stuttered response came in staccato. "Um. I...I'm...I don't remember."

Rage engulfed Henry. What could he have done to his sister that would have been so terrible that her young, innocent mind blocked it out? His thoughts moved immediately to grave images. He forced them from his mind. He drew in a deep breath and exhaled in an attempt to mask his angst.

"Try," he begged. "Just try. Did he hurt you?"

"Yes."

Henry struggled to move. He wanted to rip the flesh from the Headmaster's face. Again, he tried to appear calm. "Where are you hurt, Belle?" He silently prayed for an unexpected response. The next few minutes seemed an eternity. Finally, Belle replied.

"My head hurts. My arms hurt. My feet tingle. My back burns."

Relieved that she echoed Henry's pain and nothing more, he fought tears.

"Anything else?"

"Henry?" Belle's voice began to quiver.

"Belle, don't cry. Please don't cry. It will only make things worse."

"I can't see."

Henry felt as if someone shoved a sock into his mouth. All saliva left his mouth and throat. He tried to speak, yet could not. After clearing his throat a dozen times, he managed to speak.

"W...What?"

"I can't see. Everything is black. Can you see me?"

"No, Belle. It's totally dark in here."

"So I'm not blind?"

Henry's release came as a hoarse wheeze. "No, you're not blind."

"But how do you know?"

In times such as these, Henry's realization of Belle's naivety became apparent. Their mother sheltered Belle from many things that Henry had not, making Belle's life-view more innocent than most. That thought evoked a strong sense of guardianship within him that he had yet to experience. He vowed at that very moment to protect his little sister and baby brother, wherever he was in this awful place. He noticed a thin line of light appear under the door.

"Shhh, Belle, someone is coming."

The sound of the opening lock brought little comfort to both Henry and Belle. The obvious outline of the Headmaster's body made Henry swoon.

"Are you two ready to follow the rules or do you need more time to decide?"

Neither child had an immediate answer — Henry because he struggled to control his anger and Belle because her distended bladder caused her excruciating pain.

The Headmaster's black silhouette remained fixed with one hand on his hip, the other resting on the doorknob. He waited for a reply, although he knew none would come. "Okay then." He closed the door.

Belle cried out at the sound of the fastening lock. The shadow of Enoch's feet soon moved from the door and both Belle and Henry listened to his soft footfalls move away from the closed door. The silence seemed deafening.

Belle immediately began to whimper. Henry tried to console her.

"Henry, I can't..." She sobbed uncontrollably.

"Can't what, Belle?"

Within seconds, the smell urine left no doubt of Belle's unspoken confession. Henry's eyes filled with tears thankful that the darkness covered his emotion.

Belle felt the warm liquid gather under her backside, creep to her waist, shoulders and then finally settle around her neck. The thought of lying in a puddle of her own fluid made her shiver.

Henry's soft whisper offered little comfort. "It's okay, Belle. You gotta go when you gotta go."

It was not until the following evening that Enoch came to release their restraints. He allowed them to return to their rooms only after they cleaned and sanitized both wooden slabs of their urine.

7

Rule #3—No child may exit his or her room until the
light of day.

Belle sat straight up in her bed. Her bedmate filled
the night's emptiness with soft, steady breaths that
normally would have lulled her back to sleep, but
baby Willy stole her every thought.

It seemed hours before the room held any light.
By the time Belle saw the faint outline of her bed,
she tossed off the covers, dressed as quickly as her
battered body allowed and tiptoed to the door.

Although certain "the light of day" meant at least
after the sun rose, Belle interpreted it differently.
She pattered down the stairs and bounced into the
common area. To her surprise, it was empty. Normally, her Matron tidied the room in preparation for

the early morning lull before breakfast, but Belle obviously rose before her.

Belle liked her Matron, Miss Betsy. Her age suggested her title of 'Miss' to be grossly misinterpret-
ed and better suited as 'Mrs,' but by her self-intro-
duction 'Miss Betsy' stuck. Her pale skin, wrinkled
and loose, quivered with every movement. Her short
stature, barely surpassing five feet, made her the
perfect counselor for the young girl's cottage, ages
two through eight. Outside of caring daily for her
group, she baked the reception cookies for the visitors and/or new guests. Judging from her full figure,
Miss Betsy sampled many of her creations prior to
arranging them on a serving tray.

She baked a different cookie seven days a week.
The children favored her snicker doodles, chocolate
chip, peanut butter, and sugar cookies, while the staff
savored her lemon bars, and date nut pinwheels. The
rolled raisin filled cookies, which she baked on Sat-
urdays, went straight to the desk of the Headmaster.

Normally, Miss Betsy recklessly battered her
coffee cup to wake the household, serving as her
make-shift alarm clock. The children then rushed to
dress for the day and hurried to the dining room to
find a seat. The last children to arrive stood to eat
their breakfast due to insufficient seating. The girls
quickly learned the lesson of tardiness. Miss Betsy
made certain of that.

Belle walked through the empty room disappointed. She wanted to talk with Miss Betsy about Willy.
She wanted to know where he was. She wanted to see
her baby brother, hold him, kiss him, and whisper
that everything will be okay. Her desire to be there

for him, as Henry was for her, pushed her to look for the Matron.

A floorboard groaned behind her. Belle spun to meet Miss Betsy, but to her dismay, the Headmaster stood in her place.

"And why are you out of your room?" He groaned through his clutched jaw.

"But it's morning." Belle's finger shook as she pointed to the whisper of light coming through the window.

"Morning, huh?"

"Yep." Her short answer, cut by her narrowing throat, choked out any additional information.

The Headmaster stared into her innocent face. Without the need to look toward the window for the morning light, he leaned closer to her filling the air with the stench of his smoker's breath. His body tensed and his eye began to twitch.

Somehow, Belle found her voice and a bit of courage. She spoke rather calmly despite the trembling of her body.

"Where is Miss Betsy?"

Stunned by her casual response to his intimidation tactics, his body sprung into an upright position. Even his clenched fists opened.

"She...she," he stammered. "She is under the weather today." Regaining his composure he added, "It is I whom will be overseeing you today."

"Oh," Belle replied, her eyes filled with obvious disappointment.

"Why do you ask?"

Without a thought, she responded, "I wondered if I could see Willy. I don't know where he is."

Immediately, her face flushed wishing she had not uttered her thought. She watched as the corners of his mouth turned into a perverted smile.

"Dead," was all he offered.

Belle swooned. She felt nauseated. Tears flooded her eyes and rushed over her colored cheeks. She moved her mouth but no sound befell.

"Oh child, do not cry," he attempted to mask his pleasure with sentiment. "The child arrived weak, neglected, and near death. He died within hours."

Belle's sobs woke several children. Soon many stood in the hall and listened to Enoch's story.

"When Miss Betsy brought him to the nursery, she immediately called for our nurse. With his pale complexion and low vital signs, she feared the worse. Worried that his ailment may in fact be contagious, she made the decision to transfer him to the hospital by way of the in-ground passage saving all the children from exposure. On the journey, his cough settled to a deep wheeze. He struggled to breathe on his own and within a few hours, he no longer had the strength to fight." He elevated his voice to ensure it carried over Belle's cries. He added, "We buried him in the cemetery the day of your discipline."

Enoch lifted his head and shouted to the gathering group of awe-struck girls, "Breakfast in ten minutes. Run along and get yourself dressed."

A thunder of footsteps filled the hall. Within minutes, the dorm room buzzed with chatter loud enough to fill Belle's ears. She never heard Enoch's demand until he shouted inches from her face.

"I said, for the third time, wash your hands."

She stumbled toward the stool. Before she placed her weight and second foot on its surface, she accidentally flipped the stool to its side and fell flat on her face.

Enoch pulled her to her feet by pulling on her ear. "For heaven's sake," he spit. "Get control of yourself. No amount of crying will ever bring Willy back."

She stepped on the stool as he handed her the stiff brush. Barely able to see out of her swollen, tear-filled eyes, Belle masked her break down in a spray of water. By the time she scrubbed each fingernail, she was soaked to her waist.

Enoch did not call attention to the pool of water that covered the sink and his feet. He simply waited until Belle finished the required task, extended a bucket and rag and said, "Now clean up your mess." As he walked from the room he added, "If any food is left from breakfast, you may eat. If not, your first meal will be lunch."

Belle crumpled into the puddle of water and silently added to it unsure of how she would ever survive in this place called "Home."

With the news stealing her appetite, Belle waited in the kitchen of the main house for everyone to finish breakfast. A few of the older girls pattered into the room to perform their dish duty and jumped with delight to see Belle tackling the chore alone. Sophie, the eldest girl in cottage #7, slid beside Belle to help. Both remained silent until all of the children left the house.

Sophie wiped the last plate placing it on top of the growing stack. She placed each dish in the cupboard. She looked at Belle, crumpled to the floor, with great pity. She also had lost a brother from a high fever.

"I'll go with you to the cemetery if you would like." A thread of tears slid down Sophie's cheek.

Belle could not speak. Tears and soap-less dishwater covered her. Finally, she shook her head, accepting Sophie's invitation.

Sophie lifted Belle to her feet as she peered out of the kitchen window. Many of the children gathered in the courtyard for a game of tag. She gently pulled on Belle's arm.

"Come on, Belle. Let's go find Henry."

When Henry saw them approach from the distance, he knew something was wrong. Belle's eyes were red and her skin blotchy, a sure sign that she had been crying. His first thought was to blame Enoch, but after a brief explanation from Sophie, the three embraced and cried together.

Enoch watched the sad exchange from the window in his office. He felt a slight twinge of compassion and shook his head to remove the thought. He was thankful that the baby had not suffered long under his care, yet more thankful that Willy's ailment would not spread to others. He watched the trio disappear as they walked over the hill toward the cemetery. He picked up a bell that sat on his desk and shook it. Within seconds, a young woman poked her head through the door.

"You rang?"

Enoch sat at his desk, with his glasses clinging to the tip of his nose. He lifted a stack of paper and thumbed through them without looking up. In an automatic tone he asked, "Mrs. Twill, would you see that those three make it back from the cemetery?"

She looked out of his window and saw no one, yet only after a few months experience, she did not question. She replied, "Yes, sir," and excused herself from his presence.

Janet walked out of the main building, across the expansive front lawn toward the northwest corner of the property. Surrounded by trees on three sides and the road on the fourth sat a small cemetery. Its headstones, modest and simply carved with the names of those laid to rest.

The first marker that Janet passed made her shiver. It read:

Joseph K.

Although his death happened prior to her employment, most of the staff still whispered about the cow trampling. She shook the conjured image from her mind and walked quietly toward the sobbing children. The pathetic sight made her cry. She stopped at a distance.

"Poor baby Willy," Belle repeated incessantly with her face burrowed into Henry's chest.

Henry hugged his sister, too sad to offer words. Nervous sweat soaked his forehead and clothes.

Sophie sat quietly beside her brother's adjacent marker. She plucked a few blades of high grass that covered his memory — Jimmy Aikerman — Aged seven. She tossed the thin green slivers one by one into the breeze mindlessly watching them float back toward the ground. She seemed to block out the Gates' grief.

Henry tried to lift his sister's spirits. "Belle," he offered, "Willy was so sick. He didn't have a chance." He lifted his eyes toward the Home. Only half of the third floor windows and chimneys were visible from their position. He wanted to run. He wanted to spew all of his hatred for his father, the Headmaster, their situation and circumstances, but he kept them hidden. It was then he noticed the Headmaster's secretary. He urged his sister to her feet.

"Let's go, Belle."

Belle sensed his apprehension. With innocence glossing her eyes she whispered, "Go where, Henry?"

Aware of Janet's presence, he hung his head. "Home, Belle. Let's go Home."

Henry and Belle walked together with their arms wrapped tightly around each other. Henry struggled to walk upright, limping from his recent beating, yet he managed to fill the role of big brother to his broken baby sister. Reassuring her, he squeezed her shoulders.

"I'll always take care of you, Belle. I won't let anything happen to you again."

Belle knew what he meant. So did Sophie and Janet.

8

Rule #4—Each child will evenly share all work
duties without complaint.

After their "discipline," Henry and Belle became in-
separable; only when the afternoon shadows grew
long did they reluctantly separate. They never spoke
of their two-day punishment to each other or anyone else.

Henry's raised abrasions slowly began to heal although the hearing in his right ear never fully returned. His sister blocked the beating from her memory. Henry's feeling of helplessness, coupled with
the Headmaster's excessive force, fueled a hatred
that foamed deep within him. Outside of his abrasions, the only visible sign of their introduction to
the Fairmount Children's Home was the permanent

scowl on Henry's face. He rarely smiled at anyone outside of his sister.

The loss of innocence that once beamed from Belle's eyes slid to barely a flicker of contentment. Daily, she prayed for her father's return despite the consistent denial from Henry.

When Henry and Belle's father dropped them off at the Home, the spring planting had long since occurred. The Home's vegetable garden occupied four of the one-hundred-fifty-three acre property. The children bore sole responsibility of the planting, maintenance and reaping of the bounty. Once harvest arrived, the staff helped the children can, freeze, and preserve the crops.

The field corn, grown mostly for livestock feed, covered half of the farmed ground along with alfalfa and timothy occupying the second half. The Home's hired farmer supervised the hay baling process three times a season. It was a tough, dirty, and often sweltering job, especially stacking the hay in the mow, but with the use of the Home's tractor and two hay wagons, most of the high school boys seemed to enjoy it. At the very least, the work excused them from their school studies.

The first time Belle stepped into the garden, she stood amazed at the quantity of sweet corn rows. They seemed to stretch for miles, disappear over a hill only to reappear and spread for another imagined mile. Of the four acres the children planted, sweet corn occupied half of them. The crop stood one foot in height. It seemed to take the better part of a week to weed all of the rows.

Belle preferred to work among the radishes, lettuce, turnips, and cucumbers. The tomato worms made her shiver, yet only half as much as the potato bugs, although she despised the yellow and black corn spiders the most. Many of the children mocked her screams when she walked through an unseen web. No matter the child's preference all had to take a turn caring for each crop.

"If you are going to share in the harvest, you must equally share in the work," the Headmaster repeated as he inspected the children's progress.

The cool early days of June quickly melted into a scorching summer. The older children, fourteen through eighteen, held the responsibility of drawing water from the hand-dug wells and carrying it to the struggling plants. Some of the older boys made carts in their spare time to aid in this chore. All welcomed the sound of a summer rain, giving the children a much-needed rest.

Belle especially enjoyed the days of harvest although with the variety of crops it seemed to never end. Cucumbers seemed to be the earliest taxing chore. Depending on the variety and size, she helped sort each day's harvest into three categories – eating, dill and sweet pickles. Although standing for hours in one place slicing the cucumbers into spears or rounds made her back, legs and arms ache, she enjoyed the smell of the spices, sugar, and vinegar. The bread and butter pickles were her favorite.

Henry helped the older boys with the watering and construction of the windmill-watering wheel. Designed out of necessity rather than pleasure, this combined invention allowed the children to discard the old pulley system and increase the speed in which the water was disbursed. The Headmaster seemed pleased with the boy's ingenuity although he expressed no compliment.

Henry stood before the harvest calendar and sighed. Tomorrow was July 4th, his birthday. Although he knew there would be no celebration, he did not expect to spend the day harvesting garlic. He chuckled to himself.

"What's so funny, Henry?" Peter asked as he peered over his shoulder.

"Huh?" Henry stumbled. He thought he was alone. "I was just looking at the task for tomorrow."

Peter looked at the words "Pull Garlic" written in red ink. He scrunched his face and asked, "Pulling garlic is funny?"

Henry unwilling to spend any more time in explanation shrugged his shoulders and began to walk away. He did not want to tell his roommate that tomorrow was his birthday. For the first time since their arrival, he fought tears.

John, the bully of the triplets, mocked Henry's down turned face. He rubbed his eyes and pretended to cry. "I don't wanna pick garlic on my birthday. Boo hoo hoo."

Henry snapped. He lunged at John and pushed him easily to the ground. A flurry of punches came without warning. Belle stood in horror as the Headmaster pulled the boys apart. One of Henry's jabs connected to Enoch's cheek in the tussle leaving a distinct red mark.

The Headmaster forced the two boys across the lawn toward the main house. All knew what happened next, especially Belle. The Gates children lived at the Home for just over one month and the vision of her brother going through another beating made her head swoon. Belle collapsed on the ground. She did not see Henry for two days.

Henry's third beating came barely a week after his second and his fourth the following month. Belle tried to encourage him to avoid the troublemakers, but they seemed attracted to Henry and soon the majority of the boys' fights involved Henry in some fashion. On occasion, even after Henry's professed innocence, he received punishment.

9

Rule #5–Infractions require discipline.

Henry barely became accustomed to sharing his bed
with Jack when the third boy, Joey, returned home
from a summer's stay with his aunt. Joey had been
away from the Home since the middle of May, and
the moment Jack saw him walking across the play
area he groaned, shook his head, and walked away
from his group of friends mumbling. Jack's friends
pointed and mocked Joey, but the young boy paid
them no mind.

Joey was a small boy for his age. His sun-bleached
hair seemed to glow a bright orange in the failing
summer light. He walked with a slight limp favoring
his left leg. He had a backpack slung over his shoulder, which he struggled to carry. Clearly overstuffed,

the stressed seams looked as if they would rupture at any moment. He disappeared into cottage #2 without a single person welcoming him Home.

It was late evening when Joey appeared at Henry and Jack's bedside. He carried a brand new pillow, an apparent present from his loving aunt. He offered the fluffy white puff to Jack without question. Jack snatched the pillow from Joey's hands and replaced it with his. Joey accepted the yellow-stained flattened cushion and settled into the opposing position between the boys.

With the obvious enjoyment of his new head support, Jack fell asleep immediately, while Joey and Henry jockeyed for positions. Twice, Joey accidentally kicked Henry's ribs. He whispered, "Sorry," so softly that Henry questioned whether he really heard it.

Henry struggled to fall asleep long into the early morning hours. He forced thoughts of self-pity from his mind too often to count. He tried to remember the life of his mother.

Her frail frame hid her inner strength. Her demure manner, often mistaken as naivety, commanded respect from other women without words. She was kind, resolute, and playful with her children. Both children inherited her ash-blonde hair and sense of humor, although only Belle presented the humor in a playful manner. Henry felt it necessary to hide it from others.

He lay in his bed thinking of the daily mundane things that he treasured about his mother — peeling potatoes, darning socks, hanging sheets on the clothesline, running from spiders, building a make-shift teepee from old wool blankets, and his favorite — her perfume. If he closed his eyes and drew in a deep breath, he could smell the essence of lily of the valley.

Thoughts of her brought him peace. He smiled in the darkness finally calm enough to drift into dreams of her when he felt a warm wetness creep through the sheet under him. He moved his hand over the fabric between Joey and himself. The pungent smell left no doubt. Joey had wet the bed in his sleep.

Henry groaned inside, pulled the top cover from their bed, and rolled onto the floor. He grabbed his pillow in mid-slide. Dry and safe from the growing onslaught, he thought he heard a second whispered confession as the covers settled around him, but his sleep came immediately.

Jack woke up with groans of disgust. "Again, Joey?"

Joey groggy from a deep, restful sleep shook his head to clarity. "Huh?"

"You peed the bed again." Joey jumped off the soaked sheet. "We just got these last night."

Jack's verbal onslaught caught the room's attention. Two other beds experienced similar situations.

"Ugh!" It came from the bed a few feet away.

"That's gross!" echoed from across the room.

Soon the Matron rushed into the bedroom and shouted to the three perpetrators. "Grab your wet sheets and come with me." Joey and the other two boys hurried to pull on yesterday's clothes, while the Matron continued to call for them. "Hurry up. I haven't all day."

With their urine-soaked sheets rolled into a ball in front of them, the boys marched single file out the door, down the staircase onto the grass. All eyes in the room watched as they stood in a row in front of the cottage.

"Arms out wide," the Matron yelled. "Sheets over your head." She waited until the young boys settled into the scarecrow position. A thin smile appeared through her pursed lips. "You may come in when your sheet is dry. Then, you can remake your bed with the dried sheet."

Henry nearly stumbled to the floor. He turned toward Jack. "What? We sleep on the pee dried sheet?"

The scowl of Henry's disdain made Jack laugh. He clutched his stomach and doubled over attempting to gain control. The idea of sleeping in the dirty, stained, air-dried sheet was not comical; it was the look on Henry's unsuspecting face.

Jack slapped Henry's back. "Don't worry. It doesn't happen every night."

That statement did not ease Henry's thoughts. He silently cursed his father. He wondered how he could ever stay.

"Why can't we just get a new sheet?" His innocence in the Home's frugality of operations would soon be shattered.

Jack's smile morphed into a grimace. "Because they are too cheap to wash them more than once a week."

He began a rant that soon gained momentum. Its rhythm seemed more like a tuneless song than an angry vent. It did not take long for several boys to add their own lines.

Baths on Saturday. Three in a tub.
Scrub, scrub, scrub
Until you wash off the mud.
If you are lucky, you'll be the first.
Even if second, it's not the worst.
But if you're third, oh my word,
You'll be as clean as a stinkin' turd.

Use it up. Wear it out.
Keep it clean, or go without.

Five little angels around my bed.
One at the foot and one at the head,
One to watch and one to pray..."

One by one, the boys filed out of the bedroom. All dressed for the day's work and play without Henry's detection. The boys' chant enveloped him.

Henry fumbled to slip into his shorts. He ran down the staircase pulling his shirt over his head. He nearly fell out the front door. He wanted to hear the mantra in its entirety. The muffled last stanza came just as the line of boys wound their way through the ones who stood on the lawn with the stained fabric draped over their heads.

"...And one to take my soul away."

Henry froze. He could not breathe. The odd measures of the crowd puzzled him. Their emotions seemed distant, guarded, automatic, and nearly robotic.

He shook his head to clear the images and found himself standing in the middle of the three boys. The pungent scent of urine made him cringe, yet his conscience ached. The humiliating public display was beyond cruel. He grabbed the dry edges of one of the sheets in front of him.

Joey jumped when Henry's head appeared under the sheet. He managed a pathetic grin, although he really felt more like crying.

Joey rarely gained control of his bladder beyond his diaper days, which he wore until he turned five. His deep sleep prevented his wake senses to work properly and alert him of his full and often leaking bladder. Even after the bed became soaked, he slept peacefully until the others woke him. Immediately, shame clouded him.

After arriving at the Home, fear became the only other emotion that Joey felt on a daily basis. His roommates, especially Jack, taunted and bullied him. Often, Joey felt his only friends to be the two boys who shared the same bladder problem as he, and yet they rarely spoke through the blanket of damp fabric that covered them.

"Grab the other end," Henry demanded.

Once Joey followed his order, Henry began to fan the sheet. Unprepared for the tug, the fabric slid out of Joey's hands and skirted the ground.

"Aw, hang onto to it, Joey. Fanning it will help it dry faster."

Stunned at the unsolicited offer, Joey tried to choke back his emotions. Unable to hold his outward show of gratitude, tears covered his freckled cheeks.

Henry felt more embarrassed for Joey than before. "Oh come on, Joey, don't cry. I've gotta sleep on this sheet too, you know."

Joey wiped the tears from his face with his forearm, jockeying for a better grip as Henry gently floated the sheet up and down, mimicking a soft spring breeze. After ten minutes, he finally gained enough confidence to speak without the fear of a quivering voice.

"Thank you," were the only words he managed.

With Henry's ingenuity and help, their sheet dried in one-third of the normal time. The boys gathered the fabric together, paying no mind to the yellowed center.

Joey carried it upstairs to their dormitory and covered their heavily stained mattress. He tried to avoid looking at the other two uncovered beds, but felt compelled to share in his fellow bedwetter's shame. He shook the notion and the sight of their disgrace from his mind and raced down the flight of stairs.

To his surprise, Henry stayed to help one of the other boys. Without hesitation, Joey knelt to the ground and picked up the edge of the last sheet. Together in silence, the four boys fanned the fabric until they dried.

Belle watched from a distance. Her heart filled with pride.

"Good job, Henry," she whispered.

One of the high school girls tossed an insult as she walked by Belle. "Yep, Henry, good job for peeing all over the bed."

"He didn't do it. He's helping the boy who did."

The girl fanned her hand in the air and laughed. "Oh sure. That's why he's standing there. Because he didn't do it." Again, she laughed.

Belle tried to explain, but the more she talked, the louder the girl laughed. Belle ran to her brother with tears in her eyes.

"What's wrong, Belle?"

Belle turned and pointed to the girl, now standing among several others. The girls covered their mouths and laughed.

"That girl..." she cried. "Thought you were the one who made this..." Belle hesitated, suddenly aware that the three boys with the bed-wetting problem all lowered their heads. Belle swallowed the rest of her words.

Henry covered for his sister. "It's okay, Belle. It doesn't matter what they say." He winked at his sister. "Some kids don't know how to be anything but mean."

Belle straightened her stance at the statement. Those words came from their mother. She whispered them to her children when they fell victim to another's cruelty. Belle's face flushed. Again, pride filled her.

As the two boys finished remaking their beds, the breakfast call came. The grounds soon were covered by a flurry of children running toward the main building.

When Henry, Belle, Joey and the other two boys entered the dining hall, only a few scattered seats remained, with the exception of one young girl seated alone amid seven empty chairs. She had a large piece of yellow material wrapped around her head. From the looks of her hunched position, the load was heavy.

Henry nodded a silent hello to the young girl. She made no response outside of her staring into her lumpy bowl of oatmeal. She pushed the paste around with her spoon never lifting it to taste the contents.

Just as Henry sat in the chair beside her, the familiar morning fragrance filled his nose. He shot a quick knowing glance at the seven-year-old. She did not lift her eyes.

Belle's Matron used a different method of public humiliation to deal with her bed wetter. She made the young girl wrap her wet sheet and place it on her head. It took much longer for the fabric to dry, so the children wore their crown of thorns most of the day. Often in cooler weather, the sheet still held a bit of dampness at bedtime.

The table ate in silence. Henry gulped his oatmeal in record time. Belle offered her bowl to him, but he refused. She slid it in front of Joey and he gladly accepted. Both of the Gates children took their pear with them.

Just before walking out of the door Louise, the substitute Matron, approached Henry. Her wide smile covered her face even though the distant expressions of the other Matrons expressed grave disapproval of her actions. Their body language — arms crossed, faces twisted while leaning against the wall — echoed their pretense.

"Henry?'

"Huh?" Henry hesitated, stunned by the forward advance.

"I just want to compliment you."

"On...on what?" His nose wrinkled.

"On how you helped your friends this morning." She watched as Henry's face flushed. Smiling as she continued, "I saw you from the windows in cottage #7." She leaned into him and whispered, "I thought it was most kind."

Henry's reaction, surprise mixed with the growing fear of the other Matron's approach, made him shudder. He could not find words or manage a reply. He wanted to flee quickly. His back burned at the thought of another "discipline."

He shoved the hard pear in his mouth and mumbled, "Thank you." He pulled Belle out the door.

10

Rule #6—Each child must be involved in an extra-
curricular activity

The band director, Davis, lived in the original farm-
house between cottage #3 and the cottage duplex of
#4 and #5. The aged slate roof leaked in the early
spring damaging much of the director's personal belongings. The Board of Directors decided the fate of
the one-hundred-year-old structure and set the date
for demolition in September.

In the weeks prior to the Gates' children arrival,
the older boys had helped the band director finish
his new living quarters within cottage #3. This de-
layed much of the band's practice days, but did not
hamper the director's attitude.

As a former inmate, Davis's reputation grew stronger with each passing year. His talent as an artist and musician paled in comparison to the love and respect given to him for his kindness. The children adored him and followed his orders without question or complaint.

He proudly accepted the position of band director after graduating high school and never left the Home. He did not speak of his birth family, but referred to the people at the Home as such. Even the Headmaster liked Davis.

The band's uniforms, donated by local businesses and charities, were made of a wool/polyester blend that allowed the material to resist wrinkling. The long black jacket had a large white shield-shaped panel attached to the front by a series of gold buttons, which echoed the pair of buttons on each collar. The front panel, adorned with an oversized red letter "F," became the centerpiece. A wide black satin stripe adorned the outside seam of their black slacks.

An exaggerated pillbox form was the base for the headdress. Being mainly white, the black band around the top coupled with the black bill, made the black feather plume at the top the focal point. The white chinstrap kept the top-heavy hat in its proper place through their rigorous marching maneuvers. The glint of the gold star between the bill and top black band connected the shimmer to the gold buttons on the jacket.

The majorette's uniforms differed greatly. A large white letter "F" adorned their sleeveless black top and mandarin collar. Their shorts made of black corduroy boasted of the same wide satin piping.

Their hats and white shin-height marching boots, ornamented with a thick black tassel, were the only common uniform pieces they shared with the marching band.

Davis's uniform was pure white. He wore a black bow tie, white captain's hat, and white shoes. His jacket's decorations looked similar to that of a uniformed Major with multiple cords and stripes on his shoulders and sleeves. Black satin piping outlined his pants and jacket pockets, and pins of awards from year's past adorned his hat.

A spotted black and white pony named Star pulled a cart and served as the band's mascot. She was a mild miniature and by far Belle's favorite of the Home's ponies. Often, Belle kept her uneaten apple and offered it to the mare. She giggled at the tender way Star pulled the apple off her open hand.

After the conclusion of baseball season and tournaments, if the Fairmount team qualified, the baseball field became the practice arena for the marching band. Although the ground had an aggressive slope, it served better for the band than for baseball. Fairmount hosted no Home games on the property. Practice was its only use.

Belle and Henry watched the band rehearse from outside the perimeter with several other children. Henry tapped his foot to the rhythm as they played. He picked up a large rock and a few twigs and fashioned his own set of drums to play along. Often his tapping continued long after the song ended. They listened to the band practice three songs for nearly an hour before the band director approached Henry.

"I hear you over here drumming, Henry." Davis said with a smile. "Why don't you go over to the storage building and grab a drum?"

"Huh?" Henry answered, stunned.

Davis knelt to the ground and placed his hand on Henry's shoulder. "You have great rhythm. Have you ever played an instrument before?"

"No, sir." Henry straightened his stance.

"I'd like to see you try with a real drum and sticks. I think you would be great, if you want to try it."

"Yes, sir." Henry jumped up and ran toward the storage building.

Belle laughed at her brother as he bounced across the lawn, carrying a snare drum. A wide smile covered his face. She clapped her hands as he approached.

The director placed Henry in the center of the line up. The two boys on either side shuffled to make room for the new drummer. All of the children surrounding Henry patted his shoulders or head as an outward sign of acceptance.

The band practiced for an extra hour with the newest member and no one complained. Henry had no problem learning the beat of the three songs. Even the scorching summer sun could not dampen his mood. The smile never left his face even through the interruption of lunch and redundant bowl of stewed tomatoes.

Something wonderful happened to Henry the day he tried on his band uniform. For one of the first times in his life, he felt pride. In that moment, he enjoyed life. If his father had not placed him in the

Home, the opportunity to play drums let alone be a part of the band would have never presented itself.

For the next several weeks, the band practiced twice a day. They worked hard in the morning on their formations and marching to the beat. All carried their instruments, but did not play them; only the drummers tapped their sticks together to create the proper timing of their steps. They stood in their formations — a star, the letters FCH, and the children's favorite the word "HELLO."

"Knees up. Point your toes to the ground," Davis repeated multiple times as he clapped his hands to the beat. On occasion, he blew his whistle and the marching ceased just long enough to hear him say, "Again."

After lunch, the band began to play their tunes. The final twenty minutes, they practiced the entire routine – formations, marching, timing and music – from the top. After a few short weeks, the director felt they were ready.

The day before their first performance at The Alliance Fireman's Festival, Star began to act up. Belle spent most of the day in the stall trying to calm her. Belle gave her fresh water, oats, hay, and Star's favorite treat, an apple. By dusk, the pony seemed in better spirits and began to act normal.

It was not until a few days later Belle discovered what happened. A few of the high school boys had gathered a bit of freshly-mowed grass to give Star a special treat. Unfortunately, among the grass were a few wilted cherry leaves. She reacted violently causing an emergency visit from the veterinarian. After a shot and Belle's special care, Star made a quick recovery, just in time for the next day's events.

The following morning the band members busied themselves packing the bus with their instruments for the day's performance. Belle stood a distance away watching the activity.

The band director walked toward her. "Thank you, Belle for taking such good care of Star." They both watched the pony walk onto the back of a trailer. "She really likes you."

Belle smiled. "I like her too."

"I know you are a bit young to ride in the pony cart for the performances, but perhaps you could be our assistant?"

"And do what?" Belle asked enthusiastically.

"Help us take care of her, feed her, and groom her." He winked at Belle. "And maybe sneak her in a few treats every once in a while."

Belle's face glowed red. She opened her mouth to defend her actions, but decided to remain quiet.

Davis laughed. His eyes twinkled with each word, but when he laughed, everyone felt his warm spirit. He placed his hand gently on Belle's shoulder.

"It is okay with me, Belle, if you give Star your apple." He leaned closer to her. "However, I feel it to be more important that you eat yours. I will find some apples that you can give to Star. I do not want you to go hungry. Is that okay with you?"

"I...I don't mind giving mine to her."

"I know you don't mind, but I want you to grow up strong, so you need to eat it for your nutrition. Believe me; we will see that Star also gets an apple, just not yours. Agreed?"

"Okay, Mr. Davis. I'll eat mine." She rushed to add, "And come to you for Star's."

"Great. That's the best solution." He patted her shoulder. "Thank you for your help." He cupped his hand around his mouth and yelled to the driver who stood by the open door. "Are we ready?"

"Yes, sir," called the driver.

He looked at Belle. "Well, Miss Star's assistant, are you coming?"

Belle clapped her hands and jumped up and down. "Yes. Yes. YES!"

She ran toward the bus with Davis close behind her. Heads and arms extended from every operable window as one boy played Reveille. Wide grins appeared on everyone's face, especially Belle's.

When the bus pulled into the parking lot, the rowdy children grew silent. A few mouths dropped open from the first-time experience, but the seasoned children's anticipation stole their words. Davis exited first, calling to the groups of players by their instruments.

"Reeds."

A large group of children carrying clarinets, oboes, flutes, and a lone piccolo hurried through the cushioned seats toward the door. After a few minutes, the band director repeated his call.

"Reeds?"

No one moved. Davis jumped onto the bottom step of the bus. He poked his head over the chrome railing. "Saxophones, are you coming?"

The three boys looked at each other. "I thought we were brass."

Davis repeated, "Saxophones, come!" He waved his arms in the air and added, "You are woodwind instruments. You use reeds. Therefore, you are Reeds, not Brass."

The bus erupted in laughter. The boys held their instruments in front of their faces hoping to cover their embarrassment.

"Percussion!"

Henry was the first to jump to his feet. His excitement was obvious.

Belle shouted, "Good luck, drummers!" as Henry walked down the bus steps. She spied the horse team as they began to harness Star and decided she would leave with the percussion group to help. The cymbals bumped her as she stood. The loud clang fueled the rumble of laughter.

"Brass!" Davis called.

Belle, happy to have exited the bus prior to the tubas, quickly ducked out of the way to give the large instrument players the much needed room. Head bumps and shoulder scrapes made the seated children groan until all of the tubas, trombones, and trumpets were safely off the bus.

"Entertainers!"

Up popped the majorettes. They carried their batons far above their heads to ensure an easy exit. They were always the last group to exit.

Davis gave the marching order. The drummers began to tap their sticks in unison. First, it sounded like, tap, tap, tap, and then quickly escalated to tappity tap tap, tappity tap tap. The band marched to the edge of the bleachers and waited, anxious to begin their performance.

Davis held up his hand and blew his whistle with three short bursts. The drummers spun into action and the band began to move across the field. Belle watched on the sidelines. Her feet danced to the rhythm.

A hush fell over the crowd as they waited for the Fairmount Band to begin. Davis lifted his hands and blew his whistle one last time. All of the children raised their instrument ready to play.

The trumpets played the first long note. One of the boys hit a sour squeak and the audience giggled, but then settled into hushed silence when all the instruments joined the brass. The symbols clashed and the drums thumped the beat. The members marched from their long straight line into five letters as they played the song.

It was a wonderful sight to see and hear. Belle clapped her hands and danced to the beat of the song she had heard dozens of times in the past few weeks. She watched the performance on the baseball practice field until she felt she could also march in step with the group. Deep pride bubbled within her as she watched the band perform in their uniforms, boot tassels swinging with each exaggerated step and hat plumes bouncing, as the majorettes' batons flew through the air. And, Henry stood smack dab in the middle.

At the conclusion of the song, the spectators roared with laughter. The Fairmount Band stood proud in their letters — O-H-E-L-L. Soon they began to shout to one another, shuffling their feet, and swinging their instruments. Their exaggerated play-acting of the misspelling brought the crowd to their feet. The children in the "O" ran past the others and settled on the far end, changing the word to H-E-L-L-O. Again, the standing crowd whistled and cheered vigorously. Once the crowd settled, the band took a long bow.

Davis once again lifted his white-gloved hands, whistled, and the children began their second song. They played three selections in total. Once the performance ended, the crowd jumped to their feet and clapped. The band took their final bow, as did Davis, which elevated the noise of acceptance. Star was the first to exit the field. All else followed the mascot, marching to the beat of Henry's lone drum.

11

Rule #7–Each child must maintain a C average.

Once the calendar page of August found its way into the trash, September opened with a flurry of activity. The hectic harvest of the late fruits and vegetables seemed simplistic compared to the start of the school year.

Belle entered the Fairmount school in first grade at the age of six. Although she was the youngest in her class, her studies came easily.

Henry tested above the ninth grade level, but the staff decided that due to his young age of eleven-years-old, he would settle best into eighth grade studies. They wanted to keep him challenged in hopes of keeping his fighting to a minimum while keeping him away from the rowdy ninth grade boys.

His triplet roommates, green with jealousy, needled Henry incessantly about his advancement of two grades.

Henry and Belle's mother pushed her children to study, read, and write at early ages. She understood the importance of a well-educated adult. Forced to drop out of college due to her family finances, she decided then that if she had the privilege of raising children they would not suffer her same fate. Her tenacity paid off in both children.

When Belle walked through the tall wooden door of the schoolhouse, the sea of desks in the oversized room took her by surprise. Two teacher's desks, one table height and the second podium style, sat at the front of the room directly behind the wall of chalkboards. A tall, thin woman with dark hair drawn back into a tight bun greeted the children as they came through the door.

"Good morning, students. Welcome back to the Fairmount School. I want you to form nine lines, one for each grade. And, yes, before any of you complain, I know the eighth grade class is by far the largest, which is why you students," she pointed to Henry, "will line up in the back." She clapped her hands, "Hurry, now. Time is limited. Get into your lines." She pointed to the floor at her feet, "First grade is here." She took two steps to her right and pointed to the floor, "Second grade is here." She repeated the process until all of the students settled into their appropriate line.

Henry's roommates — Peter, James and John — caused a bit of a ruckus. It seemed that Peter and John were jealous of their brother James advancement to the next grade and leaving them behind. The three boys complained about their situation.

"But Miss Adelade," Peter whined. "I'm smarter than my brother. Why does he get to go to the seventh grade?"

The teacher's automatic reply came without emotion. "If you are smarter, Peter, why did James receive better marks?"

Peter's eyes shimmered from his crooked grin. "I did his homework."

James' face burned hot from Peter's lie. He entered the room proud of his accomplishments of graduation from sixth grade, but after listening to Peter's tale, he lost control. James lowered his head and slammed it into the stomach of his unsuspecting brother. Peter fell to the floor, gasping for air.

Soon the room of curious children rushed to see the fight blocking the teacher at a safe distance. James threw one punch after another, while Peter lay on his side clasping his hands around his throat.

Henry remembered Peter pulling the paper stick from his lollipop and tossing it on the ground knowing the teacher strictly prohibited candy, gum, or food inside the school. Henry knew that Peter was in trouble. He pushed John out of the way, forced Peter to his knees, wrapped his arms tightly around his chest, and pumped. With the second squeeze out flew the lodged sucker ball.

The ring of students watched in silence. Henry helped the coughing Peter to his feet and slid his arm around his waist. They walked through the parting crowd.

Miss Adelade rushed toward Peter. "My goodness, Peter. What happened?"

He stuttered and coughed a lie. "He just knocked the wind out of me."

Henry made no mention of the candy that blocked his windpipe. He acted on instinct and felt reasonably certain that had he not been there, Peter may have choked to death, yet Henry wanted no attention.

The teacher grabbed James by the collar and pulled him to his feet. Red blotches covered her cheeks and neck. Her voice came as a strained squeak.

"You are coming with me, young man."

The room gasped. All knew what to expect.

As soon as Miss Adelade disappeared with his brother, Peter rushed toward Henry. "Thank you, Henry. You saved my life."

Henry nodded but spoke no words. Belle stood beside him, physically patting her brother's back.

Peter looked down at the floor, "I...I owe you."

Again, Henry only nodded. He wondered if Peter's loyalty would last.

Once the teacher returned, the line up resumed until all the children stood in their grade line. Belle had ten in her class, while Henry had thirty-eight, the largest eighth grade class since the opening of the Home on October 20, 1876.

"First grade to the front," she commanded.

Belle looked down at her worn brown shoes. She felt reasonably certain she wore boy's shoes as they slid off her heels with each step. She tripped twice, nearly falling into the little boy in front of her. Before she sat in her assigned seat, her heels burned from the forming of a blister.

Students received a workbook appropriate for their grade level, although the younger students received the majority of the teacher's attention, the children labored through his or her workbook at their own pace. This posed a bit of an attention problem for those who advanced quickly through their grade.

The ninth grade class, only thirteen in number, left the building for the basement of the main building, adjacent to the staff's kitchen. The majority of the younger students sighed in relief when the Freshmen left the schoolhouse. The eleven boys consistently caused trouble, but their actions became amplified if the pair of girls led the charge. Even the older students, who attended classes at the local high school, happily created distance from the instigators.

By the end of the first day, Belle's head ached. She struggled to remain focused on her individual studies when the teacher worked with the older students. She found the second and third grade studies to be more interesting. She closed her workbook and began doodling on its cover.

The teacher's escalated shouts made her stop. Nearing the end of the school day, some of the students became restless. A fifth grader kept interrupting the students around her. She talked out of turn and refused to comply. After multiple unheeded threats, the teacher walked to the girl's desk and pulled her to her feet.

"Attention," the teacher screamed at the young student. "I will not tolerate disruption. You will speak only when spoken to! You will only answer when asked! You will be quiet when told!"

Her face twisted and flushed. She shook her head and pounded her feet so hard that a few strands of hair fell from her tight bun. She brushed the annoyance from her face twice before tucking them behind her ear.

From where Belle sat, it appeared as though the teacher pushed the girl against the wall. She unwrapped a cake of lye soap in such a flurry that the string and waxed brown paper floated toward the floor. Without warning, the teacher shoved the soap into the girl's mouth. She knelt to gather the litter and used the string to tie the girl's hands behind her back. With escalated frustration, the teacher crumbled the brittle paper into a tight ball and tossed it in the wastebasket.

"Any questions?" she chastised the classroom. All glances slid toward the floor.

Belle lifted her head and stared at the horror on the young girl's face. Her eyes watered from the fumes. Her lips turned red. A wide band of pinkish saliva covered her chin and dripped onto her light yellow cotton top. The stain grew wider, deeper with every drop. Belle felt sorry for her. Suddenly, the teacher pounded her fist on Belle's desk. She flinched.

"Stop staring at her!" screamed Miss Adelade.

Belle lowered her eyes and head without question. She watched her own tears dot the surface of her desk, thankful they ran clear.

When the bell rang, Belle ran through the door, across the yard and into her cottage before Henry could gather his books from his desk. She threw her body onto her bed and sobbed into her pillow. Her workbook lay next to her.

"Did you draw these?" Madeline, her bed partner whispered.

Belle managed to pull her face from the dampened pillow. She wiped her nose with her hand. "Yes," she answered between sniffles.

"From memory or were you looking at it?"

Belle sat up and propped her head against the headboard. She watched Madeline's hand run over the dragonfly etchings as if she was petting the insect.

Belle shrugged. "I just drew it."

"You weren't looking at it?"

"No." Belle wrinkled her nose uncertain of her question.

Madeline pointed to the two dots that Belle added to the dragonfly's tail. "What are these?"

"Two white dots on his body." Belle's face remained furrowed.

Belle looked toward the window where she first saw the dragonfly. She took Madeline's hand.

"Follow me." They walked to the window. Belle pointed to the window weight settled into the lower corner. "He sits here. Sometimes, he is here all day. Sometimes, I don't see him at all."

"So did you sit here and draw him?"

Belle laughed. "No silly, I drew that picture today at school when..." she lowered her voice. "When that girl got in trouble."

A group of older girls walked into the dormitory interrupting their conversation. They surrounded the soap girl from school. With her lips swollen and face covered with red blotches, Gayle struggled to speak.

"I can't believe that witch made you do that," one friend said.

"What can we do to help you, Gayle?" Another girl asked.

"I think we need to teach that teacher a lesson," added a third.

"I know just who to ask," the last said. "Come on girls. Let's go talk to the Freshmen."

The three girls walked out of the room leaving their friend to suffer alone. Belle wanted to approach her, but was uncertain of what to say. She decided to keep her distance. After all, she was in seventh grade, quite a bit older and non-approachable in Belle's eyes.

That night, Belle struggled to sleep. She wondered about the punishment Gayle received. She thought it to be excessive.

Gayle's circle of friends whispered tales of revenge far into the night. No one seemed to notice the number of coughing fits that befell Gayle. Her eyes burned, itched, and wept. Her eyelids began to swell. Her irritated throat caused her voice to rasp.

Long after her friends fell asleep, Gayle struggled to breathe. She thought she might feel better if she walked a bit, perhaps drank some water. As soon as she stood, the room began to spin and faded to black. Her body hit the floor with a loud thud.

The room awakened to a loud scream. Gayle convulsed on the floor while her friends stood helplessly over her.

"Get some help!" One girl screeched.

The Matron entered and flooded the room with light. She reacted quickly.

"Grab her feet." She directed an onlooker. "Lift her head." She pointed to another. "Get the nurse." She turned to Belle.

Belle ran so fast down the staircase, out the door, and across the lawn to the hospital that she felt as if she floated. She began to yell for the nurse before she entered the building, so by the time she touched the doorknob the nurse met her with an opened door.

"Come quickly. It's Gayle. She can't breathe."

It was then Belle felt the pain from her ill-fitting shoes. The blisters on her heels made her skin feel tight and swollen. She struggled to catch the nurse, watching the distance grow between them with each step.

By the time Belle stepped onto the front porch, the nurse carried Gayle through the door. The Headmaster appeared without a word and carried the unconscious girl to the hospital.

"It's a reaction to the lye." The nurse explained. "She must be allergic to it."

The girls were hushed to immediate silence. The Matron reassured Gayle's friends that all would be fine, although her words lacked confidence.

Belle heard one of Gayle's friends cry long after the Matron ordered sleep. Belle silently prayed for Gayle's recovery.

The young girls' cottage hurried to join the other students at breakfast. Gayle's friends seemed especially anxious to talk with the Freshmen. The small group gathered at the end of a long table warning others not to join them.

"This is a closed meeting," they announced at least six times.

News of Gayle's allergic reaction traveled through the Home like fire through a rainless forest. By the time most finished eating their oatmeal, a dry hush blanketed the room. Only the Freshmen chatted, led by the pair of girls. When the Freshmen stood, all stood, and when they left the dining room, all followed.

With the high school students departed nearly an hour prior, no one stood in the way of the eldest students on the property. The thirteen seemed larger, taller, more daunting outside of the absent shadow of the seniors, juniors, and sophomores.

When the Freshmen led the charge toward the schoolhouse, no child questioned why they did not go to their classroom in the basement of the main house or why one boy stayed behind.

The large student body entered the schoolhouse. Thick tension coated the air leaving the light to appear strained and reduced to a near shadow. Revenge bent the feelings of frustration and anger. Miss Adelade would certainly pay for her error.

To the surprise of all, a tall, gaunt, bald-headed man stood in the front of the room. He cleared his voice several times before speaking.

"My name is Mr. Carl. As of today, I have accepted the position as your tutor. Miss Adelade," he covered his mouth with his hand and coughed again. "Miss Adelade is no longer assigned."

The students groaned. The news should have calmed the situation, but the opposite occurred. The Freshmen boys slammed desks together and shouted words unknown to Belle. Their red faces, warped by uncontrolled hatred, looked as though they would explode. Voices escalated. Many younger students huddled in the corner covering their ears and faces from the onslaught of flying books, pencils, chalk and erasers.

In the mayhem, no one noticed the entrance of the Headmaster until he pounded his fist on the chalkboard. A loud crack reverberated through the room. The students froze in mid motion. Some held objects in the air, while others stood in a wind-up stance about to hurl the object drawn behind them. Immediately the room fell silent.

Belle stared at the damaged chalkboard. Enoch's fist made a deep depression into the half-inch thick slate creating a web of erratic fissures. His second strike rattled the board until a large piece fell to the floor. The slate shattered onto the floor in one-hundred grey shards.

"CLEAN THIS UP!" His voice rattled the windows.

He snatched every Freshmen boy and one of the girls by the hair, ears, and clothes. He threw them against the wall.

The new teacher, wide-eyed and awe struck, stood motionless as the younger students gathered the sharp pieces of slate from the floor under his feet. Drops of blood from the pieces speckled the floor. No one made a sound or made mention of his or her pricked fingers.

The Headmaster shoved the Freshmen out the door. When the children heard the slamming of the front door, all exhaled together. The sigh helped relieve the tension, although the pressure was too much for the new teacher. Without a word, he gathered his books, papers, and personal belongings, placed them into his bag and left the room.

Slowly the students started to move. They reorganized the desks, chairs, books, papers and pencils. Belle picked up the chalk and erasers. No one spoke over the squeaks, pops, and chirps of metal scraping across the wood floor. Soon all was in order. The children sat at their desks and opened their workbooks. No one dared to speak.

Without warning, the missing Freshman entered the room. The students buried their faces into their studies pretending not to notice him. He slid a wooden crate to the left of the doorway and stood on it. He pulled his fists to his chin and waited.

Enoch never saw what or who hit him. When he passed through the door, the boy punched Enoch in the face with all his strength. The Headmaster hit the floor with a thud.

In the days to follow, a third teacher came. Enoch beat and pressured nearly half of the classroom for the name of his assailant, but the children banded together. No one broke. No one gave in to Enoch's force. The Headmaster had begun to lose control.

12

Rule #8–All strangers must be greeted with respect and cheerfulness.

"Craig is awake!" The loud cry filled the building. "He's awake."

Belle watched the girl's long blonde curls bounce with every stride. She ran through the dining room shouting the news repeatedly. Within minutes, she disappeared through the door.

"Who is Craig?" Belle asked the little girl sitting next to her.

She shook her head and shrugged her shoulders. "I don't know."

Belle asked several people surrounding her, but no one seemed to know the answer. Far in her peripheral vision, she saw Sophie, arms flying, and echoing the other's news of Craig's awakening. Belle rushed to Sophie to hear more. Sophie grabbed her shoulders and shook Belle's little body with uncontrollable excitement.

"He's awake." Tears streamed down her face.

"Who's Craig?"

Sophie's posture stiffened at the question. Smiling warmly, she remembered the accident happened before Belle and Henry arrived.

"His parents work here. His mother works in the kitchen and his father oversees the farm and the equipment. Craig is their son and the most adorable four-year-old you would ever want to know."

"He loves to play games especially with us older girls." She laughed, "And we love to play with him. Honestly, Belle, wait until you meet him. He's so sweet."

They walked out of the dining room just in time to see the girl with the long blonde hair run out the front door with Craig's mother.

"Come on," she motioned for Belle to follow her. "Let me show you something."

They walked to the center of the circular staircase. Sophie stopped below the rotunda and pointed to a stain in the center of the carpet.

"What's that?" Belle bent over to get a closer look at the discoloration.

"Blood," Sophie answered automatically.

Belle gasped and placed her hands over her mouth. She felt queasy.

Sophie patted her shoulder. "It's okay now. We can talk about it. He's awake."

Sophie told Belle the story of the accident, being certain to explain every minute detail. The pair sat Indian style on the worn carpet with the bloodstain between them.

"It was late morning, not quite lunch time," she began. "It was raining so we could not play outside. Craig's parents, who were also dorm parents, told us to use our imagination and make up our own games and their little boy loved to be the object of our games.

"That particular day we were playing a game of tag. We were not supposed to play on the staircase, but we did it anyway. The house was loud with everyone playing their own imaginary games, so we thought we could bend the rules a little.

"I was near the bottom of the staircase and everyone else was near the top. Craig was in the middle and running toward the top as fast as his little legs would go. One of the other girls was closing in on him. He was about to be tagged and he knew it.

"Nearly out of breath as he neared the top step, he began to squeal. He knew he would be "safe" if he made it to the landing. Just as he was about to make it, he was tagged. She only meant to touch him, to tag him, but it ended up to be more of a push. Little Craig lost his balance and went over the top railing."

Belle hung on ever word. She gasped at the thought of the little boy falling three floors. She drew in her breath and held it until Sophie continued.

"He wore long pants that were a bit large for him. When he fell over the banister, his pant leg caught on the metal support bar up there." Both lifted their faces to see the metal structure supporting the

99

staircase. "It twisted his body changing his direction to head first." Sophie pointed to the stain. "He landed right here."

"It happened so fast, there was nothing any of us could do. I was the closest so I came to him first." Sophie covered her face and tried to shake the horrid memory. "There was so much blood. He looked so tiny, so frail. We ran to get help as quickly as possible." Sophie lowered her voice. "He suffered a skull fracture. He's been in a coma for weeks."

Belle could feel her pain, her concern, and mostly her guilt. She tried to sound cheerful. "But Craig is awake."

A thin smile covered Sophie's face. "Yes, he is. Thank you, God. Craig is awake."

They sat in silence for a few minutes. Finally, Sophie added, "I just hope he can move."

When Belle retold the story to Henry, her eyes opened wide in the middle of the story. "Henry, we saw that little boy in the hospital. Sophie said she and her friend, along with his parents, took turns sitting with him. That is why there was a chair in there."

Within the next few days, all of the children celebrated Craig's full recovery. It was nothing short of a miracle. Nearly the entire Home stopped by his hospital bed to wish him well. Some shared their fruit, bread, or bits of fresh veggies they had stolen from the garden. A few smuggled some cookies to him. That treat was Craig's favorite.

Belle visited him often over the next few weeks. They became fast friends. She shared her story of the first time she saw Craig. Remarkably, in her young age, she knew not to mention the amount of blood.

It was not long before Craig began to play again with the older children. They invited Belle to join them. She happily accepted.

His parents warned the children constantly. "Be careful. Not too rough. He's still recovering. No more stairs." His mother, rightly so, seemed especially anxious. She murmured often about leaving the Home to keep Craig safe.

A few weeks later, one of the Matrons gathered the older boys and called for a surprise inspection. She clapped her hands and chased them into their cottage.

"Quickly, now. Wash up a bit, and put on your best clothes. When you are ready come to main house." She hurried down the stairs to ready the inspection room.

She rushed into the large empty room and fanned the curtains to shake off the cobwebs. A shower of dust flew into the air and caused her to sneeze. A few older girls giggled in the far corner. They sat upon a large rolled rug.

"Out you two go," she said. "This room is to be ready for a special boy's inspection."

Knowing inspection to be a code word for a possible adoption, the girls scrambled off the rolled-up rug and peered around the receiving room corner for a peek at the adoptive couple. The pair sat close together in silence. The man had his arm placed around the woman's shoulder. She stared out the window.

When the front door opened, one by one, the boys marched into the adjacent room. The couple watched the parade while the two girls continued to snicker.

Once the boys settled into a long row, the Matron gave her final advice. "This is important. You know it is not very often that we have a request for an older child. This couple has a very sick son and needs help on their farm. Left with only a daughter, they find themselves in an awful situation. Rather than indenture a young boy, they have applied for adoption of a more mature boy."

She shook her finger in the air. "This is a great opportunity for one of you. Be on your best behavior. It may be you that will be leaving with them and traveling to their Salem, Ohio, farm." She placed her hands on her hips. "Smile. Be courteous. Luck may be yours today."

She walked through the open doorway and summoned the man and his wife to join her for the inspection. She introduced the couple to the children in the room, took a few steps backwards, and wrung her hands as they walked through the line.

Henry was the fourth boy in the line up. Having never been a part of this ritual he stammered in place. The Matron's silent glance scorned him and his immobile feet fell asleep.

He managed a smile as the couple looked closely at him. He felt their eyes move over every part of his body. Following the routine of the three prior, he stepped forward, turned around, and held out his arms. He felt the woman's fingers brush his hair. It sent a stiff chill down his spine. His position remained fixed.

The boy to his right nudged him in the ribcage and motioned for him to turn around and move back into the line. The couple stopped in front of Jack, who stood two boys left of Henry.

They called Jack to step forward. The man felt his shoulders, arms and legs. He inspected his teeth, ears, and eyes. He asked a few simple questions about Jack's farm knowledge. Jack managed nervous answers through a forced grin.

The man turned toward the Matron and pointed to Jack, "This one."

Just like that, Jack was adopted. The new family left the room without looking at all the boys. Low murmurs and grumbling came from the end of the line.

"What's wrong with us?"

"Yeah. Do we stink or something?"

The two girls, who witnessed the event, giggled as they entered the room. They paid no attention to the solemn attitude.

"Out of the way, boys," they demanded.

They waved their hands to move the crowd away from the rolled rug. Both picked up the edge and held fast.

"Ready? One, two...three."

They snapped and shook the rug as quickly as they could. Little Craig rolled out of the center, soaked with sweat, for having been rolled up too long in the heavy wool rug.

The children erupted with laughter. The mood quickly moved from somber to celebratory. Everyone tousled Craig's hair and looked into his smiling little face. His sparkling eyes made every boy forget their rejection, at least for the moment.

13

Rule #9–All money made is the property of the
Fairmount Children's Home.

"Pick one." The leader of cottage #2 held up six
blades of grass, flush at one end. Each of the six
boys selected a piece. After comparing their choices,
Henry and Joey came up with the two shortest pieces.

"Haha. You two get to climb over the fence." The
leader's chant made the other three boys laugh.

Henry's face flushed. "Fine," he spewed. "But
whoever finds the biggest one gets a piece of bread
or fruit from the others tonight."

The smirks that once covered the boy's faces slid
to dejected frowns. Henry bit his lip to suppress
his grin.

"Agreed?" Henry shouted. His stomach rumbled in hopes of extra food.

After murmurs of agreement, the boys walked toward the pumpkin patch. The responsibility of selecting, picking, carrying, and stocking the market for the upcoming Halloween season fell on them.

"Why is it every year we are the ones who have to do most of the work?" one of the boys grumbled.

"I guess it's because we are good at it," Joey added trying to sound cheerful.

"Button it up, Joey," he scoffed. "You can't pick up a fly."

Henry shot Joey a warning look and shook his head. He mouthed the words, "It's not worth it" as a final punctuation. Henry did not feel like fighting today.

The boys walked through the sprawling vines and sticky leaves. Each kept their own count while Henry and Joey scrambled over the pasture fence to inspect the straggled tendrils.

"I've got twenty three."

"Seventeen here."

"Thirty one more over here."

"I have nineteen, so far."

Henry walked through multiple vines pulverized under the cattle's weight. A few scrawny trailers survived the onslaught of hooves and mouths, but the pumpkins suffered severely from the lack of nourishment.

"Stupid cows," Henry whined as he hacked through the half-dead plants.

"Yeah, can you imagine how many more we could have had?" Joey added.

"How many do you have over there?" Another boy from the patch asked.

Henry responded, "Five."

Joey added, "Seven and one huge one."

"Really?" The four boys replied in unison. They scrambled to the edge of the fence for a look. "Hold it up, if you can." They laughed.

Joey knelt to the ground and began to moan. The boys watched with vested interest. They observed as Joey struggled with the heavy weight. Soon, he cleared the leaves from their view and held up an orange pumpkin about the size of a softball. They groaned from the trickery.

After careful inspection, the boys counted over one hundred pumpkins, many bright orange and ready for harvest. The oldest boy found the largest pumpkin and all groaned of the lighter dinner they would have tonight for accepting Henry's proposal. Yet, no one felt more disappointment than Henry. He needed that nourishment to feed his growing muscle mass.

They pushed the cart close to the vines and began to gather the choice lot. With the cart filled beyond the top, Henry and another boy pushed it toward the market situated directly in front of the Home. Forcing the cart through the last few feet of the gravel parking lot proved the most strenuous, but together the boys managed to reach their goal.

The girls finished stocking the baskets with tomatoes, turnips, parsnips, kohlrabi, peppers, and onions, while the boys filled the three large bins with pumpkins, each bin priced according to size. Henry brought the final cart half full across the lawn by himself. Joey rested under the shade of the nearby maple tree while the other four boys teased the girls.

The last four pumpkins on the bottom of the cart were twice the size of the others and Henry decided they should command a higher price. He positioned them beside the mum and hay bale display.

"How much for that big one?"

The man's voice made Henry jump. "Uhhh. A dollar more than that one." Henry pointed toward the bin filled with the largest pumpkins.

The man laughed. He pulled out a few bills from his pocket and gave them to Henry. "I'll take all four of these big ones."

Henry wiped the sweat from his brow and wished the man had decided before he unloaded them. He drew in a deep breath and began to load them back in the cart.

"No need to cart them. I'll have my boys carry them to the car." He whistled to his sons. Two boys ran to their father's side. "Take these to the car boys while I look around at the rest of the produce."

The man patted Henry's arm. "You do a fine day's job, young man. A good day of hard labor will keep you strong of body and mind." His smile was warm.

"Thank you, sir."

Henry looked at the money in his hand. The man gave him an extra dollar. Immediately, he wanted to put that dollar into his pocket and save it for a movie, but the moment he thought of his own pleasure, he flooded with guilt. He ran to the man's car.

"Sir! Sir!"

The man looked at Henry curiously. His smile grew wider. "Yes?"

"You, um, you gave me too much money." Henry held out his hand exposing the moist, crumpled bill.

"No," he whispered. "I believe I did not give you enough." He winked and placed an additional dollar in Henry's palm. "Honesty is the best policy, I always say, and I will reward you for that."

Henry stood with his mouth open and feet frozen in place. He would never forget that man's kindness and generosity. Henry caught sight of the Headmaster walking toward him.

"What did that man say to you, Henry?" His voice quiet and accusatory.

Henry straightened his stance. "He paid me a compliment."

"Oh?"

"Yes, he said I was a hard worker."

"Anything else?" The gap in his teeth made his question sound like a hiss.

"Yes." Henry hesitated, smiled and held up a dollar bill in his hand. His voice, slightly louder with pride, echoed through the market. "He gave me a tip."

Enoch reeled at the comment. He saw Henry as only a troublemaker, certainly not a young man of value. He wrinkled his face to a frown.

"Well, do you remember Rule #9?" He held out his open hand, waiting.

Henry clenched his fist and watched the frown on Enoch's face shift to a twisted smirk. Once again, he got the best of Henry. Henry slapped the wrinkled money into Enoch's hand and walked away.

Henry wiped the nervous, hate-filled sweat from his forehead. An odd sneer covered Henry's face as he shoved his hands into his pockets and walked back toward the pumpkin patch. He squeezed his hand around the extra dollar, generously given and craftily hidden.

Later that evening in the dining room, the pumpkin patch pickers sat in silence. No one complained as each boy surrendered a piece of bread. The victor smiled at his growing pile. "Hey, no one is giving up their apple tonight?"

"Not I." Henry tossed his comment over his shoulder, sinking his teeth deep into the apple's skin.

"Me either," added Joey. "You can have the stinking old bread. It's stale anyway." His confidence grew with the added comment.

Henry chuckled at his friend. Since the day Henry helped Joey dry his sheet, the two had become good friends. Henry ignored most of the derogatory comments from the older crowd. Part of him hated the fact that he was lumped in with the rest of the "watering cans" or "pee team," but the bulk of his being felt sorry for Joey.

Joey's buckled posture accentuated his weak exterior. His red hair and freckles seemed to draw only negative comments, although his natural resolve thwarted them. His stark difference from Henry's strong, erect physique cast suspicion on those who saw their relationship as odd. Yet Henry respected Joey – for his inner strength, his ability to unhear what had been said, to shake off the insults, and move not only past, but also beyond their ramifications. Their friendship became mutually beneficial.

Henry's stomach rumbled for an hour after his head hit the pillow. Soon thereafter, Joey turned to face him in the dark.

"I can't sleep, Henry."

"Why?"

"Because your stomach is keeping me awake."

Henry placed his hands over his belly. He felt the growls of hunger move beneath his fingers.

"I'm sorry," he whispered. "I'm starving."

"You shouldn't have made that bet then." Disgust laced Joey's tone.

"I planned to be the winner," his voice echoed through the darkened room.

"Shhhhh...." came a voice from another bed.

Henry lay on his back, twisted to his left side. He threw the covers from his body and then quickly repositioned on his stomach, hoping the mattress would muffle his hunger grumbles.

Finally, after another fifteen grueling minutes, Joey whispered, "Okay, Henry. What can we do about it?"

In the calmness of the room, a soft light glimmering in the distance made Henry smile. Faint whispers drifted across Joey's unsuspecting ears.

"I have an idea."

Joey sat straight up in their bed. He loved Henry's adventures. He threw the covers from his body and planted his feet on the floor.

"I'm ready," he whispered.

Henry knelt under his bed and felt the exposed bedsprings. The coolness of the flashlight handle made his fingers tingle. He tugged on the object until it released. He grabbed Joey's arm and tiptoed out of the room, down the stairs, and out the front door.

"Where are we going?" Joey asked, although no reply came.

They walked across the graveled play area toward the boiler room in darkness and silence. Joey struggled to keep pace with Henry's stride. He bumped into his back after a sudden stop.

"Where are we going?" he asked again.

Henry turned to his friend and placed his index finger over his lips. "To get something to eat."

They entered the tunnel in the boiler room and followed it toward the main house. They slipped past the door leading to the "dungeon" ignoring the captured runaway's pounding and cries, until they crept deep into the tunnel.

Henry turned on the flashlight. Twenty rats ran from the light, disappearing overhead and around the next corner. Joey struggled to suppress a scream, but did not want to reveal their covert mission. When they reached the main house, Henry turned off the light. They made their way toward the food storage room.

Greeted by an oversized lock on the door, Joey groaned. Henry quickly chastised him and pulled a piece of pipe out of the back of his pants. He lifted it in the air, placed it into the middle of the hook and pulled it toward the floor. The lock's snap barely made a sound. Both boys smiled.

A pathetic squeak came from the door as the boys opened it. Henry pulled it closed behind them and turned on his flashlight once again. To their surprise, the shelves were nearly empty.

"What the..."

"Shhhh..." Joey chastised. "What was that?"

A sound that came from the tunnel rattled through the basement. They froze. Henry's hands began to shake, although he managed to turn off the flashlight. Their hearts pulsed in their throats. Henry struggled with the rising bubbles, while Joey struggled to catch his breath. In the darkness, the boys thrust their last ditch effort fueled by insatiable hunger and lunged at unknown food objects. They opened the door and ran through the dark tunnel ignoring the squeal from an occasional trampled rat, each clutching their prize. When they reached the door in the boiler room, they collapsed. Several minutes of taxed breaths passed before either managed to speak. Finally, Joey held up his prize in the dim light. Surprised at his find, he nudged Henry to look at his box.

"I got bran flakes."

Henry hurriedly turned on his flashlight. The clear jar felt cool in his hands. The light-colored contents remained solid as he shook it.

Raising his voice, he said, "I've got..." He spun the jar to read the label. "Mayonnaise," his tone fell like a weight. He wrinkled his nose and then shrugged his shoulders. His stomach rumbled.

Joey, overcome by the need to encourage Henry's choice, said, "I like mayonnaise."

Henry smiled at his friend's attempt at optimism and wondered what they could do with the strange combination of their midnight raid. He unscrewed the lid while Joey attempted to open the box quietly. The boys took turns plunging their hands into the jar coating their fingers with the mayonnaise, and then repeated the dipping action into the box of bran flakes. Henry turned off the flashlight and the two boys spent the next ten minutes filling their empty stomachs by licking the concoction from their encrusted fingers. Not a bit of mayonnaise or bran flakes remained.

Joey snuck the evidence to the trashcan in the kitchen. He placed the jar inside the box, removed several objects from the garbage can, and replaced them to cover the evidence, confident that their raid would go unnoticed and prayerfully unpunished. They tiptoed back to their bed and attempted to sleep.

As their stomachs wrenched, they need not worry about the consequences for their theft. The taste served as punishment enough.

14

Belle stood in the open basement doorway peering into the darkness. An odd fragrance surrounded her. She thought she heard distant thumping. She slipped through the entrance and crept quietly down the basement steps.

Alone in the dark, she waited for her eyes to adjust. Slowly, a dim light in the tunnel begged her to enter. She slipped off her clumsy shoes, pattered down the corridor, and listened for the root of the sound. She followed the tunnels to each building. She doubled back twice, mistaking the origin as it grew more distant. Occasionally, when the thumping halted, she sat on the floor and waited for it to commence. Certain the noise was not something mechanical due to its irregularity, she grew more determined to find the source. She imagined it to be someone in distress.

The pounding gained strength as she followed the hospital tunnel. She reflected on her time spent there and whispered a quick prayer for Craig's full recovery. Her feet led her to a closed door. She pressed her ear against it and listened. A large bump from the other side made her jump.

"Who...is...in...in there?" She hesitated. Her voice came barely above a whisper.

"Me." A surprised boy answered.

"Me who?"

"John."

"John? What are you doing in there?"

"Being punished," he spit the hate-filled words.

"For what?" She asked with innocence.

"For running away."

"How did you get here?"

"They found me and brought me back."

"Why?" Belle tried to make sense of his story.

"I guess they thought I'd be better off here."

His angry tone frightened Belle. She stammered for a reply. She could think of nothing to say.

"Who are you anyway?"

Feeling the sudden urge to flee, Belle struggled with her response. Since he did not know who she was maybe she should run. John was a troublemaker as well as the reason for at least two of Henry's beatings. Tears of frustration fell from her eyes.

"Hey," he shouted. "What did you do? Leave me here to die?"

"No," She retorted without thinking. "I'm still here."

"Well, are you gonna help me or not, Belle?"

She jumped at the sound of her name. She wished she did not have a curious nature.

"Belle?" His voice softened. "I've been in here for two days. Please, please, help me."

"What can I do?"

"Look around. Is there a lock?"

Struggling to see in the dark, she used both hands to aid her sight. She felt a long strap hinge plate. At its end was a ring with a long piece of wood shoved into it securing the door.

Confident in what she felt, she whispered. "No lock, John. Only a piece of wood stuck in a metal ring."

"Really?"

"Yes. Just a piece of wood."

"Great! Pull it out."

Belle struggled to reach the purposeful elevated mechanism. "I can hardly reach it."

"Look around for something to stand on."

"Okay. I'll be right back."

"Belle, don't leave me."

The desperation in his voice made Belle tear. "I... won't," she whispered. "I just need to find something to stand on."

She raced up the stairs to the main floor of the hospital, hoping no one would hear or see her. Her elevated heartbeat throbbed in her throat. She held her breath as she opened the door. It was dark.

She ran room to room looking for something, anything to help her reach the object. She found several boxes but they collapsed when she tested them. Desperation pushed her forward. She rounded the last corner and tripped over a small bucket in the center of the walkway, spewing water onto the floor. She felt a drip on top of her head.

"A roof leak," she chuckled. "What luck."

She picked up the bucket marked with an oversized red letter H, dumped the remaining water, and ran back down to the basement. Pride lifted her spirit. When she reached the door, it was quiet. She struggled to catch her breath.

"I...I found a bucket."

"Great." John sounded relieved. "Now pull that wedge out."

Belle placed the bucket on the cement floor and stood on it. She had to move it several times for the best position. John encouraged her from the opposite side. After barely a minute of pushing, pulling, tapping, pounding and anyway else Belle could think of, she hung her head in defeat. John grew anxious in the silence.

"Did you get it?"

Belle started to cry. "I...I can't. It won't move."

John wanted to scream. He pounded his fist on the door. He listened to her sobs. Then, he remembered the spoon. He ran to the back corner of the cement-block room and rummaged his hands over the dirt floor until he felt the cold metal. He ran to the door.

With his spirits lifted, he tried to encourage Belle. "Don't cry, Belle. I found something that may help."

"Huh?" She wiped her nose.

John dropped to the doorway and started to dig a space beneath the door. The shallow cup of the spoon helped him move the hardened earth at the entrance.

Finally, after removing a small bit of dirt, he pushed the utensil under the door.

Belle jumped when the spoon handle appeared from the other side. She pulled. Inch by inch, the spoon moved until with the final tug, she had it in her hands.

"I got it!" Her loud voice echoed through the tunnel. She froze.

"Belle?"

At the mention of her name, Belle sprung into action. She tried the handle first, with little success. Then, she tried the bowl with less success and returned to using the handle. The wedge began to move.

"I'm getting it. It's moving."

"Great. Keep trying."

After another minute, Belle pulled the wedge from its place. "Got it."

She swung the door open. Her mouth dropped at the sight and smell of the room. John's face, ground with dirt, beamed at his helper. He threw his arms around her.

"Thank you, Belle." He shook his head. "Thank you."

The sound of a slamming door overhead changed their faces. Suddenly faced with the gravity of the situation, they began to run. After a few steps, John grabbed Belle's arm.

"Where's the wedge?"

"Huh?" Her heart raced. Horrified by the thoughts of a second beating, she could not understand his question. She stood with her mouth hanging open. Her frightened stare made John push for the answer.

"The wedge. Where is it?"

Belle lifted her hand without a word and opened it. John grabbed the wedge from her open palm and ran back toward the dungeon.

"Go! Run! I'll catch up."

Belle watched him run into the darkness and disappear from her sight. She listened until they stopped. She turned and raced through the hospital channel until it intersected with the main tunnel. She ran without recollection of the flight, breath, or sight. When she made it to the basement of her cottage, her shoes were gone.

Fear of certain discovery made her shiver. She wet her pants. She cried. She tried to listen for John. She heard nothing. Her lungs screamed for air. She burst into the washroom, filthy, dusty, and bleeding.

She pulled off her bottoms and ran to the sink to wash her face, hands, and any body part that she could. The spoon rattled in the bottom of the porcelain bowl. The running water washed the mud and dirt from its surface. The long silver handle, covered with embossed flowers and vines, gleamed like new. Carved in the oval bowl was the main house of the Home along with the words — Fairmount Children's Home Alliance, O.

"What are you doing?" Gayle asked.

Belle tossed her pants in the sink to cover the spoon. The water soaked the fabric. The smell of fresh urine filled the room.

"Huh?" Guilt lit Belle's eyes.

"Baths aren't until tomorrow." Belle's roommate announced.

"I know, but," Belle looked down at the blood on her leg and hands. "I'm bleeding," she said more to herself than to Gayle.

"I see that. What happened?" Gayle looked at Belle with great suspicion. "What were you doing?"

"Huh?" Belle's innocent face revealed her poor attempt at lying. "I was, ummm, playing in the dirt."

"Where?" Gayle placed her hands on her hips. "I didn't see you anywhere."

Belle could only think of one place that many would not see her, and that place happened to be, "The barn."

"What were you doing in the barn to get so dirty?" Gayle wrinkled her nose, "What's that awful smell?"

"Pee," spilled from Belle's lips without a thought. She quickly added, "I was playing with Star and she peed on me."

"Oh, yuk." Gayle stuck out her tongue. "That pony is gross."

Belle suddenly defensive added, "No she's not. It was my fault really."She lowered her voice.

"Where are your shoes?" They both looked at her bare, dirty feet. Gayle waved her hand in front of her face. "Oh never mind. Don't even tell me she peed on your feet."

Belle shrugged her shoulders.

"Get cleaned up. I won't tell anyone you used water." She started to walk out the door. "I wouldn't want to sleep covered with pony pee either."

"Thank you," Belle called to her disappearing friend.

15

John ran back to the dungeon door. He closed it as quietly as his adrenaline allowed. He fumbled with the wedge, dropping it twice, until finally securing it in position. He grabbed the handle of the bucket and ran back the tunnel.

When he reached the intersection into the main tunnel, he ran the opposite direction as Belle. He ran past the pathways that led to cottages #3 and #2, until finally resting at the entrance to cottage #1—the high school boy's dorm. He slipped through the doorway and ran up the stairs.

Just before stepping out onto the main floor, John paused at the door. He listened for any movement, any sound, and when he heard none he opened the door. Two boys sat in the common area, both with their backs to him. He quietly placed the bucket in the back hall and left the way he came. Knowing the Freshmen's reputation for mischief and trouble, he felt no guilt placing the incriminating evidence in their cottage. Happy with his detective work, he slowed his pace a bit.

He followed the main tunnel back to the main building. He walked up the staircase and down the hall toward the front door. The children who saw him paid no attention, and neither did the staff. Just before stepping out the front door, he gathered a throw and decorative pillow from the receiving room. With his bedding in hand, he slipped under the front porch. There he would wait for his brothers or Henry.

His stomach ached, but his body moved beyond the hunger pains he endured while alone in the dungeon. He waited for the sound of children's voices for nearly an hour. His eyes began to droop. He laid his head on the pillow and fell fast asleep.

When he woke, it was dark and very quiet. He crawled to the edge of the porch and looked across the front lawn. He saw no one. He tried to find the moon, but the clouds covered its face. He guessed the time to be nearly midnight. He was wrong.

Wondering his next move, he sat out on the open lawn. The autumn grass smelled sweet and felt cool. He spread out on the dew and enjoyed the smell of fresh air for only a few moments until he heard approaching voices. He crawled back under the porch, rustling a few of the bushes.

"Who's there?" a boy asked as his voice squeaked.

John held his breath and crawled back against the stone foundation of the house. A rat slid across his hand. He cupped his mouth to suppress any sound.

"I said, who is there?" The voice drew closer. The rustling bushes echoed his announcement.

A distant boy called, "Ray? What are you doing?"

"I saw someone crawl under here." He pointed under the porch.

John's instincts begged him to run, but fear kept him bound. He held his breath, awaiting his discovery.

"Aw, come on, Ray. We've got work to do." Disgust filled his tone. "You always look for a reason to get out of work."

"But, I'm telling you there's someone under here."

"Yeah, yeah, yeah right. No one ever believes you. You tell too many stories."

A second boy joined Ray by the edge of the porch. John counted their feet. Sweat beaded on his forehead and slid down the front of his face. His eyes burned from the salt and dirt. He dared not move. He dared not breathe. He prayed for them to leave.

"What are you guys doing?" A third boy chastised. "I am not doing morning chores by myself. We have eggs to fetch, cows to milk, pigs to feed, and you two idiots are just standing there." His voice elevated with each word.

"But..." Ray began.

"I'm not asking. Get over here, now. Or I'm going to cook all of the eggs for myself."

The thought of eating eggs made all of their mouths water, including John's. He could not recall the last time he ate eggs. Used on rare occasions in the kitchen for baked goods, they were mostly gathered and sold in the market to raise money for the Home.

124

John placed his hands over his rumbling stomach. The thought of fresh cooked eggs made him restless and anxious to follow the boys.

Since dawn appeared to be at least thirty minutes away, he felt comfortable following them under cover of the darkness. He crawled from under the porch and slipped behind a large maple tree.

The three boys joined at least four more, although it was difficult to count the true number in the faded light. Once the group moved a safe distance away, John ran quietly behind them, ducking behind trees, bushes, or buildings along the way.

One by one, the boys entered the chicken coop. John waited for what seemed thirty minutes until finally they emerged, each carrying two large baskets overflowing with eggs.

"Eggs," he whispered as he licked his lips. "Now, how do I get some?"

Just as the thought crossed his famished mind an opportunity presented itself. One of the boys stopped directly behind the silo.

"Come over here." The leader demanded.

"But why?" Someone asked. "We always put them over there." He pointed to his left.

"Because if we keep repeating the pattern, we will get caught, stupid." He shook his head. "Do you want to lose your food source?"

"No."

"No way."

"Nah."

"We would starve."

"Okay, then," the leader continued. "Listen to what I'm telling you. Put them here in the weeds.

We will come back after we slop the pigs and milk the cows." He shook his finger at them. "Remember what I told you. We are gonna split up. No clowning around." He lifted his finger in the air. "Today it's all business and we will do it fast. And our reward will be a dozen eggs to split between us."

John listened with great interest. He wondered how the Freshmen boys seemed to have more energy and better strength than the rest. Now he understood. They were stealing food. It was genius.

The leader continued, "I have a small fire burning in the field corn. I took a one-gallon can from the garbage pile and have it ready to use as a pan. Sam stole a few potatoes too. Ray, don't forget to grab a piece of the salt lick. We're gonna need it for the potatoes." He clapped his hands. "Everyone ready?"

All joined in the answer, "Yes."

"Okay, then. Let's get this done, so we can eat like kings this morning."

They picked up their slightly lighter baskets and walked them into the main building. John waited until they reappeared and split into two groups. The smallest group of three went into the hog barn to feed the pigs. The rest went into the milking parlor. Soon the sounds of happy animals filled the air.

John used the noise to cover his moves. He ran to the egg stash and grabbed as many as he could without stopping and ran toward the cornfield. He followed the smell of the fire until he found it.

Among the second swath of grass that grew above the field tile a ring of stones appeared. In the center burned a small fire. John found the can and potatoes, just as the leader described. He looked at the four eggs in his hands, wishing he had more. He knelt to the ground, gathered all of the fingerling potatoes, and secured them in his shirt. He walked toward the east and sat on the ground twenty or so rows away from the site and waited. After five minutes, he began to munch on the raw potatoes. They tasted like heaven. He counted his eggs for the third time while the sky grew brighter with each passing minute.

When the group arrived, they created a ruckus. Their voices were angry.

"Where are the potatoes, Sam?" His accusatory tone left no mistake the boys did not trust one another.

"I...I left them right here. Honest."

"Then where are they?" The leader screamed.

"I dunno."

The corn stalks rustled as the rest of the group joined them. Ray began to speak before he broke through the field.

"We found two of the eggs smashed by the edge of the cornfield."

John counted his stash for the fourth time. He did grab six eggs. His heart sank at the news.

Ray continued, "There are only seven left."

All of the boys groaned. "Ugh."

"So much for eating like kings," one sarcastically added.

"Must have been a coon." Ray offered as a solution. "No kid would have let two eggs go to waste when all we ever get to eat is stewed tomatoes or mystery soup."

All agreed with Ray's comment. John felt worse than before. He pined for the two lost eggs as he nibbled on the last bit of potato.

Soon the air smelled of fresh eggs. The boys chattered with excitement, and then all fell quiet. Within a minute, the babble continued followed by another spell of silence. This happened three times until all of the eggs were cooked and eaten.

A splash, followed by a sizzle, formed a thick line of smoke that signaled anyone who knew that the raid was over. The Freshmen's bellies were as full as one egg per boy would allow. They ran back through the field corn to avoid suspicion. Today's incursion joined the past thefts as a success.

John heard the leader triumphantly yell, "Twenty-one!" as they exited the field and ran toward the main house to join the others for breakfast. He wondered if that meant this was the twenty-first incidence or a covert code for another escapade. He daydreamed of becoming a Freshman.

He waited for only a few minutes longer as he watched the thick smoke trail settle to a thin line. John knew the fire's warmth waned and hoped he had enough hot coals to cook his eggs. When he reached the ring, he removed the stack of fresh leaves lying on top of the flame. Immediately, the flame blew out. Placing his hand above the center, he smiled. The fire held plenty of heat.

He saw the large tin can lying off to the side in the first row of corn. Cut in half, the folded edges were pounded flat to eliminate any sharpness. The metal, still hot, burned his fingers, but he endured the pain. John carefully placed his eggs on the ground and picked up the make shift pan with his shirt. It continued to sear his fingers through his damp shirt. When he tossed it on the white coals, ash flew into the air. He watched the powder float toward the Home. Suddenly, he became nervous and wondered, "What if he got caught?"

Driven by what he felt was certain starvation he cracked the eggs, one by one, into the metal pan. A few pieces of shell floated among the yolks, although he paid no mind. He waited until the edges turned white and solid. He wrapped his shirt tight around his hand, and forced it onto the metal lip. He ran into the cornfield with his stolen meal.

By the time he reached his waiting spot, the eggs had cooked completely. He struggled to lift the hot mixture from the bottom, but attacked it without caution. He ate in record time. When he finished, he felt full for the first time that he could ever remember.

He waited in the field for most of the day, struggling to stay out of the sight of the farmer and his staff, yet he managed. When dusk set in and the grounds were empty, he slipped back under the porch for another rest on his stolen blanket and pillow.

The following morning, he woke to the sound of a multitude of feet pounding on the floor above his head. His sound sleep gave him much-needed rest. He wondered how long it would be before he was discovered missing from the dungeon. He laughed to himself, wishing he could witness the look of shock on their faces. He crawled to the edge of the porch and waited to catch sight of Peter, James, Henry or Belle.

He saw Belle first. She was his first choice. Obviously, she could be trusted. She kept his secret. No one seemed to be looking for him. If John were the Headmaster, the front porch would be the first place he would look. It was easy access in or out, and it sat at least four feet off the ground, leaving plenty of room to maneuver or sit erect.

He lay on the ground nearly exposed. "Belle." He slid back into the shadows.

Belle turned around, but saw no one that seemed to be calling her name. All those surrounding her hurried to prepare for their school day. After looking in all directions, she turned to walk away.

John called to her again, "Belle! Come here."

Belle looked a bit confused but walked toward the voice. "Where are you?"

"I'm here." John called a bit softer, careful not to draw the attention of the flock of children on the lawn.

"Where?"

John waited until she came within a few feet of him. "Pssst, Belle," he whispered. "It's me, John."

She walked to the edge of the porch and started to kneel down. "Are you...."

John cut her off. "I'm under the porch." He watched her kneel. "Don't move." She froze in mid-stance. Her naive reaction may have been comical in any other situation. "I mean, don't come any closer."

Belle stood awkwardly a few feet from the front porch. A few older girls ran past her tossing quizzical glances, but did not stop. Her feet pranced in nervous anticipation. When most of the children had passed the area, John began to speak.

"Over here, under the porch."

"I wondered what happened to you."

John felt no need for small talk. He needed help.

"Can you bring me something to eat?"

"But, we just had breakfast."

"I know, but I haven't eaten since yester-day morning."

"Where did you get the food?'

John ignored her question. He needed to have a quick conversation, without raising the staff's suspicion.

"Belle, listen. Tell Henry and my brothers I am here. I need food." He shook his head wondering why she was his first choice. "Don't let anyone hear you. If they find me, they will beat me until I'm dead. Got it?"

"Got it," Belle whispered.

John hoped she did. He watched her skip toward the schoolhouse. She was the last child to enter the building.

The brothers, Henry, and Belle fed John for two days until one morning he was gone. No one ever saw him again. He was twelve years old when he left the Home.

16

Enoch sat at his desk in his office. He folded his hands in his lap while his secretary hurried to follow his dictation. Once concluded, he waited only a few moments before pressing Janet.

"Did you get it all?" he demanded.

Her pen nervously fluttered over the paper. Her hands felt clammy making the task a bit more cumbersome. Finally, she finished.

"Yes, I believe I have it." Pride filled her statement.

"Good. Read it back to me."

Enoch folded his hands behind his head and closed his eyes. He leaned his body deep into his plush leather chair forcing it to tilt backwards.

Janet held her scribbled paper in the air and cleared her throat. She began:

To our esteemed Board of Directors:

As you know, we at Fairmount believe in equality of rights and opportunity for all of our children, and it pains me to admit that many of our students are unable to share in the privilege of summer vacation with their loved ones simply due to the fact of their family's nonexistence or apathy. I am thrilled to announce I may have a solution.

When I accepted the position as Headmaster, I surrendered my life to this noble cause. I believe, collectively, we are making an enormous difference in the lives of those less fortunate and gladly left behind my home and property in Bucker, Ohio, to answer this servant calling. I have visited my property two weeks this past summer while on furlough and find it failing in my absence. It pained me to see this once lush land suffering from a lack of intentional function.

As I returned to Fairmount, the thought of sharing this restful place with the children who have no family brought me hope and much joy. Before merrily sharing my idea with the staff, I felt it would be best to propose the idea to the Board. I would only require a small consideration for use of the property as a summer camp for our less fortunate ones, as it would require staffing, supervision, food rations, and the like.

If it would please the Board, I would be honored to share my home and property with the children, so each youngster could experience equal value in the absence of his or her family for a summer vacation.

Please consider this humble request as another way that the children of Fairmount can experience the Board of Directors acting on their behalf as an extension of our family.

I trust this letter is sufficient for a vote in your upcoming annual meeting.

Sincerely,

Enoch A. Rumsted, Headmaster

Fairmount Children's Home

Enoch's crooked smile lit his face. "That sounds grand. Thank you, Miss Twill. See that it is properly completed and mailed today. The Board meeting is at the end of the month."

Janet rose, straightened her skirt, and hurried to her desk to transfer her scribbles into a typed version. She quietly closed the door and immediately began to work.

Enoch snatched his calculator and pounded on its keys. He worked every possible financial scenario that crossed his mind. By allowing the children to use his home and property, the extra funds should cover his mortgage on the property.

After unlocking his bottom desk drawer, he placed his hands around the top handle of a grey metal box. He listened for the rhythm of Janet's typewriter keys. Satisfied after the third systematic ding, signaling the end of another row, he opened the lid of the box.

Inside laid stacks of money. He counted his stash until the total matched the amount written on a scrap piece of paper placed on top. He pulled a few bills from his pocket. After counting eleven paper dollars from today's egg, produce, and pumpkin sales, he removed six dollars and added that to his embezzled total. The other five dollars and miscellaneous coins, totaling six dollars and fifteen cents, he added into the Home's ledger as the day's profits and placed it in a separate money box. He placed his private money in the bottom right drawer and the Home's funds in the bottom left, along with the ledger.

This daily habit, which began shortly after coming to the Home, became an automatic part of his day. Guilt had long passed. After the first month, followed by an annual audit, Enoch came to think of it as part of his benefits and succeeded in concealing the missing money.

Janet's keyboard grew silent. Soon, she rapped on his door.

"Mr. Rumsted?"

"Yes, Miss Twill?" Enoch fumbled with the drawer's lock.

"I have finished the draft. Would you like to proof it before I send it?"

"Yes, just give me a minute." His steady hand successfully turned the key. "Come in."

Janet presented the letter to him. He read it twice. It was flawless, in both Janet's typing and his cunning persuasion. Again, he smiled.

"Nicely done," spoken to Janet, but more of an open compliment to himself. "Would you mail it, please?"

Janet, blushing from the uncommon praise, hesitated a bit before replying. "Yes, sir. I will mail it immediately."

He watched her walk through his door. The sound of the lingering silence as she closed the door caused

Enoch to daydream. He thought of the day he would arrive at the bank with his box of funds to satisfy his mortgage. He dreamed of leaving the Home, of fishing in the trout stream in his back yard in Bucker, and mostly of being free from the whine of hundreds of children. He grinned at the assurance the Board of Directors would buy into his scheme.

"That," he said triumphantly, "would take many years off my payments."

Since Enoch's induction, he had pilfered money from the food fund leaving minimum means for provisions. Outside of the livestock and crops produced on the property, little meat, if any, came to the Home. Occasionally, a butcher or meat packing company supplied turkeys or hams around holidays. After the initial meal, the meat reappeared in several soups and stews by Enoch's insistence.

Since the majority of the Home's funding came from outside private sources, it became a taxing ordeal to manage the finances throughout the year. October and November proved the largest challenge. Most businesses and charities relied on the public's good will and generosity spurred into action by the Christmas holiday season. Corporations withheld donations until the year's end to capitalize on their tax benefits.

Late fall also created havoc in the chicken coop. Egg production slowed to a crawl during the cooler weather, forcing the slaughter of many foul. This put a damper on Enoch's private fund, so he required more sacrifices from the kitchen. All baking and sweet treats ceased until the holiday donations began to fill the barren shelves.

The kitchen staff, forced to be creative, used the only abundant source of food available – tomatoes. The Home seemed to have an over abundance of the fruit every year. Besides making juice, sauce, stewed, whole, fresh, canned, or frozen tomatoes, the home sold as many bushels as the children could gather. Enoch skimmed the profits from the top.

The livestock's food situation echoed the children's. April through October the cattle ate only field grass. Corn and hay silage supplemented their pasture diet when available and grain, supplied by a local feed mill, came only once a year and it mostly sat in the storage room of the maintenance building. Only the rats benefited from its hiding place.

The pigs seemed satisfied with scraps from the dinner plates, although they quickly developed an aversion to tomatoes. They laid untouched in the slop yard until pulverized by their cloven hooves, becoming part of their sludge.

The chickens remained cooped for most of their lives. With the egg production directly correlated to the amount of feed they consumed, they were the only group properly nourished. If not, Enoch's fund thinned considerably.

Enoch sat alone many hours in his office conjuring plans to increase his filch. Three years prior, he devised what he determined as an ingenious plan to capture a large sum of money. He demanded the children yield their shoes at the conclusion of the school year and suffer through the summer without, only to receive a used pair come September. Church attendees found an exception, but only for the few hours spent off the property.

Most of the children did not mind going bare-
foot during the summer months, but the coolness of
the spring posed a different feeling. Enoch watched
many boys stand in the midst of fresh cow manure
to warm their chilled feet as they carried out their
morning chores. They stomped and squished the
steaming cow patty between their toes until the
numbness in their chilled feet subsided. Enoch never
realized he caused the children's discomfort. Selfish
gain remained his sole thought.

The only salvation in the autumn months came
from the market sales. Pumpkins returned a good
cash profit. As long as Enoch reported daily sales,
and listed increasing funds on the Home's ledger, he
remained safe from detection, or so he believed.

Afflicted with many bad habits, Enoch's princi-
pal downfall proved his inability to hold his tongue
when he beat his subjects. The Freshmen first suspected Enoch's illegal activity. The group's inherent
knack of creating trouble caused them to spend the
majority of time in the dark room. During their punishment, they began to piece together a case against
the Headmaster.

17

Enoch walked down the basement stairs and through the main tunnel. His heart lightened a bit by the hope of financial relief. He feared certain foreclosure on his Bucker property if the Board turned down his plan. He stood before the wooden door without re-membering the stroll to the runaway dungeon.

"Have you had enough time to think about your infraction, John?" He waited patiently for a reply. None came.

Immediately, he felt his head would explode. His fractured nerves raced with the sensation of burn-ing fire. He worried that he left John imprisoned too long. He fumbled with the wood wedge until it slid from the ring. He flung the door open. It bounced off the wall and sprung the hinges. He turned on his flashlight and raced the beam around the room. It was empty.

He felt dizzy. He staggered to the open doorway gasping for fresh air. The damp, stale odor of urine made him nauseated.

"John? Where are you?" His voice echoed throughout the tunnels.

Frustration colored his face. He raced up the stairs toward the hospital and ran from curtained room to curtained room, pushing and pulling at the fabric forcing them to echo his torment. He swirled about the room in tornado fashion. When his tirade ceased, he gasped for air and watched the curtains settle into disarray. He turned to leave, slipped on the water puddle, and fell flat on his back. The room went dark.

When he woke, a nurse hovered over him splashing cool water on his face while softly patting his cheek. He pushed her aside.

"I'm okay." He waved his hand in the air as a visual warning not to touch.

"What happened?" Her voice was filled with concern.

Enoch's face burned red. "I slipped on the water from the leaking roof." He pointed to the ceiling. He tried to stand and stumbled to his knees.

The nurse placed her hand on his shoulder. "Do not try that again," she warned. "I'll send for the doctor. He needs to look at your head."

"My head?" Enoch raised his hand to feel the growing lump.

"Stay here until I fetch him."

Suddenly aware that his clothes served as the water's sponge and soaked up most of the rainwater, he whined, "But I'm sitting in water."

The nurse stood. "I said, don't move." She shook a warning finger in his face and left to find the doctor.

When the doctor arrived, he helped Enoch to his feet. They walked together to a hospital bed. There he stayed for twenty-four hours. By the time Enoch walked out of the hospital door, his body pulsed with rage. He immediately walked to cottage #1.

The Freshmen scattered like rats when Enoch burst through the front door. He managed to grab two boys before they moved outside of his reach. Before he spoke, he saw the hospital bucket sitting in the corner of the room. That was the only proof he needed. Rather than identify the perpetrator, he decided to punish them all. He pulled the first two boys across the lawn to the barn.

Without a word, he snatched the two horse whips that hung by the door. He swung at the boys in mid run. The first strike welted their bare arms; the second lashed their faces. By the time the boys turned their backs to him, splatters of blood speckled the floor.

Enoch struck until his arms went limp. He left the boys clutching to the vertical barn beams, brutally beaten, with no strength to speak.

He walked directly toward the Freshmen's cottage and found three boys gathered in the communal space. He found another cowering in the shower. He spoke not a word, only motioned for them with the curl of his finger. They boys obeyed silently.

141

They followed Enoch into the barn aghast by the scene before them. He began to whip the four without warning. Refueled by anger, Enoch found renewed strength to complete the task. When he finished, he left the barn to search for the next group of Freshmen.

It took four sessions before each ninth grader suffered punishment for a crime he did not commit. Only Jane had the courage to speak against the Headmaster. She suffered greatly for her insurrection.

Thirteen Freshmen lay flat on the barn floor. Two passed out cold from the abhorrent beating; the remaining eleven sat silent wondering the cause of Enoch's outrage.

Enoch felt no remorse for his actions. He grew increasingly tired of this group of troublemakers causing havoc in the Home. His anger bubbled in his throat. With nearly deafening volume, he berated. "I will not tolerate this mockery. If this disrespect for authority continues, you will all be removed." The statement brought a smile to a few faces, which made Enoch lose control.

Once again, he swung wildly. The sound of the whip as it cracked in the air made one girl wet her pants. Eleven children scattered in all directions, ducking behind anything that would save them from another onslaught. Unfortunately, the two unconscious boys received no mercy.

The farmer rushed into the barn, dodging the untamed whips. He wrapped his arms around Enoch's exhausted body. The children wept from relief.

"Get control of yourself, brother," he shouted into Enoch's ears. "What are you doing?"

Enoch collapsed into the man's strength. He glanced around the room at the damage he had caused. His eyes reflected no regret.

The farmer did not wait for his reply. He withdrew his arms. Enoch fell to the floor. The children slid behind the safety of the hay bales.

He ran to the first boy sprawled out openly on the barn floor. He placed his fingers on his neck feeling for a pulse. Happy to find one, he moved to the second boy. He moved his fingers to multiple positions. Growing concern covered his face. He slid his arms under the boy's body lifting him and ran toward the hospital.

"Call the doctor!" he screamed to anyone who could hear. The staff in the lawn scattered to different buildings in search of the doctor. The farmer cries, "Be quick!" and "Hurry, before it's too late!" echoed throughout the barn. "I need the doctor, NOW!"

The slam of the hospital door resonated throughout the property. Everyone knew this boy was in grave danger.

Within minutes, one of the farm hands carried the other boy to the hospital. Although he walked rather briskly, his pace was somewhat slower. The boy's arms swung limply at his sides and his head tilted back at an odd angle. Many wide eyes watched from behind the hay.

News of the "Lashing of the Thirteen" ran through the cottages like wild fire.

Henry, Belle, Peter, and James listened and struggled to hide their guilt. Multiple stories for the cause of the mass beating aired throughout the dormitories long after dark as the four maintained their silent distance.

Warnings from Henry, "Don't say a word and all will be okay," blanketed their dreams. By morning, news of Ben's death filled all with horror.

Henry advised Belle to remaining silent. He reassured her that she had done the right thing by releasing John from the confines of the dungeon.

"He could have died in there, Belle," he said more times than he could count.

"But, Henry, a boy died because of what I did. How can I ever forgive myself?"

"By never telling anyone what you did."

"How would that help?" she whispered through her steady stream of tears.

"What do you think would happen to you if you told the Headmaster that you were the one who let John out?"

"I don't know," she managed through her sobbing.

"I'll tell you what would happen. You'd be beaten to death." He raised his voice in frustration, "Then I would be visiting two siblings in the cemetery." He lowered his voice. "Is that what you want?"

"No." She cried harder.

Henry placed his hands on his little sister's shoulders. He softened his tone. "Listen, Belle. This was not your fault." He sighed, "It was Enoch's. He lost control. He was the one who beat Ben to death and nearly killed Billy in the process. It wasn't your fault."

"But why did he beat all of them for what I did?"

Henry shook his head. He could not get through to his sister and it frustrated him. He turned at the sound of someone running towards them. It was Peter.

Nearly out of breath, Peter struggled to bring them his news. "He found...a bucket. In...the... Freshmen's...cottage, a bucket," he forced each word out simulating Morse code.

Henry became more agitated with every word. He finally spit, "What are you talking about?"

Peter drew in a deep breath, trying to make his delivery clearer. "The Headmaster found a bucket in cottage #1."

"What does that have to do with anything?" Henry wrinkled his face at the comment.

"A hospital bucket."

As Henry's irritated words smothered Peter's response, Belle's mouth dropped open. She whispered, "That's what I used to stand on. To get that wood thing out of the door. A bucket from the hospital." Her words trailed off, "That's what I used...."

Both boys stood wide-eyed and stared at her in silence. Once again, her eyes flooded with tears.

"See, Henry," she blubbered. "It is my fault."

"Why did you put it in cottage #1?"

"I...I didn't." Belle sobbed.

"Then who did?" added Peter.

The three of them whispered the revelation together, "John."

It took Henry, with Peter's help, to convince Belle that John had set the Freshmen up to take the fall. Although Henry did not say it, he was grateful that John went to such extremes to protect Belle.

18

The next day felt oppressive. The air, stale and hot, inside and out, stifled any positive thought. Dark clouds lingered above the treetops, spilling gallons of rainwater. Murky mud puddles gathered on the unused play area, separated at first, but with each falling raindrop, they grew closer to one another until the area became a shallow pool.

The children followed their school lesson plans without complaint. Only two Freshmen attended class; the rest recovered in the infirmary. Not a hint of laughter lingered in the Home's halls; all of the children remained busy in the kitchen, dorms, or bathrooms. No one dared enter the barn, not even Belle.

Jane woke early in the hospital. Her comrade's moans filtered out from their exam rooms. She rolled her eyes in disgust. She tried to move, but the restraints made it difficult. She screamed aloud for all to hear, "I promise to get even. I promise to bring justice. I promise to do everything in my power to bring down this monster." She hesitated, drew in a deep breath and added, "Who is with me?"

"I am!" screamed Curt.

"Me too," followed Lucas.

"I am all in," cried Tom.

"And I," added Ray.

One by one, all but the unconscious Billy pledged to rid the Home of Enoch's wrath. Jane fell silent after her expelled energy, happy to rally the boys. Just as the group settled into their hospital stupor, a weak voice sliced the air.

"And steal all of his dirty money." Billy joined the conversation.

After a few brief, weak cheers, the Freshmen smiled, each fantasizing how to follow through the pledged task. No one noticed the sound of the closing door as the nurse scurried out of the hospital.

At mid-day, a black limousine drove up the winding drive and stopped in front of the main house. Two cars immediately followed. Six men in black suits walked into the front foyer. Janet Twill greeted them nervously.

"Good afternoon, gentlemen. May I take your hats?" She extended her arms.

The men surrendered their dress felts to her. One added his damp overcoat to the growing load.

She pointed to the woman standing at her side. "Cookies?"

Most of the men denied the request. Although one man took two.

They walked up the grand staircase toward Enoch's office. Hushed conversations ensued behind his closed door. No one entered or exited for nearly three hours. After the frictional chirp of multiple chair legs, the door swung open. All but Enoch exited.

Janet followed the suited men down the staircase. She excused herself for a moment to retrieve their belongings and escorted them to the front door. She closed the door behind then and placed her head on it. Pausing for only a moment, she exhaled a deep sigh and sauntered toward the Headmaster's office.

She knocked on the open door jamb. Enoch, seated on his chair with his back toward the door, watched the three automobiles wind down the long drive departing the Home.

"I trust it went well?" Janet asked, forcing the knot in her throat to remain calm.

Enoch shook his head and spun his chair to face her. "As best as the situation would permit."

She wanted to ask what he meant by that statement, but assumed since he still sat in his chair and remained on the property surrounded by his personal belongings, that his position remained secure. She waited a minute longer. The silent stare forced her to clear the lump in her throat. Obviously, Enoch was not about to divulge the specific details of the Board of Director's meeting. She forced a smile, lowered her eyes, and excused herself from his presence. She began to close the door when he spoke.

"We received approval to use my Bucker property as a summer camp."

Janet felt as though she swallowed her tongue. She found no words to reply. She nodded and closed the door behind her.

Rumors of Enoch Rumsted's possible suspension or termination coursed through the staff. Small groups gathered in secret places and hoped for a change in management.

Janet left Enoch's office in a daze. She walked down the winding staircase without memory of it. When her feet touched the floor, she walked toward the kitchen. She stopped just outside the door, listening to a hushed conversation.

"I am certain he will be fired," one cook said.

"I hope you're right," whispered another.

"I don't know," contested a third. "He has the Board of Directors eating out of his dirty hands."

"But how could he talk his way out of a death?" spit the fourth.

"I agree," added the first. "He can't talk his way out of this one. Not when he is to blame."

Round and round the conversation went. Janet, who also secretly hoped for a dismissal wanted to rush in and join the gossip, but fear of punishment held her from entering. Instead, she crept back to the corner, turned, and retraced her steps forcing the sound of her heels to announce her approach. When she entered the kitchen, the four women hurried to appear busy with food preparation.

"Good afternoon," she addressed them with reserved emotions.

The women replied, "Good afternoon," in unison and quickly turned their backs.

She wanted to blurt out that not only was his position safe; in fact, it was strengthened. She wished she had been able to hear the conversation between Enoch and the Board.

She walked over to the plate of sugar cookies and took the last two. It had been two months since the Home smelled of cookies. She took a bite and immediately spit it out. The cookies tasted like the freezer.

19

The following day, hope lit the sky with a rainbow of purple, pink and blue. The dawn of the new day whispered promise to all who rose early enough to hear it.

Belle finished her task of polishing the banister, treads, and risers. She straightened two of the dust guards in the corner of one stair and whisked the lint into her dustpan. Happy with a task well done, she danced down the remaining steps. Her smile fell to a frown when she saw Sophie kneeling on the floor.

Sophie sat with a bucket of warm, soapy water and a stiff scrub brush. She rubbed the same area on the carpet until some of the fibers stuck to the bristles. She looked up at Belle.

"I can't get it out." Her words echoed defeat.

Belle looked at the ground-in stain on the carpet. "Is that...?"

Sophie interrupted, "Where Craig fell."

Belle felt the pain that Sophie carried within her. She wanted to say something that would make her feel better. She tried to remember some of her mother's wise sayings, but realized that a little bit of them slipped away every day. Soon, she feared, she would remember none. She already forgot the sound of her mother's voice. Belle's eyes filled with tears. She could think of nothing to say.

Sophie stared at Belle, pleading for a word of encouragement, anything that could help soothe her guilt. She smiled at her young friend.

Suddenly, Belle found her voice. "But Craig is doing well!"

"I know, but he's gone. His family left because of the accident."

Belle squinted. "I thought his father got another job."

"Really?"

"That's what I heard," she blurted out so quickly her words jumbled together.

Sophie's countenance changed. Maybe it was not her fault after all that Craig's parents left the Home. Maybe, just maybe, Belle was right.

Belle helped Sophie try to remove the bloodstain for the final time. When the water held a faint hint of pink, Belle added, "See it's coming out."

They worked a bit longer and decided together they had removed all that was possible. Belle helped Sophie carry the water outside and dump it in the bushes. Belle avoided eye contact with Sophie, ashamed of her lie.

The sound of gravel crunching under car tires made both girls turn. A long black car sat idling in the driveway. An elderly man stepped out of the passenger's seat and walked around the rear of the car. They watched him open a large oversize door. With the driver and two other's assistance, they carried a wooden casket up the front steps, across the wide porch, and into the front hall of the main house.

"I guess Ben just came Home," Sophie added with a shrug.

Soon, the empty inspection room flooded with people. The staff hurried to reposition rugs to accommodate the upcoming procession. They placed two large bouquets of flowers on tall columns - one at the head and one at the foot of the casket. Once they finished the arrangement, they waited for the Headmaster to arrive before opening the lid.

Enoch entered the room in eerie silence. The small staff clustered around the casket blocking Belle and Sophie's view. After a bit of discussion, the consensus was to open only the top half of the casket.

"It seems to me that since this will be the first wake for many children, that a partial view of the body would be best." Enoch's statement sounded alarmingly tender.

"Yes, but," Janet began, "I feel it may be more traumatic to only see half of the body." She added quietly, "You know how children are. They will create horrific stories if something is left to the imagination." She continued, rolling her eyes. "I can hear them now...They chopped him off at the waist...They cut off his legs...He was so badly beaten...."

Enoch interjected, "I believe we get your point, Miss Twill." He cleared his throat, attempting to ignore her accusatory expression. "And while I believe personally that half shown is best, I feel that Miss Twill's comment may have some merit. May I ask for a general show of hands?" He held up his hand. "How many feel half is best?" One other joined him. "How many feel all is best?" Everyone else meekly raised his or her hand. He huffed, "Then all it will be."

He walked toward Ben's casket and opened the bottom half. He straightened the blanket that covered his feet as well as his coat and shirtsleeve. Pressing his hand on Ben's chest, signifying the required action to say goodbye, he walked out of the room.

"Gather the children," he tossed over his shoulder.

Outside, the mournful church bell rang. The children settled in a long straight line without prompting. Those that had been through a prior wake knew what to do. If this was the child's first experience, they followed the lead of the others.

The line formed in age groups, the eldest first. The echo of the Headmaster's sentiment was a requirement to show proper respect. The older children felt the mandatory touch to be a morbid act. They maintained that the younger children would not understand, although the main issue seemed to be their recollection of their own first experience. Many children remembered their first touch - cold, clammy, a nearly plastic feeling of the embalmed body - and faulted the Headmaster for his firmness. To most, it seemed cruel at best.

Absolute silence was the other requirement. Random spouts of "Shhh..." echoed through the room covering many repulsive utterances. After the first touch, many of the young children withdrew their hand and shook it in the air, trying to force the sensation from their hand.

Belle watched those ahead approach the casket, including Henry. He touched Ben and moved on without a flinch. She prayed her reaction would be the same.

When she arrived at the casket, Ben's hand was out of her reach. She stood wide-eyed looking for someone to help her. She mouthed the words, "I can't reach him." Finally, Sophie took notice. She walked to Belle's side and lifted her in the air until her hand touched his.

Belle drew in a deep breath and swallowed her gasp. She looked at her hand as if it immediately infected.

Sophie held fast onto Belle's hand. She pulled Belle down the stairs and into the bathroom and helped her wash.

Horror filled Belle's face. "That felt awful! He didn't feel real." She looked at Sophie. Innocence surrounded her. "Was that really him?"

The comment made Sophie smile, although she, along with every other child in the Home, remembered the reaction of the first touch. "Yes, it was him."

"Why did he feel so...so...." Belle rubbed her wet fingers together, closed her eyes, trying to find the right word to describe what she felt.

"Plastic?" Sophie asked.

"Yes, plastic and hard, like a doll."

A doll. Belle thought about the one she received from her parents one year for Christmas. It was an extravagant present for the family finances. The doll had long blonde curls, much like Sophie's, blue eyes, and a bright yellow dress. Belle loved that doll. Today was the first time she thought about her. Belle envisioned the doll sitting on her bed awaiting her return.

Sophie was in mid-explanation of why Ben felt that way when Belle returned to the present. At that moment, the strange sensation spurred by the required touch no longer mattered to Belle. She wanted her doll.

That evening, Belle lay awake on her bed. She tried to remember her mother – her voice, laugh, face, smell, words, touch, hugs, and kiss. She tried to recall her features - face, eyes, nose, chin, hair, smile, teeth and lips. She squeezed her eyes tighter hoping it would somehow aid in the memory. It did not.

Belle thought about her own bed – a twin, made from pieces of a discarded double bed. Her father carried home the broken frame, cut, glued and mended several splintered boards until he finished it. She remembered the day her father carried her to the barn. "Close your eyes. I have a surprise for you," he proudly explained. When he told her to open them, she thought the bed was the most beautiful thing she had ever seen. Its warm stain gleamed enhanced by the fresh coat of varnish.

"Now, you can get out of that crib," he said with a wide grin.

That memory was the first Belle could recall. She was three years old. The following Christmas she received her doll.

Belle's mother had sewn a quilt for her daughter's bed. She used old scraps of clothing that either belonged to a member of her family or friends. The main color of the spread was yellow. For the extra touch, she made a dress for Belle's doll to match.

Belle smiled at the memory while she wiped the tears from her cheeks. She missed her mother and her father. She whispered in the darkness, "Until we meet again," and fell fast asleep.

20

By mid-October, the children were busy with their school lessons and the final harvest of the onions, peppers, and never-ending tomatoes. The children stored the onions in layers of straw in large crates, much like the apples, pears, and potatoes in the fruit cellar. The room was dry, dark and cool — an ideal environment to store their bounty.

Over the past few months, Henry associated more with the Freshmen and less with Joey. He found Joey to be too weak, mentally and physically. Although there was an age difference, the Freshmen viewed Henry as a solid eighth grader and sought his attention for a possible replacement for their fallen one, Ben. This posed a bit of a problem for the Headmaster.

Henry's initiation came without warning. The Freshmen heard of Henry's covert laundry room raids and wanted to hear first hand if the rumor was true.

After sneaking into the middle cottage just after midnight, two of the Freshmen, Curt and Jane, crawled over to Henry's bed. Curt covered Henry's mouth with his hand. He woke with a start. Jane held her finger over her lips and Henry relaxed. He liked the fact that Jane came. Both motioned for Henry to follow them. They tiptoed through the sea of beds, down the staircase, through the tunnel, and into the maintenance building before anyone spoke.

"We have a question," Curt began, getting right down to business.

Henry, now fully awake, became agitated. "You woke me up to ask me a question?"

Jane jumped in, thinking her approach may seem softer. "We heard that you have been raiding the laundry room."

Henry crossed his arms in front of him. "Is that so?"

"Yes," Curt sarcastically added.

Jane shot Curt a disapproving glance and returned her attention to Henry. "Look, Henry. We don't care at all. We just want to hear your side of the story." She rolled her hand in the air.

Henry stood firm, ignoring her signal to speak. He pulled his arms tighter against his body.

Curt groaned. "Look! We need another Freshmen. Are you in or out?"

Jane snapped her attention toward Curt. "I want to hear his story first, Curt." Softening her voice, she looked at Henry. "Go on."

Henry felt important. His calloused attitude served him well as a possible recruit into the Freshmen's club. He smiled on the inside, although remained careful not to outwardly reveal that emotion.

"Well, you know I sleep with a bed-wetter," he opened.

"Yeah, that's disgusting," Jane interjected.

"After the first night, I realized that this could be a serious problem." He started using his hands to magnify his story.

"I helped Joey dry the sheets the first morning and actually several mornings after that. But, the day the Headmaster made him stand in the rain, totally naked, with a tin can tied around his waist and told him that he couldn't come inside until he peed in the can, I knew something had to be done. So, I devised a plan."

His small audience sat speechless, begging Henry to finish. He tilted his head backward and laughed.

"You should see your faces!" He laughed harder. "Anyway, I waited until the laundry staff left for lunch. I ran into the room, grabbed two fitted sheets, and smuggled them into our dorm. I lifted the box springs and tucked them between it and the slats, beside the flashlight. I always kept at least one fresh sheet under there." He winked, "You never know when you're gonna need one."

"So what did you do with the dirty ones?"

"Burned them."

"Where?"

"Behind the slaughterhouse." Henry smiled. "No one suspected a thing."

"But didn't the Headmaster become suspicious when the sheets went missing?" Jane asked.

"No, that's the funny part." He put his hand beside his mouth. "He thinks he cured Joey with the tin can thing." All three laughed. "He's so stupid," Henry added and spit on the floor.

"But that still doesn't explain how you account for the missing sheets." Curt's comment sounded accusatory. "Or how you burned them."

He narrowed his eyes and moved closer to Henry's face. Henry remained stoic.

"Oh that's simple," Henry began, "I am in charge of burning the trash. I hide the dirty sheet somewhere behind the barn, silo, or hog pen. I never use the same place twice. That way, I don't get caught. Once the fire is good and hot, I throw the stinking thing on it and let it smoke. No one suspects a thing." Henry's smile turned into a frown. "Hey! How did you know I smuggled sheets?"

His sudden visual concern made Curt laugh. Jane jumped in to answer the question. She did not want Henry to feel threatened.

"Joey told us." She smiled.

"We had to pressure him," Curt added with a wider grin.

Henry remained steady. "Ah, Joey's all right. Weak, but all right. He needed someone to look out for him. I guess that was me." He shook his head. "It was either that or I slept in pee for the rest of my life!"

"Okay, well, I guess I'll ask you again." Curt stood up. "Are you in or out?"

161

"I'm in!" Henry's response came with great enthusiasm. It felt good to be a part of something even if it was the troublemakers.

The following morning, Henry's duty switched from trash burning to cow feeding. He wondered if one of the Freshmen ratted him out. Faced with the fact that he must design a new disposal plan, he walked into the maintenance building looking for an outlet. He walked into the storage room on the second floor and opened the door.

"Ahhhh!" he screamed. A flurry of rats scurried across the floor, feedbags, and his feet. He stomped on a few wounding them and then delivered the crushing head blow. Rodent squeals surrounded him. He grabbed a crow bar that hung by the door and started to swing. He killed four more.

"What's going on up there?" the farmer yelled from below.

"RATS!"

"Ah, let them be. They won't eat much," he said as he walked away.

Rats were a normal part of life at the Home. They lived in the tunnels during the day and came out to an unusual extent at night. They chewed on the children's clothes if their pockets held any crumbs from smuggled food. They jumped from floor to bed, bed to bed, and bed to floor searching for something to eat. They hid in the silo, barn, and especially in the maintenance grain stash. After a few days of the new chore, Henry could not stand them anymore. He devised a plan—his first adventure as a Freshmen.

On Friday, October 21, Henry led the way with the twelve others to the storage room. Armed with baseball bats, the boys stood poised in batter position, while the girls followed closely with pencil and paper.

"Everyone ready?" Henry whispered.

"Ready!" they replied.

Henry opened the door. Rats scattered in every direction. The girls screamed. The boys pounced.

"I got one!"

"Me too."

"Two!"

"Me too."

"I got four!"

"I got one."

"Finally...."

"I got two!"

"Five for me!" Henry squealed.

"That's not fair! You know where they hide!"

"Six!"

"Three."

"One...finally."

"I can't see any!"

"Ouch! That was my foot!"

"Four!"

"LOOK OUT!"

"Three! I got three!"

"Big deal!"

"Two!"

"Cut it out!"

"Five for me!"

"None...for me."

"Two!"

"That was mine!"

"No way, that makes four for me!"

"I hit it first!"

"I killed it!"

"One...one...I GOT ONE!"

"Seven!"

"Someone tie his hands! This isn't fair!"

"That was a double whammy! Yahoo!"

"I got six!"

"Stop hitting me!"

"Four!"

"Ten!" Everyone stopped. "Just kidding!" Henry laughed.

"They're getting away!" The girls squealed, dropped their paper and ran down the stairs. More than two dozen rats followed them. "They're down here!"

The boys ran down the steps swinging. Their bats hit the metal railing and rattled their teeth. They laughed all of the way back through the tunnel. Henry could not imagine a time when he had so much fun.

The following evening, Henry received blame and of course punishment for masterminding a siege of rotten tomatoes on an unsuspecting passersby. One couple, out for an evening ride, were pummeled with the slimy red flesh. One tomato blew out their front windshield. The man stopped his automobile out of the boys' sight and crept up the hill on foot. He crested the knoll a few feet from their battle station. He chased the boys toward the Home, but lost them in the thick brush. Standing before the Headmaster, the only child the man pointed out was Henry, who had been asleep in his room the entire night.

That was Henry's final beating of the year. It was particularly hard on his battered body. As the Headmaster drew back for his final strike, Henry vowed to get even. He spent three days in the dark room.

21

Visitor's day came the last Sunday of every month. In October, it fell just a few days prior to Halloween.

The coolness of the morning quickly warmed in the cloudless sky. Many people arrived with picnic baskets filled with food and candy. Some brought Halloween costumes and masks to aid in the afternoon's gaiety.

Henry watched with frustrated jealousy. He followed every visitor with his eyes, dismissing one at a time until there were no more.

"Yep, just as I suspected," he sulked. "Father is not coming." He spoke only to himself. "This is the fifth month and no Daddy. Useless!" He stood and spit on the ground.

It took a dozen or so steps before Henry managed to work out the stiffness in his muscles. His back, heavily marked from Enoch's tirades, created additional discomfort. He felt like an old man. He hung his head and walked into the barn.

Belle greeted him cheerfully. He scowled.

"What's wrong?"

"Nothing," he spewed. "Why do you think something's wrong?"

"Because you're a grouch."

Her automatic reply made Henry smile. Belle's pleasant countenance, sweet smile, and ooze of innocence consistently brought Henry back to reality. Despite the fact he grew bitterer each day they remained, his sister became his bright spot.

"What are you doing in here?" he asked, intending to shift the focus off his discontent.

"I was feeding Star." She pointed to the show pony. "I just finished."

Wanting to capture and adopt Belle's positive attitude, Henry asked, "Want to do something fun?"

"Yes. What?" She jumped up and down like a pogo stick.

"It's kinda a secret," he whispered.

"Okay...." She hesitated, begging for details.

"Can't tell you. I have to show you." Henry pulled on her arm.

"Now?"

"Yes. Now!" He shook his head. "You have other plans?" Sarcasm had become Henry's best defense.

"Well, no...but," she hesitated. "I wanted to wait for Father."

Henry felt a deep burn grow inside him. His chest hurt. First, his neck burned and then the heat moved up to his face. He broke out in patchy blotches. His hives tingled. A burst of anger flew from his mouth, "HE'S NOT COMING!"

Belle stumbled backwards. "Why do you always say that?" She screamed though growing tears.

"Because it's true!"

"No it's not!" Belle threw her hands by her side and stomped away from her brother. She mumbled a frustrated conversation with herself.

Henry's eyes filled with tears. He wondered why he constantly made his sister cry, why he harbored so much hatred, and why she refused to see that they would live in the Home until they were old enough to leave.

He sprinted out of the barn into the cornfield. The dying stalks ripped at his unprotected skin, yet he continued with an unquenchable fury. With momentum building with every step, he pushed, pulled, and yanked at the hanging ears of corn. He threw them into the air with blind rage. Several fell at his feet causing him to stumble, but he continued until he finally broke through the last row of corn. Doubled over with his hands on his knees, he gasped for air. After several deep breaths, he straightened.

Before him stood a large maple tree split nearly in half by a lightning strike. The dead branches clung to the trunk for life support to no avail. The leaves, shriveled and brown, drifted to the ground in the absence of a breeze.

Large rectangular holes riddled the bark. Chunks of dead wood formed small piles near its base. A pileated woodpecker pounded its bill deep into the crevices. Its distinct call seemed to warn Henry to keep his distance.

Henry watched the eighteen-inch bird for several minutes. It repeatedly used its long neck to pull far back from the tree. It magnified the strength of the blow by also pulling with its feet. The strike sounded like a heavy thunk, and Henry marveled at the speed and strength with which it moved. The distinct red crest on its head, split in two by a band of white that began at the base of the beak and trailed deep into bird's side and wing, echoed the dominance of the black eye band. The bird looked like a trouble-maker – a red headed bandit.

One by one, the bird pulled carpenter ants out of the heartwood of the dead tree. Occasionally, it stopped with a wiggling insect stuck to the end of its barbed tongue and played peek-a-boo with Henry, ducking is head behind the tree only to pop it out on the other side. Without announcement, the bird took to flight. Its warning cry of "wuk, wuk, cuk" settled Henry's anger. He laughed aloud.

Henry kicked around the base of a tree scattering the chunks of fallen wood from their neat piles. A few ants scurried away, safe to live another day. He walked back toward the corn and kicked a few of the tantrum ears that lay before him. He fumbled with the box of matches in his pocket. A deviant idea prompted a smile.

Belle dried her tears under a large shade tree. She watched several groups of children picnic with their families, relaxing on a large blanket or red-and-white checked fabric spread on the ground. Disappointment shadowed her face as she looked for her father.

"Henry is right," she moaned. "He's not coming."

She picked up a stick that had fallen from the tree and began to pound the ground until it broke into several pieces. She looked at the broken bits before her and sighed. She found it difficult to admit that he no longer cared.

Laughter from the largest crowd snapped her back to reality. An elderly woman sat in the center of a homemade quilt. Its edges, wrinkled and tattered, went unnoticed by the crowd of children seated around her. Belle unconsciously counted the children.

"Thirteen!" she exclaimed.

She crept under the next shade tree bringing her closer to the group. She realized they were the children that arrived the day Belle and Henry left the hospital. She recalled the nurse's conversation:

"Out you two go. We need every one of these beds."

"Who are all those people?" Belle asked looking over her shoulder.

"A large family just arrived."

"How many are there?" Henry pressed for an answer.

"Eleven." The nurse's tone was automatic.

"Eleven?" echoed the children with disbelief.

"I don't think I even know eleven people." Henry mused. "That's a huge family!"

"There are three more."

"What?" Henry shouted immediately aware of his volume. Lowering his voice, he added. "Why aren't they here?"

"Too young," was all she offered.

Belle counted again. There were fourteen people including the woman. As she eavesdropped on a bit of the conversation, she realized that two of the small children came with her. Belle heard one of the girls call the woman "Grandma."

Depression set in as she watched their interaction. Belle never knew her Grandmother and witnessing the woman hug and kiss each child repeatedly became too difficult to watch. She stood to walk away just as the group fought over who would wear the Halloween mask next. She covered her ears, muffling their laughter, and decided to look for Henry in the barn.

"Henry!" she called just inside the door. "Are you in here?"

"Nope!" he laughed. "I'm right behind you."

Belle turned to see her brother standing there, his arms covered in dots of blood and red welts. His face dripped with sweat.

"What happened to you?" She pointed to his arms.

"Huh?" Henry lifted his arms and inspected the corn stalk wounds. "Oh, I ran through the corn." He shrugged. "They get brittle when they start to dry up." He grabbed her hand and pulled. "Come on. I have something to show you."

They walked through the field of corn until its end. Henry relayed the story of the woodpecker as Belle inspected the holes in the tree. She watched a few black ants crawl around the base of the tree.

Henry gathered the wood chips left by the bird and made a small pile on the green grass. He pushed the dry leaves away from the wood and then decided to crush them on top of the wood chips instead.

"What are you doing, Henry?"

"Making a fire."

"Why?"

"You'll see." He pointed to a stone pile situated at the edge of the field. "Grab some of those stones and bring them over here." He made a circle with his fingers about half of the size of a basketball. "Get ones about this big, if they aren't too heavy to carry."

Belle made several trips, carrying one rock at a time. Henry began to build a ring around the wood chips. Anxious to start his fire, he helped Belle collect the stones. Soon, the ring surrounded the kindling. Henry struck a match and nestled it deep into the dry timber. He blew gently on its center. A band of smoke rose from the pile.

"Where there is smoke, there is..."

"Fire." Belle finished one of her mother's sayings. "She used to say that when she lit the stove," she proudly added, forgetting the saying until that moment.

Henry stoked the fire and added a few dead twigs. The fire cracked and popped forcing a few hot embers to spew from the flame. He jumped to stamp them out, thankful for his shoes.

They stared into the dancing flame as it mesmerized them. Belle immediately felt sleepy. Henry felt content.

Interrupting a sense of peace, Henry asked without lifting his eyes from the flame, "What else do you remember about Mother?"

Surprised by the question, yet eager to respond, Belle began to replay all of her previous thoughts. She talked non-stop for ten minutes while Henry listened. Her words added to the serenity of the moment.

Suddenly Belle jumped. "Henry, the fire's going out!"

"It's just how I want it."

He placed a rusted tin can that he found in the rubbish pile on the hot coals. The smell of hot metal burned off quickly. Belle wrinkled her nose showing her distaste. Henry assured her.

Several field corn cobs, shriveled and dry, lay beside him. He pulled the kernels off the cob and dropped them into the hot can. A few fell directly on the fire and expanded immediately with a pop. The flaming seed landed in the grass and fizzled. Henry picked it up and ate it.

"Needs butter!" he joked as he pulled some half-melted butter pats from his pocket.

Belle's eyes opened wide. "Where did you get those?"

"From the dinner table."

Belle helped Henry peel the yellow squares from the cardboard bottom and waxed paper top. They placed all of the butter pats on top of each other until the corn finished popping. After most of the corn popped in the can, Henry picked up a forked stick, wrapped the V around the can, and pulled it off the fire.

Belle tossed the butter into the tin and listened to it sizzle. It smelled heavenly.

Henry picked up a different tin can. It was small and full. He shook it vigorously and tossed it onto the white coals.

"What's that?"

Henry grinned. "You'll see."

When the corn can was cool enough to touch, Henry placed it before him. He pulled a salt lick chunk from his pocket and scraped it against the side of a stone. Salt dust fell onto the dark kernels. When he seasoned it to taste, Henry shook the can to coat the popped corn with both butter and salt.

Henry lifted the can to his sister. "You first."

Belle pinched a few warm, slippery kernels between her fingers. After Henry's nod, she placed them in her mouth. The corn was blackish in color, a bit salty, and chewy.

Henry waited patiently for her approval. "Well? What do you think of parched corn?"

Belle smiled. Her teeth were black and filled with bits of the corn that stuck like glue. "It's pretty good!" She picked at kernels wedged between her teeth.

They devoured their illegal treat in a matter of minutes. Belle asked for more, but Henry had another plan in mind. He pulled four apples from his pocket.

"But we have apples everyday!" Belle whined, "I'm sick of apples."

"Oh I assure you that you will love these apples."

"Why? What's so different?" She took one from his hand and inspected it closely. "Looks the same to me." She opened her mouth to take a bite.

"Wait!" Henry warned. "I have something to go with it."

Belle pointed to the expanding tin can that rested on its side among the ash. "That?"

"Yep."

"What is it?"

"Almost ready."

174

"Okay, but what is it?"

"Just be patient. It's a surprise!" He watched Belle scrunch her nose. "Trust me. You will love it!"

Henry pushed the can off the coals. He held a screwdriver above it. "Ready?"

"Ready," Belle echoed.

He forced the tip into the lid of the can. Golden brown liquid splattered over his hands, arms, and pants. Immediately it blistered. He wiped the hot liquid from his skin and pulled the fabric away from his body.

As comical as it was, Belle dared not laugh. She knew her brother had been burned, although not too badly.

When Henry sat down on the ground, he had three blisters on his hand, one on his arm, and one on his right leg. If the treat had not been worth it, he may have complained, but enjoying freshly picked apples with warm caramel made from a can of condensed milk trumped the pain. He enjoyed the act of rebellion. It suited his taste.

22

With Thanksgiving fast approaching, the children hurried to prepare for the big celebration. The junior and senior boys placed large tables end to end in the dining hall, while the girls spread brown craft paper donated from the butcher for their tablecloths.

It was during this first Gates' attended holiday that the staff discovered Belle's artistic talent. Although only six years old, her skill far surpassed her young age. She covered the brown paper with turkeys, pilgrims, Indians, corn, platters of bounty, and women stirring the contents of steaming pots. She drew flowers at the center of each table and trimmed the edges with live greens, pods and cones from the fields and woods. Her presentation was beautiful, even the Headmaster said as much.

With the tables set and the scent of turkey in the air, the children's spirits rose to a new level. Since meat as a main course was a rarity, even the staff joined the excitement.

Belle sat amazed at the amount of food that passed before her. One of the Matrons carried the overweight platter of turkey from table to table. The children passed warm rolls, green beans, and mashed potatoes. The sweet potatoes smothered in candied marshmallows were Belle's favorite. She took an extra helping and no one noticed.

Due to the overwhelming amount of food preparation, the Thanksgiving meal took place at three o'clock. The children, starving from the absence of breakfast, gorged themselves until they felt their bellies would pop. Some left a little room for a narrow slice of pumpkin pie, while most of the children hid the treat in a napkin to save for later that evening.

After washing the dishes, wiping the tables, and resetting the dining hall, most of the children took a nap. Going to sleep on a full stomach was a rare indulgence.

At six o'clock, everyone gathered in the inspection room. Everyone wrote his or her name on a scrap piece of paper and placed it in a box labeled by cottage numbers. When all finished penning their names, they waited for their turn.

"Cottage number one!" Miss Twill called.

The Freshmen, sophomores, juniors, and seniors stood in single file. Each drew a piece of paper, opened it, and read the name silently. Sophie pulled her own name, so Janet instructed her to pick another. Once complete, the group sat in silence. This continued until the high school girls, cottage #7, drew the final names.

Miss Twill cleared her throat for attention. "This year we are doing something different for Christmas. We will be making our own presents." Some of the children groaned, although Janet continued. "The name you drew is the recipient of your hand made gift." The room filled with grumbling voices. Janet held up her hand as a sign to silence the room. "Be creative. Get to know the person. Find out what they like. Think of something that you could make that would bring them joy. Also, do not place your name on it. This gift should be given freely and anonymously." She started to clap. "Go get started! You only have a month to do it!" Shuffling and shifting flooded the room. People shared their names with their friends. Some children switched names. No one noticed the Headmaster's entrance.

"Children!" The room fell immediately silent at his word. He grinned, showing his approval. "This is not a request. This is mandatory. If you do not make your present, someone will not have Christmas. Understood?"

A quiet response came from a few. Enoch's face burned. His voice echoed throughout the room. Even the windows rattled.

"Understood?"

"Yes, sir!" responded the children as they ran from the room.

Belle sat on her bed staring at the name on her paper – Dorothy. She had no idea who Dorothy was. For the first time since Belle arrived, she watched every girl enter the room, too embarrassed to admit that she barely knew half of their names.

The following morning, Belle picked at her oatmeal. Henry attempted to include her in the table's conversation several times without any response.

"You gonna eat that?" the boy seated across the table impatiently licked his lips.

Henry nudged Belle. "Do you want that?" He pointed to her bowl.

"Huh?" Belle responded more to the physical contact than to the question. Finally, she slid the bowl in front of Henry. "No. You can have it."

Henry glanced at the boy and shrugged his shoulders. He took the first bite of Belle's oatmeal.

"Hey!" shouted the boy. "I wanted that!"

Belle watched Henry shovel the lumpy cereal into his mouth, uncertain if he took a moment to chew. Suddenly aware of her distracted mistake, she attempted to smile at the boy. She wanted to explain, but became paralyzed by the inability to remember his name. Dejected by her failure, she snapped.

"I'll give it to whoever I want." Her snotty response made the boy angry.

"But, I asked you first!" He pointed toward Henry. "He never even asked for it!"

"So?" Henry fostered the protest.

The boy pounded his fist on the table. Everyone seated near jumped at his aggressive behavior.

"But I asked...first!"

Belle felt instantly guilty for causing the conflict and irritated with her brother for promoting it. She grabbed her bowl of half-eaten oatmeal and slid it over to the starving boy.

Henry, in mid-motion, spilled the contents of his spoon on the table. "Hey!" He shouted at his sister.

Belle stormed out of the room. Henry ran after her. The boy picked up Belle's bowl and gulped the oatmeal before anyone could take it from him. Nearly half of the children in the lunchroom gawked at him.

Henry ran in front of his sister forcing her to stop. "What was that about?"

"What is wrong with you?" Belle shook her finger in her brother's face. "When did you turn into such a bully?"

Henry recoiled. "What?"

Belle's face flushed. Her hands shook. She pounded her feet on the floor. "You are turning into a troublemaker!" Her bottom lip began to quiver. "Why, Henry? Why?"

Henry shrugged his shoulders. "I don't think I'm a troublemaker." His tone held indifference.

"Well, of course you don't," she scolded. "You never do."

Henry tried to explain. "That kid always mooches food off other people all of the time. I'm sick of it! Why should he have your oatmeal?" He began to shout. "I'm your brother. I'm the one who should have it!"

Belle, shocked at his demeanor, fell speechless. Her first instinct was to mention their mother, but decided against it. At that moment, she realized she had lost her brother. He had become someone else, someone she no longer liked, someone filled with anger and hatred, someone without a soul. She turned from him without a sound, ignoring his demands to return.

23

"We need a plan," Curt whispered to the rest of the Freshmen seated before him.

"Let's shoot him!" interjected Jane.

"And where are we gonna get a gun?" Curt chastised.

"How about blowing up his car?" one boy added. The gang laughed.

"Listen up," Curt fumed. "This is serious! We have to figure out a way to get rid of Enoch once and for all."

"I overheard one of the Matrons say he was on the take," Henry offered.

"That wouldn't surprise me," Jane chattered with an extra grin toward Henry. His face flushed at the show of affection.

"Yeah, Henry, I heard that too." Billy offered. "I heard he has a separate money box. Keeps all the produce money for himself." He huffed, "No wonder all we ever get to eat is tomatoes."

Lucas, the most levelheaded Freshmen, scratched his head. "We have to think of a way to drive him off. A way that he leaves on his own."

"I'd rather kill him!"

"Yeah, look what he did to Ben!"

"He's evil!" Voices began to escalate.

"He deserves to die!" The group murmured in agreement.

Curt threw his hands in the air. "This is not helping. We need to come up with a plan!"

"What? Killing him isn't a plan?" Clarence's sarcastic overtone made some laugh.

"It would certainly get rid of him," heckled another.

"What if we staged an accident?" Lucas solicited.

Everyone fell silent. Lucas rarely talked, let alone masterminded a plan. All eyes fixated on him awaiting his suggestion. It took a while for him to speak.

"I'm just saying, what if we just scared him into thinking we are trying to kill him."

"If he lives he will continue to beat us whenever he feels like it!" Clarence added, "Want to see my scars from the last time?"

"Clarence, we all have scars!" Jane tried to calm him down.

"Not like me!" He lifted his shirt, rounding his back for all to view.

"Gross!" Both girls turned their faces away from him.

Several lacerations remained infected and seeping, the surrounding skin puffed red with infection. Henry gaped; thankful his wounds had fully healed.

Curt rallied the faction. "Clarence is right. We can't afford for him to live."

"But killing him...?" Lucas doubted. "We need to just scare him."

"I did that once," Tom added, referring to the punch that knocked Enoch out in the schoolhouse. "And all of you suffered for it."

Voices erupted. Each child bared arms, backs, legs, and necks displaying some of Enoch's rage-filled antics.

Henry sat still, not interested in the battle scar show and tell. He thought about Lucas' suggestion and Clarence's point. He waited for the group to settle again into their circle.

"I have an idea," was all Henry said. The chatter ceased. Everyone held his or her breath waiting for Henry to explain.

24

Henry spent the next few weeks in the company of his new recruiters. He made no attempt to talk to his sister or acknowledge her presence. He needed to prove his loyalty to the Freshmen. The group attempted several raids on the storehouses, most unsuccessful, but their bond grew stronger with each passing day.

After Belle's devotion to the Thanksgiving decorations, she gained respect from many other children. They begged for her help with the Christmas decorations and she willingly accepted.

Since Belle's daily task required the dusting of the staircase, it seemed a natural marriage for her to decorate it as well. The farmer cut fresh pine branches – white, balsam, fir, and red. The blend of their different needles and fragrances made the garland look like a piece of art. Belle added juniper berries and rose hips for color, as well as a few sprigs of holly.

The dining hall became the hub for assembling the decorations. The children busied themselves cutting and gluing paper garland together. Bits of colored paper littered the floor and tabletops. Once finished, they draped the masterpiece on the tin crown molding.

"I think we will have enough." Sophie clapped her hands as she watched the architect on the ladder.

"I'm not sure," he quickly added.

Belle smiled. "We can always make more."

"But," Sophie pointed to the paper on the table. "All we have left is green."

"Then, green it will be." Belle waved her hands through the air as if she held a magic wand.

They finished their billowing swags with nearly three feet to spare. They decided to tape the extra bit to the top of the double door jamb. Belle clapped when they were finished. Each day the group decorated, more children offered to help. When it came time to decorate the tree, the number of members grew to fifteen.

Two seniors helped one of the farm hands select and cut a fir tree on the property. The bottom boughs posed a difficulty as they attempted to pull it through the front door. Pine needles dotted the floor as several children tugged and pulled. Finally, the limbs gave way and the children stumbled into the foyer.

Belle, the smallest of the group, stood against the wall far out of the way. As the tree bounced past her, a small bird's nest fell to the floor. Belle placed her hands around the tiny wren nest being careful not to damage it.

"It's a sign of good luck!" she exclaimed as she proudly lifted her prize.

One of the boys picked her up as high as he could. "Put it up there, Belle."

Belle selected an area where a single stubby branch protruded from the trunk barely one foot in length. She snuggled the empty nest into the branch's only web of needles. The children clapped when she finished. It made her blush.

The bulky lights adorned the tree first. Several strings, discarded on the floor, lay idle or unusable due to an electrical short in the cord. Nonetheless, the children made do with the strands that worked. Everyone danced around the colorfully lit tree.

The Home reused their ornaments from years past. A large white angel lit the top while smaller versions swung from the lower branches. Glass ornaments, mostly round with a deep inset of another color, came next. A few clip-on birds with spun glass tails filled in the tree's natural openings while beaded garland draped from branch to branch nearly skirting the floor in the lower boughs. Tufts of feathers, white-tipped pine cones, and candy canes finished the masterpiece.

A circular skirt, made of random discarded material, covered the floor under the decorated tree. The senior girls completed assembling the tree skirt only a few hours before. It was the prettiest tree Belle could remember. The wide variety of color lifted everyone's spirits.

The group quickly gathered up the empty storage boxes and hid them from sight. After they swept up the needles, the rest of the children gathered for an evening of Christmas carols. Belle barely noticed her missing brother.

The following week seemed more like spring than approaching winter. Two days of strong southern winds brought seventy-degree temperatures. The play area and lawns soon filled with children and laughter. Many played baseball, badminton, or a simple game of tag. Henry spent most of his free time in the pit.

Several years ago, a rubber company from the Canton area sent a truckload of discarded rubber bands to the Home. Being able to use any donation for a positive purpose, the older boys came up with the idea to dig a pit and fill it with the bands. The quantity and elasticity made a perfect trampoline. Since the surface held the same plain as the ground, the Headmaster felt it would be reasonably safe and approved the project.

The boys dug the hole by hand. They placed the rubber in careful layers on the bottom in opposing directions until they covered half of the hole. The rest of the bands, tossed haphazardly on the top half, aided in the spring. For one summer, the children bounced on their makeshift trampoline until one little girl suffered a broken arm.

The Headmaster burned the rubber and filled in the hole. What he did not account for was the curiosity of a young mind when Henry fell into the collapsing hole. He clawed at the soft earth attempting to climb to the top. By the time his exhausted body lay on the grass above, he discovered his restraints - two rubber bands hung from his arms.

The bands, nearly sixteen inches in length and an inch in width, disintegrated as he stretched them. He sat on the edge of the hole with his feet dangling into the abyss wondering about their purpose. He swung the broken strip around repeatedly over his head. A sly grin covered his face. He jumped back into the hole and began to dig.

Most of the rubber bands lost their elasticity long before Henry discovered the pit, but he continued to dig through the black debris hoping for a few good pieces. He walked over the entire surface until he felt a spongy corner. He bounced on the ground happy to find recoil beneath his feet. Under several layers of charred remains, he found a cluster of rubber bands untouched by the fire and protected by the elements. He lifted the first band and pulled it as far apart as his strength permitted. It snapped. The second did the same, as well as the third. Fueled by a fever to find a few salvageable remnants, he dug to the bottom of the pit. Rewarded by his tenacity, he found dozens of resilient bands. He sat half-covered by dirt, ash, and grime, elated with his find.

He slid the bands over his arms paying little attention to the quantity and began his climb out of the pit. The extra weight proved too difficult to maneuver. He separated his find into several piles, repositioned ten over each arm, five on each side, and managed to climb to the top. He sprinted toward the barn.

After three exhausting trips, he climbed into the haymow and hid his treasure. He lay on top of the soft green piles staring at the ceiling. He pulled bits of charred rubber that stuck to his sweaty face. He laughed aloud.

Belle sat alone watching the children play. More often than not, she unconsciously gawked at Dorothy. She labored over Christmas ideas wondering what she could make that may be suitable.

Belle heard distant laughter and watched the Freshmen slip into the tattered cornfield. Henry led the charge. She waited barely ten minutes before a thin trail of smoke rose in the distance. She smiled at the memory of parched corn.

With only a few corn stalks that remained standing, Belle watched the unseasonably warm breeze toss remnants of their brown leaves. They appeared to wave, beckoning Belle to draw closer. Mesmerized by the motion, she stood and walked to the edge of the field.

She knelt and gathered a few corn bits from the ground. Her hands twisted and pulled at the dry yet pliable leaves without paying attention to their results. When she reached the end of the second leaf, she held the beginnings of a corn stalk doll. Belle smiled triumphantly.

She gathered the neck tight and began to twist it into position, but instead of making it stronger, the twist weakened its ability to remain rigid. She pulled a few new pieces from a corn stalk and tried again with less success.

189

"Hmmm," she whispered aloud. "I need something stiff to make it sturdy." She pinched the neck of the would-be doll. "It has to be skinny here." She enclosed her fingers in a circle, "and rounded here for the head."

Her back stiffened at a bright thought. She turned to face her cottage, nodded her head, and ran towards the door. When she reached her cottage, she skipped down the flight of stairs into the locker area. She opened the metal door and fumbled through her stash of goodies until she felt the cool handle of the decorative spoon. Holding it tightly, she closed her locker door and began to run toward the stairs when she heard soft sobs.

Surprised at the sound because she thought she was alone, she whispered, "Who's there?"

A pathetic whimper came from behind her. Belle turned to face an empty set of lockers.

"Who's there?" she asked again

"It's me...Dorothy."

"Where are you?" Belle continued in a whispered voice.

"I'm in my locker." She began to cry.

"Which one?" Belle began to knock. "This One?"

"No. To your left."

"This one?"

"Almost."

Belle skipped a locker. "This one?"

"Back."

She tapped on the locker. "Are you in here, Dorothy?"

"Yes." She could barely speak through her sobs.

Belle opened the door and helped Dorothy stand. She stumbled at her first attempted step. Her feet tingled.

"Who put you in there?"

"I don't know," she whimpered. "I didn't see them."

"Them?"

"Yes, I heard a few voices. Maybe there were three or more. I don't know."

"And they just pushed you in your locker?" Belle gasped.

Dorothy struggled to finish her story. She fought the tears and then finally surrendered. After a few minutes, she gained enough control to tell Belle her story.

"We were playing in the yard and one of the girls broke the badminton birdie. I said I had another shuttlecock that my Grandma gave me in my Halloween pail. I ran in here to get the birdie and someone smashed the door against me, pushed me into my locker, and slammed the door closed." Tears filled her eyes again. "I screamed but no one heard me, until you came in."

"How long have you been in there?" Belle pointed to her locker.

"I...I don't know, probably at least an hour."

Belle threw her arms around her new friend. They embraced and cried together.

Belle wondered why none of her friends came to look for her.

"I just want to go outside," she said filled with desperation. "I've been cooped up in there too long. I felt like I couldn't breathe."

"That's terrible!" Belle motioned for her to follow. "Come on. Let's go out and enjoy the sunshine while it lasts."

Immediately Belle swallowed the growing lump. She heard the sound of her mother's voice echo those same words. She looked down at Dorothy's hand inside her own and smiled.

She glanced over at the spoon in her opposite hand. Its image of the Children's Home glimmered in the growing light. Had Belle not decided to keep it in her locker, or search for it for the doll's structure, Dorothy may have spent many hours crammed inside her locker. Somehow, the use of that spoon in Dorothy's Christmas doll seemed more special than a few minutes prior. Belle could not wait to start.

25

With Christmas fast approaching, Belle hurried to finish Dorothy's doll. She used discarded bits of twine from the hay bales to shape the doll's neck, arms, and legs. She wrapped several layers around the spoon's bowl for the perfectly shaped head.

She found a floral handkerchief blowing across the lawn after October's visiting day and used it for the doll's dress. She was able to attach it without the need to cut it. The finished scalloped edges of the sheer fabric gave an elegant appearance to the otherwise crude construction.

Belle used the Home's art supplies to paint the doll's face. She made her eyes blue with long eyelashes sweeping out from the outside corners, an understated nose, and bright pink lips slightly curled to form a grin. Happy with her gift, she placed the doll carefully in her locker.

Several children, widely separated for secrecy, painted their presents in the dining hall. Belle tore a large piece of brown kraft paper from the roll donated from a local butcher and began to paint her wrapping paper. She painted trees, sleighs, horses, bells, churches, stars, and a manger with baby Jesus, Mary, and Joseph, cows, donkeys, shepherds, and angels. She duplicated the pattern on the reverse side once it dried. After selecting the best side, she wrapped her corn doll in the paper gathered at the top and secured it with a piece of twine. She wrote the word DORO-THY on a folded card strung through the string. She proudly carried it under the Christmas tree to join the other presents gathered there.

Henry worked feverishly on his slingshots. He finished Joey's first, wrapped it in newspaper, and placed it under the tree. He propped the odd-shaped present against the tree trunk. The red painted letters—JOEY—drew attention. He left the room and slipped into the barn to count the remaining rubber bands.

With the weather growing colder by the day, the ground soon hardened as the snow began to build. Gathering Y-shaped sticks became increasingly difficult. Henry grinned as he wound the eighteenth band around its frame. He counted the remaining strips and decided he would save them for replacements if the original bands broke. He finished the final slingshot two days before Christmas.

The Home bubbled with excitement as the day of gift giving drew nigh. Many local churches came in small groups to sing Christmas carols. The crisp evenings made their breath freeze in a smoky haze as they belted out the Holiday's favorite hymns — Hark the Herald Angels Sing, Go Tell it on the Mountain, Away in the Manger, Silent Night, and always exiting with We Wish You a Merry Christmas. The children clapped and sang along. Even the ones who did not attend church knew the words before the season ended.

Members of the local high school club - Future Homemakers of America - baked and delivered cookies. The older children served as their tour guides once the cookie social and caroling concluded. They spent extra time in cottages #1 and #7, since many of the outsiders knew the inmates.

Christmas morning came with the age-old fever. Most of the children woke long before dawn. It became torture to stay in the dorms until first light, but most managed. Only a few snuck down to the tree, rummaging through the presents until they found one with their name.

Belle felt particularly giddy. Anticipating Dorothy's favorable response made her antsy. Only once did an unfavorable vision cross her mind. She dismissed it with a vigorous headshake.

Henry also seemed excited to share his slingshot with Joey, although of late their relationship grew estranged with Henry spending the majority of his time with the older boys. Joey spent much of his time in solitude.

Although Henry continued his bi-weekly raid of the laundry room to help his friend, his motives became mostly selfish. Last week, he barely escaped discovery, so he grabbed an extra sheet in case that may be his last. With the noticeable reduction in sheet inventory, the staff grew suspicious and carefully guarded the room. Occasionally, Henry stuffed their soiled sheet on the bottom of the pile. It was fun to listen to the scream of discovery from one of the laundry staff.

After listening to the Headmaster's repetitious banter of the rules of opening presents, Henry lost interest. He barely acknowledged Joey's excitement when he opened his slingshot, but when one of the Freshmen mumbled a jealous comment he took notice and smiled.

Immediately, the Headmaster made his way through the crowd of children, string, and bits of paper. He lunged at Joey's slingshot, although Joey had a firm grip and refused to let go.

"This is an impossible present!" Enoch screamed. The room fell silent. Even Henry sat at attention.

"Let go!" Joey demanded, surprised at his show of confidence.

"You can't have that! You'll hurt someone with it!"

Henry's deviant grin grew with every word. He thoroughly enjoyed the exchange.

Enoch's body shook as he pried the slingshot from Joey's grip. He peeled one finger at a time loosening his grip until Joey relinquished. Once the toy broke free, Enoch raised it above his head.

"Who made this?" The space between his teeth made his statement hiss.

The children erupted in excited conversation. Most began to point to the various troublemakers. The Headmaster approached the designated children and interrogated them. Once satisfied, he moved to the next. No one admitted to making the slingshot, especially Henry.

Belle glared at her troublemaker brother. The smug expression on his face spoke volumes. She knew he was guilty.

Joey ran toward the Headmaster and tried to pull his present from his lanky hands to no avail. Exasperated, he kicked his shin.

Enoch doubled over. He grabbed Joey's ear and pulled him out of the room and down the hall.

Joey repeated, "But it was my present! You said everyone would get a present!" His cries faded until they suddenly stopped. The sound of a slamming door silenced each child. No one waited to hear the sound of the whip. They scattered from the room.

Henry carried his peashooter in his back pocket. He felt a light tap on his shoulder. He turned to see Peter, his face beamed with pride.

"Do you like it?" He pointed to Henry's pocket.

"Huh?" Henry hesitated watching Peter's smile turn to a flat line. He pulled the peashooter from his pocket. "This?"

Peter found his grin. "Yes. Do you like it?"

"Yeah, sure. It's neat."

Peter waited for Henry to expand, but he said nothing more. Peter's face flushed. He awkwardly backed away from him and slipped out of sight.

Clarence nudged Henry as he walked past him. He turned around and whispered, "What a way to ruin Christmas!"

Immediately, Henry froze, worried his secret was out. "What do you mean?" he finally asked.

"I mean Joey. Getting a whippin' on Christmas day."

Henry sighed. "Yeah, really."

"It was a cool present, though." Clarence continued, "Wish I had one. I could knock out that jerk!"

Henry puffed his chest out. He motioned for Clarence to come closer. "Grab the others and meet me in the barn. I have something to show you."

"What?" Clarence screeched. "A surprise?"

"Just do as I say. Get the others." The pair separated.

Belle stumbled away from the stampede of frightened children. She looked for Dorothy, but could not find her. She sulked toward her cottage disappointed that she missed the opening of her present. Belle placed her handmade hair bow and pair of hand-stitched white gloves on her bed just as Dorothy entered the dorm. She watched her friend carefully prop her new doll against her pillow. Dorothy fanned out the dolls handkerchief dress and walked out of the room. Belle smiled, pleased that Dorothy liked her doll.

Henry waited anxiously in the barn. He retrieved the pile of slingshots from the haymow. He chose his finest creation and slid it back under the pile of loose hay. He chose twelve others and displayed them on top of the closest hay bale. He waited for the group to arrive.

Clarence announced the arrival of the clan before they walked through the barn door. "You in there, Henry?"

"SHHHH..." Henry chastised.

Once all entered the building, he stood to reveal his hiding place. He motioned for them to join him.

"I'm up here."

One by one, the children climbed the vertical wooden ladders. After climbing eight rungs on the first ladder, they tightrope-walked a few steps toward the second one, repeating the process until each stepped onto the haymow.

Henry pointed to the stacks of hay in the back of the mow. "Go pick your favorite. There is one for all of you."

The children rushed toward the hay bales. Their voices etched with excitement. Only Tom argued about his choice, but quickly found the perfect size of base to fit his hand.

Henry proudly watched. He lifted both hands and motioned to the group. "Listen up, everyone," he warned. "The Headmaster can not know about this! He will kill us all!" The crowd murmured in agreement. "We can only use these when we are together. No one and I mean NO ONE can use these on their own. Got it?"

"Got it!" They responded in unison enthusiasm.

Henry crouched to his knees in the center of the circle. "Now, if we are going to use these weapons we must practice. Tonight at midnight, we will meet here, gather our slingshots, and attempt to hit a target." Henry laughed. "I'm certain the Headmaster will be sound asleep, not expecting any more commotion today, so our practice time should be safe. Everyone agree?"

"But what if he hears us?" one of the boys asked.

"Then we run." Henry's response to the question came without emotion.

"What if someone sees us?" asked another.

"Then we run."

"What if someone else hears us?" Jane whispered.

"Then we run." Sarcasm laced Henry's voice.

"But..."

Henry exploded. "But what? You guys are acting like scared babies! We are working on a plan." He huffed, "But in the meantime, we have to practice. Get it?"

A few random responses dotted the circle. Henry shook his head. He tightened his fists and thrust them deep into his hips.

"I'm coming out tonight at midnight. If anyone wants to practice with their slingshot, show up." He slapped his thighs. "And if you're too scared, stay in bed." He kept his hands on his thighs and bent closer to their faces. He whispered, "But if you don't come, you can't keep it." He lifted his slingshot and jumped off the haymow into the lofty pile of soft hay below, shaking his head until he exited the barn.

That evening, Henry stared at the ceiling, unable to sleep. He struggled to control inflated waves of anger. Joey never returned, so Henry had the bed to himself. It seemed odd to feel alone in a room filled with sleeping boys.

He cast aside the guilt of Joey's beating. If Joey had only given it up when the Headmaster asked for it, he would be sleeping in his bed tonight instead of recovering in the dark room. He slid a second slingshot under Joey's pillow. He hoped Joey would not harbor animosity toward him for the confrontation. The idea that the Headmaster would respond as he did never crossed Henry's mind. He closed his eyes and prayed for Joey's restoration.

When Henry opened his eyes, he realized by the foul taste in his mouth that he had fallen asleep. He threw off the covers and crept out of the room, down the steps, and out onto the front lawn. His heart raced as he remembered his final words to the rest of the group. When he walked into the barn, ten boys stood in a straight line receiving instructions from Jane.

"Nice of you to join us," Clarence jeered.

"Just making sure you really wanted to learn." Henry tried to cover.

"Yeah, right," Tom chided. "You fell asleep."

Henry stood beside Jane and eyed her stance. Not only did she hold the slingshot correctly, she chose the correct size rocks. He smiled at her.

"When did you learn to use a slingshot?" Admiration filled his words.

"My Grandpa taught me...before he passed. That's why I'm here." Jane choked back tears.

Henry faced the line of boys. "Okay, then. Let me see what you've got!"

A shower of rocks sailed through the air. A few hit their intended target, although most flew in wild directions causing Henry to duck from their trajectory. When the last rock thumped against the far barn wall, the group erupted in laughter.

They spent the next hour practicing inside the barn until Henry felt they should move to an open area for the final exercise of the night. They walked in small groups toward the gymnasium. When all successfully crossed the property without detection, Henry gave the instructions.

"Okay. Everyone line up! Stones ready. Target in sight." He held up his hand. "Ready? Set. Fire!"

A shower of stones hit the broad side of the gymnasium. One struck a window. The glass shattered into a shower of glitter. The commotion sliced through the quiet of the night and immediately struck a cord of horror.

The twelve Freshmen scattered like grain rats. Each took a different path to their beds, rushing to settle in before their Matron would discover who made the racket and who bore the responsibility for the broken window. With luck on their side all made it to their beds. When the last sheet settled over their dressed bodies, the woman turned on the light.

"Everyone up!" The Matron shrieked. "I want to see who is missing!"

She counted and recounted, relieved that none of her children were responsible for the commotion. She happily turned out the light.

In the dark, devilish smiles covered the faces of the guilty. This time they got away with it.

26

Belle sat on the empty staircase, arms bent, and elbows on her knees, with her face cradled in her idle hands. After a few minutes, she stood and dusted the banister twice, taking special care to re-inspect the corners. She removed a few stray particles that gathered there. Boredom consumed her, so she resumed her seated position.

She jumped at the sound of the front doorbell. Excited for the task at hand, she ran down the staircase and threw the front door open wide. An elderly man stood before her.

"Good afternoon, young lady." His eyes sparkled as he greeted Belle.

"Good...Good afternoon," Belle fumbled.

Her eyes slid to the floor of the front porch where the two toboggans and three wooden sleds waited. Belle jumped up and down clapping her hands repeatedly. She watched the man's grin widen by the outward show of her excitement.

"Are these for me?" Belle asked while still jumping.

"Well," he laughed. "These are for all of the children to share."

A cold burst of wind blew Belle's hair and covered her face. The icy blast made her shiver.

"Come in, sir," she added remembering her greeting manners. "It's freezing out there."

"Thank you," he replied as he shook the snow from his hat.

Belle had a difficult time containing her excitement. This was the first time she saw a sled up close. Her family's meager finances did not permit many recreational luxuries.

"Where did you get those sleds?"

"Well, I own a hardware store in Alliance and we ordered a few extra." He cleared his throat. "My intentions were to bring these before Christmas, but my customers and the fluctuating weather kept me from following through." He patted the top of Belle's head. "I'm sorry I couldn't make it until now."

"Oh, that's okay. It's still the Holiday season." She pointed to the glittering, colorful decorations placed around the staircase. "We're still decorated."

"It looks beautiful." He hesitated before adding, "Who would I talk to about my...um...donation?"

"Oh, that would be Miss Betsy." Belle turned and began to walk toward the kitchen. "I'll get her."

Belle ran down the hall and nearly slid past the kitchen door. She held onto the door jamb until she regained her balance. Her emotions bubbled up in her words.

Miss Betsy busied herself with the mundane kitchen tasks. Since the cookie baking had been halted until expenses could be met, she dusted the empty cupboards.

Belle burst through the door. Miss Betsy laughed at her jumbled screech.

"Slow down, Belle! What has you so energized?"

"There's a man at the front door and he brought us sleds! Sleds! Five of them! Come on!" She tugged at Miss Betsy's sleeve. "I'll show you."

Within ten minutes, most of the children heard about the donation. They rushed to investigate the rumor, thrilled to see five new toys on the front porch. A flurry of activity ensued. Coats, hats, and gloves flew around the locker rooms. Children shouted for their boots; some gave up looking and wore their shoes with an extra pair of socks. Only a few had all the components for a warm afternoon, yet they did not care. They rushed outside and braved the cold no matter what their apparel.

The banks of the barn posed the best scenario for the runs. Although the children used both slopes, only one held a challenge for the older group. Soon, the Home split into two groups - the younger using the short, steeper slope and the older ones spending their time on the longer, more challenging course.

Henry transferred his weight from one foot to the next, anxious for his turn on the toboggan. He watched those before him fly over the encrusted snow, many taking a spill before their carriage completed its ride.

Seven groups of five rode the toboggan before his turn finally came. He settled into his predetermined position behind the curved bow. With five bodies wedged tightly together, the boy in the rear delivered the final announcement.

"Ready?"

"Ready!" everyone shouted.

The pushers placed their hands on the back rider's shoulders and gave the bunch a hard shove. Down the long slope they went.

Snow and ice formed into hardened pea-sized balls peppered Henry's face. They bounced off his eyelids, hair, and exposed teeth. He wiped his face multiple times to clear his vision.

"Lean!" he yelled to the kids crouching behind him.

All bent to the left allowing the toboggan to follow a graceful curve at the bottom of the hill. Shots of jubilation erupted from the wooden toboggan. They successfully mastered the first round of challenges.

"Okay," bellowed Henry. "The fence is next." Henry kept his eyes on the barbed wire as the toboggan picked up speed. "Ready...on my count! One... Two...Three...DUCK!"

The children forced their head between their knees, or under the preceding one's arm. Although the height of the fence posed no treat, the boys enjoyed the game. When the toboggan cleared the wire successfully, the sled team again celebrated along with the group of kids walking their sled toward the top of the course.

"Waaahooo!" they shouted, lifting their hands in the air.

206

Henry, proud of his leadership abilities, stayed focused on the last obstacle — the stream. "Almost there! Pay attention."

The waterway ran through the bottom of the cow pasture. Trampled to gradual banks from a myriad of cow hooves, it appeared to create an easy transition, yet not a single group successfully made the jump. Henry, driven by desire to be the first, coached the riders behind him.

"We're getting closer. We can do this! Almost there...ready...one...two...three...up!"

The boys forced their bodies upward, raising their hands high above their heads. The momentum proved enough. The toboggan successfully cleared both banks.

"Yippee!"

"Yay!"

"We did it!"

Shouts and cheers filled the air as the toboggan soared over the creek. In mid-air, the sled tilted to the right throwing it off balance. The cries of joy shifted to concern. The toboggan struck the ground beyond the far bank tossing the team in all directions. A shower of snow and ice exploded upwards and fell in confetti fashion.

The team, their bodies scattered and bruised, including the two that landed in the frozen creek bed, screamed with laughter. Henry jumped to his feet, holding his aching sides, and then lifted his arms and pumped his fists repeatedly. The distant crowd cheered at their display.

"Wooohooo! We did it! We actually did it!"

The boys rolled in the snow until they could no longer laugh. Tears of pride streamed down their grinning faces. They punched, pushed, and needled each other while they pulled the toboggan to the top of the run. They challenged each team to match or beat their record. No one did.

Every child had at least two rides on the sleds or toboggans before evening came. Finally, at dusk the Matrons called the crowd in from the cold. Wet, frozen, yet overflowing with joy, their chattering voices filled the Home. Even the meager dinner of hot chocolate and a crusty piece of stale bread did not dampen the mood.

By morning, Henry's winning team gained Home-wide notoriety. As each team member entered the dining hall, the crowd cheered. Henry enjoyed the attention more than the rest. After all, had it not been for his keen coaching the toboggan would not have sailed over the creek.

Before the end of January, many other teams met or surpassed Henry's team record. The children drove a stake into the hardened ground, as far as physically possible, to mark the farthest ride. After advancing the stake ten times, many lost count and more lost interest. Soon, the long lines grew shorter. Many children began to grumble about the cold, overuse, waiting time, and unfair balance that by mid-February less than forty children used the winter toys.

Henry woke early, hours before the five a.m. chore wake up call. His brilliant thought kept him from sleep. He tossed the damp sheet off his chilled body and shivered at the room's temperature. He felt certain that if he had enough light, he would be able to see his breath inside the dorm. He put on every piece of clothing within reach and headed toward the barn.

Rats scattered when he turned on the lights. Focused on his plan, he paid them no mind. His baseball bat lay in a corner.

"I know I saw it somewhere," he whispered aloud. "But that was months ago."

He walked the perimeter of the barn searching the goods stored on the lowest horizontal beam without success. Next, he checked the milk house to no avail. Frustrated at his misfortune, he retraced his steps taking extra care in his search. He moved paper bags of seed, rusted coffee cans of miscellaneous nails, and discarded rolls of material, organizing the items as he searched. He bypassed the section of mason jars, lids nailed to the bottom of the beam, being able to see their contents through the glass.

He glanced to the end of the row, only five feet remained. He held his breath, hoping to find it. He pulled on a huddle of tattered gloves wedged between the beam and barn siding. On his second tug, one of the fingers tore from the disintegrating material. He threw it on the ground and stomped on the spider that wandered out from his nest site. He yanked and pulled until finally the entire ball of gloves released. It hit the floor with a loud thud.

At his feet lay a small rectangular box. Its original moss green color faded to a yellowish-grey, but the print remained clear—Grafting Wax. Henry opened the box and slid the bar from the package. About half of the bar remained. Henry only needed a small amount. The glacial temperatures made the wax rigid. He threw it on the floor with all his strength hoping it would break. It did not.

He picked up a nearby ax and struck it. The bar sliced into halves. The ax blade stuck in the barn floor. Henry pulled the ax from its position and replaced it where he found it. He had just placed the smallest chunk of wax in his pocket when the rest of the milking crew entered the barn.

"What are you doing here so early?" one of the boys asked.

"Couldn't sleep," Henry replied, avoiding eye contact.

"Then why haven't you started?"

"Just got here," he lied.

"It's freezing in here." Tom complained.

"Come on, let's get started. The sooner we start, the sooner we finish."

Tom slapped Henry's back. "Geez, Henry. How many sets of clothes do you have on?"

"Every one I had," he shrugged. "You said yourself it was freezing in here."

The boys finished in record time. Each struggled to keep their hands from freezing to the moisture. The cow's body provided a bit of warmth, but the swirling wind cut through their inadequate clothing.

"Heat's in the work," one boy repeated each time he carried two buckets of milk. No one felt the need to reply. All wanted to get out of the drafty barn. After an hour, the boys dumped the final pail of milk. Henry shoved his frozen hands deep into his coat pocket. He closed one fist around the hunk of wax.

"Anyone up for a toboggan challenge later?" His eyes begged the group for a 'yes.'

"Maybe after the sun comes up," Tom responded. "Right now all I can think about is getting warm."

Breakfast was well under way when the boys walked into the Home. The loud chatter left no doubt that most had finished.

"Guess there won't be much left for us," Tom complained.

"Maybe we could raid the supply room." Henry whispered as he dug his elbow into Tom's side.

"Good idea!" Tom concurred. "Good idea."

27

School studies carried on, boring as usual. The children grew anxious as the February calendar page laid in the trash basket.

Henry's wax job on the bottom of the toboggan helped him regain his throne as 'King of the Rides.' He never revealed his secret to anyone.

The Freshmen continued their midnight slingshot practices until all felt confident with their aim. Despite the fact that they slipped out once a week and managed to break two more gym windows, no one was caught. Enoch suspected the group, but had no hard evidence outside of his suspicions.

Belle watched her brother from a distance with great sadness. She missed him and attempted to approach him several times in the past few months, but Henry ignored her. In an effort to divert her depression, she watched the band director paint several murals on the Home's walls. One in particular, on the third floor, just off the main circular staircase captivated her. Since most of the painting occurred in the winter months, the subject matter resonated the view from the windows.

The serene evening winter scene seemed more of a Norman Rockwell magazine series than something that should appear on the walls of an orphanage, but Mr. Davis painted with grace and style that managed to bring the children comfort. It covered most of the upstairs hall and took him more than one month to complete.

The sky, a warm honey yellow, reflected onto the moonlit snow. A horse-drawn carriage carried a couple to the distant home, beaming with bright Cadmium light through each window. A large family of all ages waited on the front porch to greet the approaching pair, smiles wide, hands lifted in greeting, even the dog seemed excited.

A heavy fresh snow clung to the bare tree branches, which appeared in all sizes throughout the painting. Their white limbs sprinkled the roadside and created a sharp contrast to the far-reaching row of pines. A few boughs of a close fir tree skirted the ground from the excessive weight.

Belle inspected the limbs carefully. "I can almost hear them creaking and groaning." She immediately felt awkward. Her face burned. "I mean it's so life-like." She sighed, "I wish I could paint like that."

Mr. Davis hurried to finish the sills around the home's windows. He never looked up from his work, but smiled in his reply. "You will never know until you try."

Belle's face flushed brighter. "But…"

He lowered his head to make eye contact with her over his low-seated glasses. "Grab a brush and try."

"Where?" She jumped with excitement.

"There." He pointed to the adjacent blank wall and then extended his can of brushes to her. "Use my brushes and paint. See how it goes. If you like it and are happy with your results, then we will get you some of your own." He put his brush down and cleaned his lenses. "Sound good?"

"Sounds perfect!" Belle nearly cried.

She spent the next few hours outlining a dragonfly. Its over exaggerated wingspan spread nearly two feet, with its body close to the same. Belle chose Payne's Grey to delineate the edges. It felt freeing to use paint first instead of carbon.

Belle twisted her face several times disappointed in her perspective. Mr. Davis told her to dampen a towel and wipe off the paint quickly before it had a chance to dry. Happy when it worked, Belle used her cloth often. When she felt comfortable in her draft, she began to add color.

"Do you think it's okay to make it a bright color?" Belle hesitated, "Like Ultramarine blue… or something?"

Laughing at her innocence, he answered, "Belle, you are the artist. Paint it whatever color you wish." He stopped to watch her first wash of blue. "If that color makes you happy, it makes me happy."

Time slipped away and soon the shadows on the wall began to cover her workspace. Unable to distinguish the hues in the failing light, she decided to quit for the day. She rinsed out her borrowed brushes and bid Mr. Davis a good night. She crawled into bed without the thought of dinner.

The following morning she raced up the stairs to look at her creation with fresh, rested eyes. The image pleased her. She sat on the top step and waited for her painting supplies. She heard his soft footfalls as he climbed the stairs.

"Well, good morning, Miss Belle." He bowed and tipped his head. "Are you hoping to finish your dragonfly today?"

"I am."

He stood in the distance and admired her work. "I have to say, Belle. That is quite good." He watched her blush at the compliment. "You have amazing talent and I am so glad we found each other. I get quite lonely sometimes painting up here."

Belle looked at his nearly finished image. It spanned the hall from door frame to door frame and covered at least ten feet. Belle did not realize until that moment that Mr. Davis's background was not the horsehair plaster wall, but a canvas glued to the wall itself.

She wondered aloud, "Are you going to leave it here?"

"Why, yes. I believe so. I think it fits rather well here, don't you?"

"Yes. I love the way the light from the window moves across it as the day goes on." Belle pointed to the south facing window.

Smiling, he added, "I agree. That's one of the reasons I chose this spot."

"And what are the other reasons?"

Startled by her question, he hesitated. He wanted to say that he hoped the painting would bring serenity to those that see it when they enter or leave the dark room. He struggled with another answer.

Belle watched his face rise and fall opening his mouth several times to speak, but leaving the hall eerily silent. Suddenly, Belle felt uncomfortable.

"I...I don't need to know." She hung her head. "I'm sorry."

"Sorry for what?" He perked up at her quick apology.

Belle did not answer. She felt unsure how to express her feelings.

His face and voice softened as he walked close to her. He knelt on the floor to meet her eyes. "It's not a secret, Belle." He lowered his voice a bit more. "I just hope my painting could make someone smile," he hesitated. "Smile on a day that they didn't think they could."

Belle's eyes flew open. Suddenly, she realized where they were. She stared at the door to the dark room, listening for any sound.

"No one is in there, Belle." He managed a thin smile. "Today is a happy day." He lifted his can of brushes for Belle to pick what she needed. She chose a one-inch wash brush, a no. 4, and a rigger. He gave her a small palette filled with a multitude of bright colors.

"Let's create a happy dragonfly. Shall we?"

Belle nodded in agreement and went straight to work. She finished the wings with a rainbow of colors — Cerulean, Crimson, Sap Green, Violet, and Cadmium Yellow. The bright colors against the

216

Ultramarine Blue body made both of them smile. She rinsed his brushes and paint dregs before surrendering the supplies.

"Today, Mr. Davis, we painted happiness."

"Yes we did, Belle. Yes we did."

Belle spent the balance of the winter months painting various images around the Home. Mr. Davis gave her a modest set of brushes, paints, and a palette. She took great care of her new present, certain to wash the paint from the brushes completely before storing them in her locker.

Mr. Davis's suggestion of "painting happiness" resonated through her brushes. Her bright colors dictated her subject matter. She painted birds, butterflies, rainbows, clouds, and trees, leaving the landscapes for the better talent.

She met several students, mostly older, as she painted the walls around the Home. A few encouraged her to paint bigger images and full landscape scenes. After much encouragement and an expanded array of colors, she decided to try a winter scene outside the dining hall.

She struggled with a subject matter until one evening she happened to see two deer standing on the lawn. They appeared as statuary, their eyes remaining fixed on Belle. She stood in the window and studied their form, placement, and colors. With a flick of a white tail, the mother warned her yearling to follow. They lopped toward the barn and slipped out of sight.

After school the following day, Belle began to recreate the image, with a few artistic liberties. She decided to change the background to the frozen creek bed where Henry captured and held the best toboggan run. Next, she added a slope dotted with a few snow-laden pine trees.

Pleased with the results, she began to outline the deer. She positioned the doe broadside with her head turned, fixed on an object behind her on her left. She added a yearling to her right standing in direct sight of the unknown distraction. She painted both of their ears standing erect as if listening intently.

Anxious to use her rigger, she painted a multi-trunk deciduous tree. Lining its bare branches with a thin coat of snow added the depth she craved. She moved the foreground closer to the viewer by painting a few clumps of reeds, altered to a brown winter whisper, at the edge of the frozen stream.

"Hmm," she rubbed her chin. "Something is missing."

She stared at her first full landscape for several minutes. Suddenly she laughed.

"Rocks. I need rocks peeking out of the ice."

She started with three different sized rocks protruding from the bluish ice. Unhappy with the trio, she added a multitude of others until they helped etch the edge of the creek.

Again, she gawked at her painting. She counted the trees and then the rocks. Both were odd numbers. She traced the form of the deer with an imaginary brush, pleased with her perspective. Yet, something about the scene bothered her. She counted the number of stones for the third time. Suddenly she realized that the thing that troubled her was the number of deer. There were only two.

"Yes," she spoke to herself. "Mr. Davis says to always use an odd number. Triangles are more interesting to the eye than a square, or in this case a line." She picked up her brush and began to add a third deer. "Yep, I need another one. Three is best."

With her painting complete, at least so she suspected, she moved farther down the hall for a different view. One of the senior girls walked past Belle as she stood with hands placed on her hips and her head cocked to one side. Belle jumped when the girl spoke.

"Looks great, Belle," was all she offered and disappeared around the corner.

"Thank you." Belle whispered aloud, "It does look great."

28

Rule #10–Every child will attend church on Easter
and Christmas, no exceptions.

Spring arrived overnight and never left. The sun
warmed the earth and left the toboggan challenges
a distant memory. Crocuses popped with a show of
white, purple, and yellow blooms. The daffodils, hy-
acinths, and tulips quickly followed.

Easter fell on April Fools Day and the Home
buzzed with the gaiety of jokes and pranks taking
center stage over the celebration of the Resurrection,
bunnies, eggs, and chocolate.

The children entered the dining hall to see the
lavish display of candy donated by a local chocolat-
ier along with several local candy stores. The solid chocolate rabbit stood front and center on his

220

hindquarters and measured nearly two feet in height surrounded by a multitude of rainbow-colored baskets. The baskets, lined with colorful plastic grasses, overflowed with hard-boiled eggs dipped and painted by the high school girls. Wrapped hard candy, jellybeans, foil-covered chocolate eggs, sugar drops on wax paper, and wax bottles filled with sweet syrup, filled four large baskets on the floor.

Many of the April Fools practical jokes continued throughout breakfast and this infuriated the Headmaster. Given a strict order that no child may eat any candy before breakfast, the Matrons flanked the candy display as sentries.

Dreaming of the taste of velvety chocolate, the children gulped their breakfast and began to form a long line. As in every Easter parade, the children could select three items from the table; the remaining treats, if any, were reserved as merits for good behavior.

The chocolate rabbit centerpiece, chopped into smaller pieces and hid throughout the Home, became the day's highlighted scavenger hunt. The reward far outweighed the risk. If you found it, you could keep it no matter the quantity. The odds of finding more than enough to satisfy his or her desire were high so when it came time for the children to select their choices from the table, the majority chose food over candy.

Having used the opportunity prior to breakfast to peruse the goodies on the table, the selection line moved rather quickly. After their choice, they ran to their dorms to prepare for Sunday services. The floors throughout the Home became dotted with bits of colored shells as many children inhaled their hard-boiled eggs on their way.

Outside of the mandatory Easter and Christmas services, the decision to go to church was up to the individual. With only one Home bus, the staff made the decision which church to attend by the time of their services. The Catholic Church remained a constant, while the second church choice fluctuated between the Presbyterian and the Methodist.

With many students preparing for church, the patience in the candy line grew thin. The children became unruly and began to shove one another. The staff quickly settled the disputes, pleased with the assertion of their authority, until one little girl approached the table.

She looked up at the oversized chocolate rabbit and asked, "Where are his ears?"

The Matron's heads recoiled like a rubber band. Shock lit their faces and immediately shifted to fear. The Headmaster, leaning cross-armed against the back wall, charged toward the table. His booming voiced bounced around the room a multitude of times before settling into a loud rattle.

"STOP!"

The children froze in mid-motion. Their eyes fixed on his advance.

"There will be no chocolate until the culprit is found!"

Enoch snatched the ear-less rabbit and walked out the door. With visions of the disappearing scavenger hunt prize, the children's choices shifted from the eggs to candy. Outside of one, most of the children went without the treat of chocolate.

Henry walked up the stairs from the basement and stood in the back of the line. The boy in front of him whispered to inform Henry of the drama.

"Someone stole the rabbit's ears," he leaned close to Henry's ear.

"Of course, that's my favorite part!" added the boy without turning back around. "The Headmaster took it."

Henry wrinkled his nose. "What's he gonna do with it?"

"I dunno," the boy answered. "Probably eat it." He shook his head.

A second boy added with great sadness, "I guess that means no scavenger hunt this year. Man, I love chocolate..." His voice trailed off.

Henry peered around the boys at the Easter display. "Looks like there is plenty of candy left for all of us."

The boys glanced toward the table. Henry was right. The basket of chocolate eggs remained half-full. With only seven in line before them, they stood a good chance of having some chocolate. The boys chattered excitedly about the taste. Henry rolled his eyes at their immaturity.

The first boy took three chocolate eggs. The second boy echoed the first, as did all seven children standing in the line in front of Henry.

When Henry, the last in line, stood before the table, he quickly chose three pink hard-boiled eggs. The color of the shell did not matter to him; it was the nourishment inside that did. Besides, he had a pair of chocolate bunny ears hidden inside his locker.

The children ran outside dressed in brightly colored Sunday dresses, suits and ties. A few girls wore hats and gloves, if they were lucky to have them, while the boys struggled to find enough dress shoes to go around. Three had to go without.

The first bus load went to early mass. The services began at ten o'clock, which meant the bus left the Home by half-past nine. Belle watched the bus pull out the long winding drive with a few heads protruding out of the open windows.

When the bus returned, a long line formed for the second trip to the Presbyterian Church. Belle was the first in line. She enjoyed the Catholic mass at Christmas, but decided she would try the other church today. She stepped onto the bus and sat in the first seat behind the driver. She clasped her gloved hands together on her lap.

Three children shared each seat save the one that was broken. The crammed children bickered and fought over seat preference and foot room, but soon settled in to a long and stuffy ride.

The morning sun had full reign of the sky. It seemed as if the sun declared that on Easter Sunday, not a cloud could cover its brightness. The heat soon rose to near summer-like temperatures warming the bus like an oven.

A few religious children sang hymns from their seats. Belle listened as they sang "He Arose" and "Crown Him with Many Crowns." Although the words were not familiar, the tune stayed with her for many days.

Belle walked off the bus and followed the others before her. They entered the vestibule and walked through an opened door near the back. A long, narrow staircase led the children to the balcony, the usual place for the Home's inmates.

Belle gasped at the stained glass windows, in awe of not only the size, but also the quantity. She asked one of the high school girls to explain their meanings.

She pointed to the one furthest from the balcony and began. "That one is the birth of Christ." She moved to the next window, "That one is The Sermon on the Mount." Moving from window to window, she shared her faith. "That one is called Suffer the Little Children to Come Unto Me." She leaned into Belle and said, "That is my favorite. I love the little lambs at His feet. Their smiles are as broad as the children's."

"This next one is the Moneychangers. It is kind of scary. The money flying off the overturned table looks real." She sighed as if lost in thought of what she would do if the money were indeed real. She cleared her throat and whispered, "The next three are the Last Supper, Peter's Denial, and the Crucifixion. The last two," she pointed toward the final windows that completed the circle of stories, "are the Resurrection and Christ's Ascension."

When she finished her explanation, the music started before Belle had a chance to ask their meaning. The organist's hands seemed to float over the keys gracefully as the pianist pounded hers. The stark contrast held Belle's attention as she moved her eyes from one player to the other. The loud music filled the room and although Belle had no idea what song they were playing, the crowd certainly did. When the duo finished, all rose in celebration.

225

Shouts of "Amen" and "Hallelujah" soon changed to the unison of one right side shouting, "He is risen" and the left echoing, "He is risen indeed." This went on for three rounds until the pastor, dressed in a white robe adorned by a purple scarf, silenced their enthusiasm. He opened with one more chant of the same and the congregation as a whole answered him.

"Let us pray."

The reverent silence mesmerized her. She watched every person bow their head and fold their hands. The pastor's prayer, heartfelt and inspirational, lifted the spirits of all in attendance. It was then Belle realized that Henry was not there. She wondered if he went to the Catholic service or if he hid to avoid attending at all.

The girl beside her jumped in her seat. She grabbed Belle's arm and pointed.

"There she is." Amy shouted.

"Who?" Belle countered.

"I knew she'd be here." She seemed to be talking only to herself.

"Who?" Again, Belle asked.

"My sister."

"Sister?"

"Yea, she's right there," she pointed toward the front on the left side. "See her?"

Belle had no idea who she was referring to, but it seemed important to her so she played along. "No," Belle questioned, "Which one?"

"Right there...with the pink ruffled dress...blonde hair. See her?"

Belle settled on a girl about her own age seated in the ninth row. She sat between her parents. Two other girls sat beside their father. They all wore pink dresses, bonnets white gloves, and patented leather Mary Jane shoes.

Amy caused a bit of a commotion in the balcony. A few adults turned to sport their disapproving glances, but the she paid them no mind. She stood and waved until finally the little girl turned to face her. Amy blew the little girl a kiss and waved.

The look on the young girl's face was nothing short of dismay. She leaned into her mother and whispered something. Her mother shook her head and turned her daughter's body around, away from Amy's view. The little girl whispered again and finally the mother wrapped her arm around her and pulled her close.

Amy seemed satisfied with eye contact and did not appear bothered by the show of horror from her sister. She wiggled with excitement in her seat for the rest of the sermon.

"That is my sister, Anna. She was adopted when she was two."

Belle gazed at Amy in disbelief. She immediately thought of Henry. How would she feel if Henry had been adopted and she was not? Alternatively, what if she found a family and they left Henry behind?

Belle felt hot, instantly overwhelmed with sadness. She fought tears. When the people stood, she sat. When they sang, she cried. She struggled to pay attention. Her thoughts were only of Henry and her father - where they were, what they were doing, and if either ever thought of her. Watching the little adopted girl sitting beside a man who chose to be her father proved too much for Belle. She hung her head and sobbed.

Belle sat in silence on the ride home. She did not care about bunnies, candy, or a scavenger hunt. She wanted to find Henry. She wanted to talk to him. She wanted a hug. She wanted to hear him tell her one more time that everything was going to be okay.

She walked off the bus and headed for Henry's cottage. Although, the children were not permitted to visit one another's dormitory, Belle entered anyway. It was empty.

She asked several boys, who rode the bus to the Catholic Church if they saw Henry. Each shook his head.

She sat on the front porch of her cottage wondering what had become of her brother. She tried to find enjoyment in the warmth of the day and the surrounding colors of spring. She swung her feet in the air and looked toward the main house, thinking of her first few weeks at the Home and how Henry took care of her. The memories made her feel worse. She jumped off the edge and walked toward the cemetery.

The row of Forsythia and flowering Quince on the far edge of the baseball field served as the perfect backdrop for the games to commence. Henry crawled out from under the front porch. He was anxious to perform. He had a reputation as a good swinger, especially when it came to rat bashing, but the idea of playing baseball seemed like the only normal thing in his Home life. Since tryouts were not necessary, any child who wanted to play became part of the team. This fact held both good and bad—good for the bad players and bad for the good players. Nonetheless, most of the boys elected to show up for the first day of practice.

The field followed a steep angle making the run from first to second downhill and second to third the opposite. The aggressive slide to home plate held the only even plane. For these reasons, the field's use was only for practice. They played their games off site on church diamonds or public parks, but the children did not mind. The bus ride to the games became as fun as the toboggan challenges.

Henry wanted to play shortstop, but the coach thought his talent would be best as a first baseman. His accurate throw far outweighed his capable distance. After a bit of grumbling, he settled into his position and played it well. The physical exercise and extra calorie consumption from the regular food raids added muscle to his lean body. He used his upper strength when he was at bat.

Henry learned to swing at the first pitch no matter what. More often than not, this became the secret to his home run success. He swung fast, and he swung hard. If he happened to connect, the loud crack of the bat left no doubt that the ball would sail far. If the backfield missed the fly, he made it to second with ease. At times, he even made third, but if he swung and missed the force of his swing racked his back. Either way, Henry felt pain the following day.

The team did not have full uniforms, only white t-shirts embroidered with the letter F and a number. The field, either muddy or dusty, made clean shirts impossible, and by washday the boy's uniform appeared well used. After the third washing, the white shirt degraded to a dingy shade of grey, but no one cared.

The Fairmount Team had a fierce reputation. Their record did not reflect their drive, but their drive resulted in fights. If the bats did not cause blisters, use of their fists did. The boys argued with the opposing team, coaches, and referees. It seemed about the only time unruly behavior went unpunished.

By mid-season, the team had an equal amount of wins and losses. Their skill set improved with each game, but their attitudes slid beyond deplorable, especially Henry's. The coach approached him multiple times, only to have Henry stand firm in defiance. The coach even threatened to tell the Headmaster of Henry's misconduct, without resulting in a change of behavior. As a final effort, the coach pulled on Henry's collar as he walked off the bus.

"A word, Henry." He spoke with a deep and disapproving tone.

"What now?" Henry retorted. He spit on the ground in front of the coach.

"Listen, boy. You have two choices—change your attitude or quit."

Henry narrowed his eyes and squeezed his fists as if ready to throw a sucker punch. He grinned, about to strike, when he caught a glimpse of Belle's long curly hair bouncing across the lawn. He loosened his grip forcing his hands to hang limp at his sides. He shrugged his shoulders and spewed, "Quit." He walked away from the stunned coach.

29

"Did you hear me?" the voice through the telephone receiver sounded irritated.

"Yes, sir," Enoch responded with a strained voice.

"You sound hesitant," he snapped.

"Charles, it is against my better judgment."

"Why? Don't you permit the children to have fun?"

Enoch's red face deepened in color. He pulled on his tie and loosened his collar. "Of course I do," he finally responded.

"Then for Heaven's sake, let them!" He chided Enoch as a Father corrects his child.

"But...dancing?"

"What's wrong with music?"

"Not a thing," Enoch quickly jumped. "It's the idea of dance that poses a problem." He lowered his voice attempting to regain control of the conversation. "You see, Charles, some of our inmates feel dancing is a sin." He cleared his throat. "I certainly would not want to be the one that causes them to stumble." He grinned at his argument.

"Then tell them not to dance."

Enoch's smirk turned to a scowl. He thought he should try a different approach.

"You want me to tell the good religious inmates that they can not participate while the ungodly, unruly ones are permitted?"

The man shouted into the telephone, "No, Enoch, I want you to allow the students to make up their own minds!" He sighed. "How do you expect to properly prepare these children for the outside when you keep them selectively harbored? You are not doing justice to the children by keeping them from the world's pleasures. That is precisely why I pushed your idea through about Bucker."

Enoch cringed at the sound of that word. He hoped the Director of the Board would not mention that subject, let alone leverage it.

"I...," Enoch stuttered, "I'm not following."

"Do I need to remind you that it was I who persuaded the others to vote through the idea of summer camps to your home in Bucker?"

"No, but I don't see how that has anything..."

The Director interrupted, "It's my grandson, Enoch. He just wants to do something nice for the children. He simply wants to come and play records for them." Charles laughed, "Believe me it will do him good to see those less fortunate than he."

An odd silence ensued. Charles waited for his friend to agree while Enoch suffered to swallow the idea of his superior's rules.

232

Ultimately, the Director spoke. "What do you say, Enoch? Can I tell my grandson that he and his friend are permitted to come to the Home to play records for the children?"

Enoch opened his mouth to speak twice, without a sound. He shook his head and surrendered to the request.

"I guess it would be fine."

"Good. I will...."

Enoch cut him short. "But only once a month...on a Saturday night...until school is finished."

Charles burst into laughter. "You win. I'll tell him he can play for the next few months."

"Two - April and May."

"April and May it is. Then, he can begin again in September if he so desires."

Again, Enoch shook his head and loosened his collar button. He dabbed his moist forehead with his embroidered handkerchief.

"If the children want it."

"Fair enough."

Enoch blurted out, "And one more thing, Charles. I want this on the record that this was not my idea and that I do not think it is a good idea...for the children."

"Done." The Director hung up.

In the meantime, Janet paced in front of Enoch's door. She held adoption papers in her hands, which needed the Headmaster's signature before the child could leave the Home with his new family. She listened to the tone of Enoch's voice and knew not to interrupt. She felt she was about to burst when she heard Enoch place the telephone receiver in the cradle. She quietly tapped on the door.

"Mr. Rumsted?"

"Yes, Miss Twill?" His tone sounded equally annoyed and sarcastic.

"May I come in?"

"What do you need?" He dabbed the sweat from his forehead for the second time.

"I have adoption papers for you to sign, sir."

"Come in."

She opened the door to the back of Enoch's chair. He stuffed his damp hankie in his pocket before turning around to face her. She placed the paper on the desk before him. He scribbled his name without lifting his glasses. She turned to walk out.

"Uh-um," he cleared his throat. When she turned to face him, he asked, "And the fee?"

She blushed. "The parents are getting it together as we speak."

"Be certain it is paid in full prior to their departure." He placed his glasses on the end of his nose just so he could look over them. "You remember what happened last time?"

Her neck broke out in hives. "Yes, sir. I...I forgot."

"And then what happened?"

Her bottom lip began to quiver. "We never received their money."

He bobbed his head in confirmation. "That's correct." He dismissed her with a hand gesture. "Be certain that never happens again."

"Yes, sir," she whispered as she began to close his door.

"Miss Twill? Would you ask the children to clean the inspection room? It seems on Saturday they will be dancing."

She closed the door. Her pursed lips softened to a grin. She returned a few minutes later with the adoption fee in her hand and presented it to Enoch without a word.

He nodded his acknowledgment. "Thank you." He scowled. "That will be all."

He waited until the door closed completely before opening the drawer to his private fund box. He opened the lid to the grey lock box and carefully placed the money on top of the other bills. He closed the lid, locked the box and the drawer, and returned the key to its secret location. He stood and walked out the door with fifty dollars more confidence than a few minutes prior.

The following Saturday afternoon, Charles' grandson and his friend rapped on the door. Enoch answered, opening it wide to allow space for their equipment and two stacks of records. The boys chattered about the latest hits from the hottest bands, but Enoch's only interest was control. He burdened the pair for ten minutes with his "rules" until he excused himself from the room. They pair giggled about Enoch's uptight attitude.

After dinner, the children funneled into the empty room and listened to music most had never heard. Some children requested a few selections multiple times until a few began to retain some of the lyrics. Their voices rose above the record as they sang along.

The two boys spun records for several hours while a few girls danced. Most of the children seated around the perimeter followed the rhythm by tapping his or her feet while others clapped. The room erupted with delight.

Music filled the Home's empty spaces, rattling the paraphernalia on Enoch's desk, walls, and door hardware. Every muscle in his body wanted to scream and toss the two intruders out of the building, but visions of satisfying his mortgage at Bucker held him fast. With his elbows firmly planted on his desk, he placed his hands over his ears hoping to drown out the annoyance.

"How much longer?" he questioned repeatedly.

As the clock neared eleven, the Director's grandson paused to make an announcement. "We have time for three more requests and then this fun evening will have to come to an end!"

The crowd groaned with disappointment, especially a few of the high school girls who displayed obvious interest in the two boys. The silence felt oppressive.

"Bring me those requests now."

The small group of giddy girls ran up to the record spinner. They twirled their hair as they shouted out their requests. Five girls requested five different songs. Unsure how to deny the five requests, the boys played them all.

By ten minutes after eleven, Enoch reached his limit. His feet pounded on the staircase as hurried toward the room, although no one heard the racket over the music. When he walked into the room, he was shocked. Multiple children danced across the floor. Both male and female shook and shimmied their bodies to the beat. He tried to shout to regain control, but the children refused to mind. He made eye contact with the Director's grandson and made a slicing motion across his throat.

Once the song ended, he announced, "That will be all for tonight, but remember we will return next month!"

Enoch groaned while the children cheered.

30

The spring planting season came and went with minimal effort. The rains came when needed, and the sun nourished the tender shoots. Soon the young plants covered the children's ankles and seemed less susceptible to disease and pestilence than ever before. The majority of the children finished their weeding chores without complaint and soon an abundance of food flowed to the tables. Everyone was in good spirits, even Henry.

Once the sun had melted the winter's snow and brought the spring greens to life, the boys led the herd to the pasture and began the daunting task of cleaning the cattle stalls. This spring break task fell only to the older boys. They removed many layers of waste, straw, and bedding and filled the manure spreader. The boys spent the majority of the break loading and reloading the wagon until the cow's quarters were dirt free and the fields were colored black with the nutrient-rich slurry.

Soon, the late days of May flowed into early June. School ended and even with the surrender of their shoes, no one complained. The ground was firm and dry.

The first group of unclaimed inmates left for Bucker the third week of June. True to form Enoch's idea of summer camp differed from the children. They painted the window trim on his house, fixed the barn siding, repaired the summer kitchen roof, and even fixed a leaky sink in the kitchen, all without complaint.

By the time Henry's week for camp arrived, it was late July. The hot summer sun hindered strenuous exercise, so when the boys climbed into the back of the farm truck they welcomed the breeze. Loose chaff stuck to their skin irritating their sunburns, but the ride away from the Home felt glorious. Henry sported a wide smile. For the first twenty miles, no one spoke until Tom broke the silence.

"Since we are safe and out of the danger of anyone overhearing our plans..." he hesitated, begging Henry with many glances to finish his sentence. When he did not, Tom grew agitated. "What's with you, Henry?"

Enjoying the purity of a silent, wind blown ride, Henry jumped at the sound of his name. "Huh?"

"What's the new plan?" Tom snapped.

"Plan for what?" Henry snapped back.

"For getting rid of the Headmaster."

"Oh," Henry shrugged. "That will work itself out."

Immediately, his face flushed. His mother used to say that. He hung his head barely listening to Tom's bantering. For the first time, he felt guilt and shame.

When the six boys jumped off the back of the farm truck, the driver pulled away. A plump elderly woman called to them from the dilapidated front porch. She looked like Henry's deceased grandmother. He suppressed the desire to wrap his arms around her thick middle.

"Look at you boys," she scolded as she pulled bits of straw from their hair. "You are a mess!" She pointed to the distance. "Go run down there and jump in the stream to cool yourselves off. Throw everything but your britches on the bank and I'll wash them up proper for y'all." She shook her head. "I swear your clothes get dingier and dingier with every group that comes."

The boys stood with their mouths hanging wide open. This woman showed more kindness toward them in five minutes than they received all year at the Home. Henry threw his arms around her waist. He could not resist any longer.

They ran toward the creek like wild animals, peeling off bits of clothing and tossing them into the air as they ran. Tom jumped in first.

"Wow! That's freezing!" He jerked his dark hair, tossing water two feet in all directions.

Henry could not wait to jump into the icy spring. Although, the outside temperatures hovered past ninety degrees, the water remained cool. After the initial temperature shock, the stream felt refreshing. The boys floated, dunked, and splashed for nearly two hours before growing weary. They crawled out

240

onto the bank and lay naked under the dappled light of the maple trees. All drifted to sleep.

The sound of the old woman's voice calling them to eat woke the boys with delight. They scrambled to pull on their damp, scratchy skivvies and ran toward the house.

The smell of a beef roast, potatoes and carrots in brown gravy filled the kitchen. A large plate of chocolate chip cookies sat under a pastry dome waiting for dessert. She filled each dinner plate to overflowing. Each boy ate two helpings and then devoured the plate of cookies.

"My, my," the woman laughed. "Don't they feed you at Fairmount?"

No one dared answer. No one knew who she was - the Headmaster's spy, wife, or mother. One thing for certain, Mae could cook. Food never tasted so good.

The following morning the boys woke to the smell of bacon. They tossed the soft pure white sheets from their bodies and tumbled down the stairs into the kitchen. Mae placed three pounds of bacon strips, curled and crisp, in front of the boys and before she finished frying the scrambled eggs, the bacon plate sat empty.

"My, my," again she laughed.

She took a seat at the head of the table and nursed her cup of black coffee. The boys ate breakfast in less than five minutes. Thankful to fulfill her ministry, she began her weekly tale.

"My church volunteered to help Enoch." She watched the boys scowl at the name. "Now, I know what you all are thinking, but let me finish before you make your judgment."

"Enoch bought this property long before he accepted the position as Headmaster of Fairmount. He nearly lost it twice." She lowered her voice as she continued. "Times have been tough around here. I know you children are a bit sheltered from the goings on outside of the Home, and I am not about to burst your bubble. I just want you to understand why Enoch is so hard."

"He has always been a quiet man, somewhat of an introvert, but he has struggled all of his life with a temper. Sometimes it gets the best of him."

Tom interrupted Mae's story, "Yeah, wanna see what his temper does?"

He started to lift his shirt. Mae tapped on the back of his hands and shook her head. "I've seen it a hundred times." She placed her hand below his chin and lifted his face until his eyes met hers. "It hurts me that he hurts you." She looked at each one and added, "That he has hurt all of you."

"I'm not excusing his actions. I'm only saying that you would be better off if you didn't provoke him." They groaned. "It's not your fault, I know. Boys will be boys and some are more of a troublemaker than others." She looked at each boy with an accusatory gaze. "You're not a troublemaker, are you?"

Each boy waited for her telling glance. Her eyes settled on the individual boys refusing to move until each shook his head "no."

Henry's silent gaze came last. When the woman stared at him, he felt as if she could read his mind. He wanted to look away, ashamed of his recent actions, but could not. Her unconditional love captivated him. Slowly, he shook his head confirming a

242

negative answer to her troublemaker question. He slid his eyes to the floor. He had lied and felt certain that Mae also knew it.

She smiled and continued, "I didn't think so. You all have kind eyes." She waved her hand in the air as if swatting at a fly.

"Anyway, our church jumped at the chance to run this summer camp. The first few groups did quite a bit of work to get this place in shape, but now it is mostly finished. The only help I need this week is a clothesline." She began to laugh, "Somehow it got torn down last week."

"I volunteered to run the summer camp this year. I have been a bit lost since my husband passed in January and when my pastor asked for help, I could not raise my hand quick enough."

"This summer has been a Godsend for me. I enjoy cooking and doing laundry. I love getting to know you children. Although, what I enjoy the most, is watching you all smile. I know there's not a whole lot of laughter that goes on there, so let's just make it another part of my job this week - to make you laugh." She clapped her hands together. "How does that sound?"

"Good!" the boys answered in unison.

"Okay, then let's get started!" She stood and wiped the sweat from her forehead. "It's a hot one already. Why don't you boys run down to the fishing hole while I clean up the dishes and gather the string for the clothes line."

Henry piped up, "I have a better idea. Why don't we help you with the dishes, put up the new clothesline, and then swim. It would be better to work now before the afternoon sun burns us up."

Mae laughed and tousled his hair. "I knew there was something special about you." She winked. "Guess you've learned a thing or two."

"Reckon I have," Henry responded. It felt good not to be a troublemaker even if it was only for the week.

The boys washed and dried every dish while Mae returned them to their proper places. They walked toward the barn.

"What do we need for the clothesline, Miss Mae?" Henry asked.

"Just call me Mae," she giggled. "It's been a long time since I was a Miss." She walked a few steps before answering Henry's question. "I suppose we need a shovel."

"I'll get that," Tom volunteered.

"And a pick."

"Okay, I'll get that," sprung Henry.

"And I guess we will need a bucket of cement."

"I'll carry that," volunteered the oldest and strongest boy.

"And a bit of water to add to it."

"I'll get that from the creek," the fourth boy joined.

"I think that will cover it, all but the two poles. And since there are two of you left with nothing to hold, I'll let you carry those."

"Will do," they chorused.

"I guess I will gather the line. Then, I believe we will have everything we need."

Mae led the group to the new site of the laundry line. The boys picked and shoveled the dirt, clay, and stones until they dug two deep holes.

"It must be below frost level," Mae warned. "That's why the other one fell. It wasn't deep enough."

Sweat poured down the boys' faces and backs. Soon, they removed their soaked shirts and tossed them out of the way.

Mae gathered the dirty clothes and walked into the house. She returned with a tray of lemonade. Tom winced at the tart flavor, having never tasted it before. The other boys gulped the glass of refreshment and begged for a refill.

Within the hour, the boys slid the poles into the holes and filled them with the cement. They patted the slurry with their hands, making it smooth on the surface.

"Let's let the stuff harden a little bit before we string the line." She stuck her finger into the mixture. "I believe it will be ready for your initials in just a bit."

They enjoyed a sandwich and another pitcher of lemonade under a shade tree. The breeze, hot and sticky, added to their discomfort. Henry picked up a narrow stick from the ground beside him.

"Think we could write our initials with this?" he asked Mae.

"I think that would be perfect." She stood and winced at a sharp pain in her hip.

"Are you okay?" Tom jumped up to help her.

Mae placed her hand over her hip. "Yes, just a bit of arthritis. Guess I shouldn't sit on the ground." She walked to the pole, knelt, and touched the cement. "It's ready, boys!"

The boys split into two groups. Each placed their initials in the bases. They giggled when they realized that no one knew each other's full name. They spent the rest of the day referring to each other by their last name.

"Hey, Gates!" Tom called to Henry. "Last one in the creek is a rotten egg!"

Mae watched the boys run toward the stream. Articles of clothing flew in every direction. "Be careful!" she cautioned, although no one heard her.

The boys jumped into the cool water. The shock seemed less intense than the day prior. They swam for an hour before resting on the bank.

"Hello there!" tossed a miner carrying his lunch pail toward the bank. "You boys here from the Home?"

"Yep," Tom interjected. "Who are you?"

"The name's Abe. I'm one of the miners." He pointed upstream. "We are mining coal up there. Quit early today 'cause the mules are tired. Guess it's too hot for 'em."

The boys listened to the man talk about the mine while he opened his pail. His skin, covered in black coal dust, seemed to flake off his body as he moved. He had a bandanna pulled down around his neck that, judging from the color difference, only covered his nose and mouth. He gummed his sandwich as he spoke with his thick accent.

"Yes, sir, this here swimming hole used to be a lot deeper. I reckon it's 'cause of all the silt we drag outta the mine, filters down stream and filled a lot of it in. Shoot, it used to be dang near ten feet deep. I suppose it's probably only half that now." He took another bite of his sandwich, not caring about the ground-in dirt on his hands. "I suppose if we got a few sticks of dynamite we could blast this into a bigger hole."

That statement grabbed the boy's attention. Each begged for more ideas.

Abe listened to their suggestions. Once he swallowed the last bit of his sandwich, he stood up and pointed up stream.

"We could pipe some of the clear water into her, but unless the hole is deeper, it won't do much good. But first we gotta get rid of some of the water." He stroked his chin looking first toward the house, and then toward the creek. He held his index finger in the air. "I gots it! I'll bring some wire from the mine. We'll hook it up to the sticks and connect it to the porch light." He looked at Tom. "It works, right?"

Tom nodded, "Yes, sir. Works great!" Excitement elevated his voice.

"Okay, then. I'll go get the stuff. You go tell Mae what we're doin'. I wouldn't wanna scare her to death! She's a good, God-fearin' woman."

The boys ran toward the small red brick house. They burst through the back door and chattered at once.

"Hold on there! One at a time, boys. I can't understand you when you all fuss at once!"

Mae listened as the boys shared Abe's plan. Henry expected her to shoot the idea in the foot, but was pleasantly surprised when she seemed thrilled to be a part of it. She followed them to the bank and found Abe busy at work.

Abe stacked several layers of rock and forced most of the water to flow against the far bank. The boys helped by pulling downstream obstructions out of the path, making the new waterway deeper than the rest while adding the rocks to the dam wall. He instructed the boys to finish the makeshift barrier while he gathered more supplies from the mine.

Abe returned with two men. They strung three half-sticks of dynamite together in pairs about five feet apart and placed them into the middle of the creek bed. With only a thin stream trickling through the center, the men wedged the dynamite into place. One man held the spool of wire while Abe pulled and the third man placed it along the ground until they stood on the front porch.

Abe started to connect the wire to the light. "Make sure it's off!" he hollered to the man at the switch. He looked at the crowd on the porch. "Ready?"

"Yep!"

"Cover your ears! It's gonna be a good one!" He turned to the man over his shoulder. "Hit it, Jim!"

Jim flipped the switch. Mae closed her eyes. The boys waited for the explosion. Nothing happened.

Abe turned toward Jim for the second time. "Hit it, Jim!" Again, nothing happened. Abe's shoulders sank, "Doggone it!"

The men jumped off the porch and walked toward the stream. The boys froze in horror.

"But...what if...." Henry swallowed his thought as the men disappeared over the bank.

Within a few minutes, the three reappeared running toward the house. They waved their arms shouting, but no one could hear what they were saying.

Suddenly, the ground shook. The sky darkened. The men burst through a cloud of dust and fell on the ground laughing. Chunks of rock, dirt, bits of fish, and snakes fell from the sky around them. The boys rushed toward the battle ground. Mae took her first breath.

The dynamite blew out not only a large section in the middle of the stream, but the temporary dam, and most of the bank as well. Muddy water rushed into the deep hole. Leaves, dead fish, frogs, and wiggling pieces of snakes swirled in the center as the cavity began to fill. The boys spent the afternoon pulling the dead wreckage out of their muddy swimming hole, while each miner drank a beer.

The following day, the water ran clear. Most of the debris washed downstream and the boys enjoyed exploring their new pool.

When Abe walked to the swimming hole after work, the boy's enjoyment pleased him. He left them with one final warning.

"Hey, boys! Keep your eyes open for unwanted floaters!" He laughed as he pointed upstream.

"Huh?" Henry cupped his hand over his ears.

"The mules!" Abe yelled over the rushing waterfall. "Watch out for their poop!"

"Ewww!" the boys crinkled their noses.

Just then, a ball of waste drifted past Henry. "Incoming!" he shouted.

The boys pulled in a deep breath and slid under water. They opened their eyes and watched several pieces of dung float by. When all of the mule's physical relief slipped past them, their heads broke the water's surface. Abe sat on the bank holding his sides. His hearty laugh filled the air with joy.

The rest of the week, the boys ate, swam, and ate some more. Not only did each child gain five pounds, but they also left with cleaner clothes then when they arrived, thanks to Mae and her talents.

On Saturday morning, Mae presented each boy with two new pair of underwear, two t-shirts, a pair of shorts, and a fluffy white pillow - gifts from her congregation. The boys stood speechless, their arms filled, with one of the best presents they had ever received. Mae cried as she kissed the boys goodbye. Henry was the last in line. He no longer fought his tears as he clung to her waist.

Henry left Bucker with a heavy heart, yet grateful for the great week of memories. The boys relived the blasting day the entire ride. The farm truck turned into the Home's driveway and everyone complained. When Henry jumped off the back of the truck, distress overcame him. He wanted to return to Bucker.

31

Henry's rancid attitude quickly returned. The physical struggle returning to meager meals left him in a constant foul mood. He ate handfuls of cow and pig feed stored for winter days, alongside the rats. Surprised at the pleasant taste, he began to experiment by alternating a bite of fruit with the grain and pretended he was eating a lavish form of oatmeal. At times, he poured it into a bowl and after his morning barn chores, added fresh milk. Only a few others joined him. "It's better than starving to death," he chided frequently.

The summer quickly faded and the colors of autumn lit the trees. Henry seldom noticed the beauty. He spent most of his time in the fields anxious to test Abe's secret to growing big pumpkins. Henry recalled the conversation.

"Dig a huge hole and put a layer of fresh manure on the bottom, then sprinkle it with'n a layer about three inches thick of good black dirt. Do this three times until its mounded up at least a foot above ground. Push three pumpkin seeds into the top of the mound and water it real good. It don't matter if'n you plant it later'n everyone else. You'll have the biggest, bestest pumpkins in the market. And you can ask a better price for 'em too. Believe me, them city folks will pay high dollar for 'em too."

Henry planted his own patch in the back of the cornfield near his parched corn pit and waited. He was both pleased and shocked when Abe's prediction came true. Henry's pumpkins were the best and the biggest. He carted his prized crop to the market and volunteered to work extra during the fall sales.

Enoch eyed him with curiosity. He thought Henry changed drastically since his stay at Bucker.

Henry guarded his pumpkin secret well. He asked an extra fifty cents over the smaller ones. Each week, they sold out completely. No one suspected Henry of keeping the extra fifty cents as well as the extra tips he received for carrying the oversized pumpkins to the client's car. By the second week, Henry pilfered over twenty dollars, just under a fourth of Enoch's take.

The following Saturday evening, October 13th, was declared as dance night. Enoch barricaded himself in his office. He held his head in his hands, wondering how he could stop this incessant nonsense. The consistent hand clapping and laughter bothered him more than the music's volume.

Henry joined a busload of boys who opted out of dancing for a night at the movies. The bus left an hour before show time and pulled into a parking lot half way between the theaters.

"I'll be right here when you get back. Don't be late," the bus driver warned. "I won't wait on you, so no fooling around." He seemed to speak directly to Henry.

Although a trip to the local movie theater happened several times a month, this was Henry's first. Since the Headmaster's requirement was to self-fund your evening, only the children who had money attended. Henry decided his past two weeks of lucrative pumpkin sales afforded him this opportunity so he spent a little of his earnings. No one dared ask where Henry received his money.

Depending on the feature, the children attended two different theatres. At one time, Alliance had three theatres, but in the recent tough times, one had closed. The two that remained worked together to ensure the public had varied selections. They took turns featuring the week's blockbuster.

Henry with four other boys split from the rest to attend an action film uptown. They walked several blocks before reaching the ticket booth. The woman took their money in automaton fashion and stated, "Enjoy the show" as she handed each a ticket. The boys wondered how many times a day she repeated the phrase and chuckled at her obvious boredom.

Henry followed the veterans to the concession counter. The smell of buttered popcorn made his mouth water. He stared at the light color and large size of each kernel amazed at the difference between it and his parched corn. He pulled his money out of his pocket. No way could he miss tasting that.

After purchasing his popcorn, a can of cola, and a box of hard candy, he followed the others into the darkened room. Red velvet drapery flanked the enormous screen and covered the side walls. The projector and film reel protruded from a balconied room in the back of the theatre. The seat covers matched the curtains and outside of being a bit sticky from overuse were fairly comfortable. Henry devoured his popcorn before the show began.

It took a while for Henry to settle in to the picture. Everything about the experience distracted him - the sound, size, food, chairs, and the screen.

By mid-show, they announced an intermission to change the movie reel. The boys ran out the door and hurried back to the food counter for another box of popcorn. Henry bought a second large.

When the second reel began, the movie intensified. The war scene appeared real as the actors moved through the bunkers. The bullets seemed to whiz over Henry's head. He ducked and dodged their approaching onslaught.

He leaned toward the boy seated beside him and whispered, "I love the movies."

Just then, the film broke. The tick, tick, tick of the film as it raced around the spinning projector made everyone turn to watch. After ten minutes of shuffling and groaning, many people walked out demanding their money back. The boys, however, sat and waited.

"Sooner or later they will get it fixed, right?" Henry asked his friends.

"Yeah, sure. We can wait. What's the worst that could happen?"

After nearly an hour and several failed tries, the diminished crowd watched the film in it entirety. As the boys began to walk out, Henry noticed a snippet of film on the floor below the projector. He picked it up and quickly shoved it into his pocket hoping to have a snapshot of the film's star actor. The boys, tired, late, and sluggish from the quantity of ingested junk food, arrived to an empty parking lot.

"Isn't this where the bus parked?"

"I think so."

"I'm sure of it." One boy pointed across the street. "I remember that sign."

"Well, then, where is he? He said he would be here."

"He also said, don't be late," Henry quickly interjected. "And I would say we are very, very late."

"Now what?" one whined.

"We walk."

"But it is miles!"

Henry placed his hands on his hips. "Anyone else have a better idea?" The boys shook their heads. "Then I'd say we better get going."

The moonless night filled the boys with gloom. No one suspected the driver would leave, even if he thought the boys were clowning around.

Only a few cars drove past the group. Once, one of the boys stuck out his thumb to hitch a ride. When the car's break lights lit, the boys thought he accepted the request, but suddenly, a deer ran in front of the car. Soon, the driver sped out of sight.

"Brilliant!" moaned the complainer. "I'm freezing!"

"Should've brought a coat." Henry snapped.

"If I knew I was walking home, I would've!" He kicked a pile of rocks on the side of the road. They skipped across the pavement and settled far out of sight.

The boys arrived at the Home long after midnight. The bus sat in the drive; its engine cold. They walked to their cottage door. It was locked.

"Now what?" the whiner grumbled again.

Henry twisted his face at the comment. "We'll get in through the tunnels."

"But..." negative nilly whimpered, "There are rats in there!"

Henry, tired and disgusted barked, "They're not gonna eat you!"

By the time the group reached the tunnel that led to their cottage, all were ready to pounce on the one boy. His constant nagging and complaining grew old before they left the parking lot. When they finally walked up their cottage stairs, the door was locked.

Henry turned to the whiner, clenching his teeth, "Don't say a word! Not a word. Let me think."

With nowhere to go except to the cold barn, the boys stayed in the tunnel. They took turns scattering the rats until the morning.

Enoch stomped through the house until he found the boys sleeping in the tunnel. His bellowing voice made them jump to their feet, save one – the whiner. Enoch bent over and pulled him by the ear. The boy screamed in pain. Henry lifted his hand to cover his deaf ear remembering the pain. He snapped.

Henry charged the unsuspecting Headmaster. The weight of his shove forced Enoch to his knees. Henry swung, punched, and kicked with insatiable hatred. In his thrashing, he somehow managed to find a piece of discarded pipe. He swung and connected often and hard.

Enoch cowered on the floor covering his head with his long arms. Within minutes, the rest of the boys joined the fight. The final blow to Enoch's temple came from the whiner.

"That's for my ear!" He bent over and spit on the unconscious man, quickly joined by the others.

"Now what?" the whiner asked.

Henry felt empowered. For the first time in his life, he felt in total control. He had been given the ultimate opportunity and he was not about to let it slip away. He looked up toward the ceiling and eyed the heating pipe.

He turned to the boy beside him, "Quick! Grab a rope, any rope."

"From where?"

"The barn." Henry watched the boy turn and run. "Make sure it's long enough." He yelled toward the sound of the diminishing footfalls, "And grab a knife!"

The other boys watched as Henry struggled to drag Enoch's body toward the center of the basement. Frustrated, he yelled to the others.

"Are you gonna help me? We need to get him out here!"

Each boy wrapped his hands around an extremity. Dragging Enoch proved difficult, but the boys

managed to slide his body into the center of the basement directly under one of the pipes.

Henry dropped Enoch's arm just as the errand
boy returned with some rope and a knife. The boys
watched in horror as Henry made a noose. He lifted
Enoch's head, and slipped it around his neck. Henry
stood, releasing Enoch's head, and watched it strike
the floor. He sat on the floor a few inches from the
Headmaster's comatose body. His internal struggle
lasted only a minute. He turned his face from the
boys' accusing eyes.

"It's gotta be done."

The sound of silence pounded in his ear until one
boy, the whiner, said, "Yep. It's gotta be done."

Enoch opened his eyes and moaned. Henry wasted no time. He bound his hands, tossed the end of the
rope over the pipe, and began to pull.

"Help me!" he begged the onlookers.

The whiner was the first to join him, but it was
not until Enoch's resistance became stronger that the
rest of the boys rushed to help.

"Pull!" Henry ordered.

The boys pulled together. Slowly Enoch's body
began to lift from the floor. The Headmaster's eyes
were wide with fear. With his hands bound, his feet
swung wildly. Finally, Enoch stretched his long legs
until his toes skimmed the ground. He became able
to support his weight.

"Higher," cried the whiner. "He can touch."

Enoch tried to speak, but could not. Again, his
eyes filled with fear. His feet lifted off the floor.

"Pull!" Henry screamed. "Again!" The boys yanked on the rope with every ounce of strength. "One more time!"

With Enoch's feet several inches off the floor, the boys tied the rope to the center beam. The elasticity of the rope stretched beyond its limit and Enoch slipped within inches of the floor. The boys turned from his flailing body and walked through the tunnel.

Belle heard the commotion as she dusted the banisters. She ran to the basement door and listened. She recognized Henry's voice. She opened the door and slipped down the darkened staircase.

She watched in horror as Enoch thrashed. Her deep disdain for the man held her feet fast until compassion overtook her hatred. She ran toward him. His feet swung in all directions and connected with her body once. She ducked, ignoring the second blow and crawled on the floor beneath him, searching for something to support his weight. She found nothing.

She looked up toward his face. Terror and disbelief filled her. Yes, he was a bad man, but this is a horrible death. His body began to convulse. Belle screamed for help. She tried to wrap her arms around him to lift him up, but could not.

His body spun in circles. His fingers stuck in her hair. Enoch held fast. The movement knocked Belle to her knees. She pounded his fist. His grip tightened. His legs swerved. Enoch's stiffened arm pulled Belle toward the floor and twisted her body backwards. She screamed for help. Suddenly, Enoch's foot slammed into Belle's chin, forcing her head backwards.

She fell limp on the floor. She thought she heard the sound of Henry's voice. "Belle! Belle...."

Henry was coming for her. The room went dark.

Present Day

32

Belle sat on the front lawn under a shade tree. She tried to find beauty in the surrounding setting, but her mood was glum. Suddenly, she jumped to her feet remembering Silver Park. It seemed ages since she went there. She peered around the trunk of the tree toward the Home searching for any staff members. Finding none, she slipped into the shadows of the buildings and began to make her way toward the park.

She tried to shake her sadness, but found it difficult to do so. She felt alone lately, isolated, and disconnected. When she lifted her eyes and saw the park, she ran toward her favorite bench, delighted to find a young boy seated alone.

"Hi," he smiled as Belle approached the bench.

"Oh, hello. How are you?"

"I'm fine. You?"

"I'm very well, thank you."

Collin struggled with the next line of conversation. "My name is Collin Sims. What's yours?"

"Belle Gates," she answered as she sat beside him.

"Do you live close?"

"Yes. I live at the Children's Home." She pointed south. "It's a bit of a walk to the park, but I love it here."

"Do you come here often?"

"As often as I can. The Home has a tight schedule." She placed her hands beside her mouth and whispered, "But sometimes I sneak out."

Shocked at her independence at such a young age he questioned, "Are you by yourself?"

"Yes. I always come alone."

"Aren't you scared?"

"No, not at all. It's nice to be away from the Headmaster."

"The who? Why?"

Belle giggled, "If you have time I will tell you all about him."

"I have time. Tell me."

Collin sat mesmerized for nearly fifteen minutes while Belle talked nonstop. She described the Home, the mean Headmaster, her rebel brother, the death of baby Willy, and her duties within the Home.

When she finished her tale, all Collin could say was, "Wow!"

Belle noticed the watch on Collin's wrist. "That is beautiful. I've never seen one on a child's wrist before. Some of the Matrons have them and certainly the Headmaster, but I don't get close enough to inspect them." She shrugged. "They ring the bells when it's time for meals or school, so there is no need to wear a timepiece on our wrists."

Collin chuckled at the word 'timepiece.' It seemed old-fashioned. He extended his arm for Belle to inspect his watch.

She gasped, "Is that the correct time?"

Collin pulled his watch to his face and looked. "Um…it's almost four o'clock."

"Oh no!" Belle cried. "I must go."

"Why? Where are you going?"

"Our Marble Champion is due to arrive at five o'clock! I must be presentable for the celebration!"

Collin sniggered again. He spoke under his breath, "Marble Champion? Who plays with marbles nowadays?"

Belle stopped and turned to face him. She forced her little hands into her hips signifying a thread of defiance. "We do," she huffed.

Collin's face revealed his embarrassment. He stumbled, "I…I'm sorry. It's just that no one plays with marbles anymore, let alone has a champion."

"Well, when you have little, you invent things to play with," she chastised. "Besides, it is quite an ordeal at the Home." She listened to his laughter swell. "Maybe you should not poke fun when you haven't tried it." She turned to walk away.

"Wait!" Collin pleaded. "I didn't mean to offend you." He lowered his head. "I don't know anyone who plays with marbles."

"Well," she forced her fists into her hips once again. "Maybe if you tried it, you would like it." She kicked the stones beneath her feet. "And then, you may be mindful of others' feelings." She tossed her long blonde curls and skipped away.

Collin called after her many times. He ran, but he could not catch her. He called, "Belle! Belle!" multiple times without a response and then suddenly, she disappeared over a knoll. He offered, "I never meant to offend you," hoping to catch another glimpse of her. He did not.

Sharon saw Collin from their walking path. He stood with his back to her, one hand on his hip and the other over his eyes. He appeared to be looking into the distant field. "Are you ready to go?" his mother questioned.

Lost in thought and hopes, he answered, "Huh?"

Sharon chuckled, "Are you ready to go home?"

"Yeah, sure," he answered. He pulled his bike from the ground and walked it toward the car.

That night, Belle filled Collin's dreams. They played marbles, tag, kickball, and touch football. Several children from the Home joined their games, and Collin enjoyed not only their company, but also the camaraderie. When the morning light flooded his east window, he scowled at the interruption. He wanted to spend more time with Belle.

He begged his mother for nearly two hours until she relented, permitting Collin to ride his bike to the park. He raced out the drive, bypassing the front gate by way of the rolling lawn, and peddled his way to Silver Park. He rode straight to the bench hoping to find her, but Belle was not there. He traveled every paved road throughout the park eager to talk to her, but he could not find her. His fevered pace slowed to a crawl as he ambled his way home.

The following morning he woke to a downpour. The rain danced on their roof and raced through the gutters. The water rushing through the downspout outside Collin's window mimicked a waterfall. He groaned at the idea of another day without seeing Belle. He pulled his pillow over his head and fell back to sleep.

He woke to the smell of bacon. The air smelled good enough to eat. He tossed off his covers and ran down the staircase. He found his mother and Bill seated at the kitchen table sharing a pot of coffee.

"Well, good afternoon, sleepyhead," Bill teased.

Collin ignored the remark. "Mom, do we have any marbles?"

"Marbles?" Sharon squinted at the odd request. "I think we do." She scratched her forehead. "Let me think what box they would be packed in." She stared out the window. "I'm guessing they would be with all the board games."

"Where is that box?" Collin pushed for an answer.

"All of those boxes are stacked in the corner of the dining room. I still have to unpack them."

Collin ran into the dining room and read the list of contents his mother wrote on the outside of each box. Luckily, the box marked 'Games and Misc' sat alone without another stacked on top. Collin opened the flaps and rummaged through it.

Sharon entered the room while he tossed things about. "Okay," she scolded. "If we are going to touch the things in this box, then let's find a place to put them away. There is no need to touch everything twice." She positioned her hands on her hips. "Got it?"

266

Collin scowled as he grumbled, "Got it."

They placed the minute stack of board games on the shelves in the front closet. The last item Collin pulled from the box was a double-pouched suede bag. The rawhide drawstring held the contents intact.

"Those were your grandpa's marbles." She sighed. "You were too young to know him." She tapped on the second half of the pouch, "The other side is filled with jacks and a few rubber balls."

"Why don't we play with them?" Collin said as he untangled the drawstring. He dumped the colored marbles on the floor.

Sharon laughed, "You never showed an interest in them before. Why now?"

"Why not?"

She rubbed the top of his head disheveling his hair. "Mr. Mystery man!"

Collin pulled a long string from the bottom of the pouch. "What's this for, Mom?"

"That's the perimeter circle string," Bill answered as he joined the pair on the floor. "You make a circle with it and then you place the thirteen regular sized marbles in the shape of a plus sign." He picked up one of the four bigger marbles, "These bigger ones are the shooters."

Collin picked up the blue glass shooter closest to him, "This one has a sheep inside it."

"No way!" Bill shouted. "Let me see that." He inspected the shooter carefully. It had a few nicks on the glass, but overall seemed in good condition. He opened his hand and extended it to Collin. He warned, "This one is pretty special, buddy. I am guessing this was Grandpa's lucky marble. It's worth a lot of money."

"Like how much money?"

"Seven to eight hundred dollars."

Sharon gasped. "How do you know so much about marbles?"

"My dad and I used to play all the time." He laughed, "Except our circle was five feet in diameter."

"Bet you didn't have a shooter like this one," Collin added.

"You are right. I had a cat's eye and Dad's was a swirl, nothing like that one." He winked at Collin. "Maybe that should be a keepsake, something to look at and not play with."

"Yeah, you're right," Collin agreed. "Can I show it to someone though?"

"Who?"

"Belle."

"Who is Belle?" Sharon teased.

"A little girl I met at the park. She plays with marbles all of the time, even has a friend that is a champion."

"Yeah, that's right. I forgot about that." Bill added, "My dad went in '52, but he lost in the second round."

The new blended family played with Grandpa's marbles until lunch. Just as they finished their BLT's, the rain suddenly stopped. Within an hour, the sun appeared.

"Mom, can I ride my bike to the park?" Collin Sims asked.

"Oh, honey, not again today."

"Looks like the rain has stopped," Bill offered as an invitation.

"Really?" Collin asked excited.

"Do you want to go?"

"It has turned into a beautiful day for a walk," Sharon replied, agreeing to the invitation.

"And a bike ride," Collin added. "Let's go!"

It took longer to pack the bike in the car than it did to make the two-mile drive to the entrance. Collin could not wait to ride his bicycle. He shifted his weight from one leg to the other while Bill pulled his bike from the back. He watched several people whiz past anxious to join them. Once Bill set the bike on the ground, Collin hopped on the seat and peddled as fast as he was able. It felt good to feel the wind in his face.

Sharon cupped her hands around her mouth and yelled, "Not too far!" It was too late, Collin slipped from her sight.

Bill patted her shoulder. "He will be fine. You've gotta stop smothering him. It's time for him to grow up."

"My head tells me you are right, but my heart says something different." She picked up her cell phone and began to dial Collin's number. She sighed, "He's been through so much these past few years."

"We all have." Bill covered Sharon's phone with his hand and shook his head. His thoughts turned toward his son's death. "Jesse would've turned thirteen this year."

Sharon placed her phone into her pocket and squeezed Bill's hand. There were no words to say.

They walked for nearly an hour and spied Collin twice – once on the swings and once on a bench. Both times, Sharon made a move to join him, but Bill held her back.

"Let him go, Sharon. He's having fun."

"But he's all alone," she protested.

"Maybe he enjoys that."

"Maybe you're right," she submitted. He did look happy. "I think he's talking to himself," she giggled.

Collin rode his bike as fast as he could. He nearly ran into an elderly couple in the picnic area. He yelled, "Sorry," but they did not hear him. He saw Belle often in various places throughout the park, but could not catch up to her. He decided to ride to the bench where he found her before.

With drops of water falling from the summer's leaves, Collin arrived at the bench drenched. He tossed his bike on the ground and positioned his body in the warm sun. Soon, his hair and t-shirt began to dry and his khaki shorts became splotchy from the evaporating water. He kept a diligent watch for Belle amid constant inspection of the disappearing water spots on his clothes.

He recalled the past few months of his life. He had experienced a multitude of changes often leaving his thoughts spinning like a top. He closed his eyes to aid in reminiscence. He settled on a memory of the last day he spent on The Great Trail, allowing his mind to wander to the days and months that followed.

Collin swung the flashlight beam over the path in front of him, relieved to have the complete necklace returned to the Indian princess, its rightful owner.

He felt proud to have given it up so freely. He was more afraid of the consequences had he not. It was hers. She wanted it. She should keep it.

With the loss of the necklace's centerpiece, Collin carved a replacement from one of his father's prized pieces of abalone. Collin's crudely carved replacement pleased the princess. He could tell by her show of gratitude.

He recalled the vision of the ancient Indian Shaman explaining the meaning of each bead of the necklace. "When the chute is opened, a helper will come. He will give you the light and show you the way. You will sing like a bird to announce your arrival. I will lift you toward the light and bring you to the gods." Those words helped Collin understand his role - he was her helper foretold hundreds of years before.

"I am the helper," he repeated aloud.

Suddenly, he landed face first in a mass of fresh pine. A fir tree, uprooted by the windstorm, blocked the path and caused him to trip. The root ball dripped with fresh dirt and pebbles soaring nearly ten feet off the ground.

Collin moved his flashlight beam over the exposed roots. Something glistened. He moved closer and retraced the tree's outline with the light. Dangling near the top of the root mass was the spiral – the centerpiece of the ancient necklace. He gasped.

He swung his legs over the tree and shimmied up the trunk. He stretched his arms to their limit but could not reach it. The unstable tree rocked. Too nervous to clamber over the exposed roots, he sat mesmerized by the illuminated spiral as it spun freely. It twirled in ghostly suspension. He slid from the trunk and walked around the opposing side.

The root ball created a deep hole filled with large rocks. A string originating beneath the ground snaked its way through the tangled mass of roots, dirt, and moss; at its end twirled the pendant.

With one quick tug, the spiral broke free. It landed in Collin's hands. It seemed much larger than he remembered. His heart raced, elated to hold it once again. His thoughts turned to the princess.

"She wanted me to find it!" he shouted.

He brushed dirt from the spiral, placed it in his pocket, and started to walk away. The fishing string pulled tight and yanked it out of his pants. He traced the line to its end.

Deep in the hole laid a metal box with part of the lid and one side exposed. Collin climbed under the root ball and tried to pick it up. It was stuck. Using his bare hands, he dug through the mud. Finally, after fifteen minutes, it broke free. He tried to lift it, but could not.

His hands shook as he struggled until the lock released with a loud crack. Collin fell backwards. Gold coins spilled from the box. They were old, very old. He dug his muddy hands through the spoil, amazed at the sight. Could this be a chest from the French soldier's lost treasure? He thought it was only legend.

Without thought, he began to gather the string. The spiral hopped along the bed of spent pine needles as it moved closer. When he closed his fingers around the spiral, he glanced at the pile of string. Puddled in his lap was the moss-green fishing line

that he had used to string the princess' necklace together. He sobbed uncontrollably.

"Thank you, princess," was all he could muster.

He knelt and gathered the heavy box, which now
seemed oddly easy to remove. He placed the string
and the spiral on the lid anxious to return home. Oh,
did he have a story to tell his mother!

He stood, shook the mud cakes from his clothes,
and started down the path toward home. His body
stiffened in place as he remembered his promise.
He pledged to keep the princess a secret. The trees
swayed in hushed agreement. They seemed to echo
the word secret, resonant of his vow. He turned to
walk home.

Collin burst through the door with excitement. No
one was home, just a note on the table in Sharon's
handwriting simply stated:

Went for a walk. We love you.

Collin washed his hands, pulled off his muddy
clothes, and changed into clean shorts and a t-shirt.
He placed the metal box on the kitchen table and opened
it to face the kitchen door. He climbed up on the kitch-
en counter and pulled three stemmed glasses from the
top shelf. He filled the champagne flutes with water.
After a quick phone call, he turned out the light and
sat at the kitchen table in the dark. His heart raced
when he finally heard his mother and Bill talking to a
young woman who had just pulled into the driveway.

"Hello. I'm Angie Wadeford from The Daily
View." She extended her hand.

"Hello. I'm Sharon Sims." She shook her hand and then extended it toward Bill. "And this is Bill Williams."

"Nice to meet you."

Sharon stammered a bit, curious of the reason for her visit. "What can I do for you?" She asked finally able to find the words.

"I'm looking for Collin." Angie looked at the frown on Sharon's face and quickly added, "He called me."

Sharon asked puzzled, "You said Collin Sims called you?"

"Yes. Is he here?"

"Um, I'm not sure. We just went for a walk and he wasn't home when we left." Sharon looked toward the dark house.

"He said it was important and that I would want to be here with camera and tape recorder."

"Are you sure you're not confused?"

Angie fumbled for the piece of paper where she had scribbled the address. After looking at it and comparing it to the house numbers, she spoke, "Even with the missing number three," she pointed to the group of numbers that hung beside the door, "Is this your address?"

"Yes."

"Then I'm not confused." She led the charge toward the door. "Shall we find Collin? Perhaps he can clear things up for us."

The trio walked toward the back door. Bill squeezed Sharon's hand tightly. Angie clutched her camera and voice recorder.

Collin's head swooned from inside the house. His heart thumped deep and rapid. His hands shook. Excited sweat dribbled down his temples. He heard the door rattle and watched the doorknob turn.

Sharon was the first to enter with Bill and Angie close behind her. She turned on the kitchen light and immediately froze.

"Collin? What is...this?" she finally asked.

Radiant with pride he blurted, "It's part of the lost treasure of The Great Trail!" He watched his mother's face stare in disbelief. "I found it, Mom! I found it on the trail!"

Angie captured the moment on tape as well as through the camera lens. She danced around the kitchen table, snapping a multitude of pictures capturing the unbelief, pride, and joy as Collin, Sharon, and Bill embraced. They laughed and cried and laughed some more. They toasted to the miracle and lifted the flutes of water to their mouths.

Collin shared his story, being careful not to mention the princess or the spiral. He thought the necklace's centerpiece held too many negative emotions to be a part of this celebratory evening. Occasionally, he patted the spiral in his pocket to ensure its safety.

The next few days, the Sims were flooded with phone calls, interviews, and requests to repeat the story. Collin enjoyed the attention, but Sharon grew more concerned with each passing day. She fielded many calls and denied comments pleading with the press for privacy. Annoyed with the invasion, she allowed the answering machine to record the *messages. Many she deleted without listening. Only one caught her attention.*

"Mrs. Sims? This is Tim Lorie. Remember me? I am in New York now and heard of Collin's amazing story. I hoped to talk with you in person. My colleagues of the Morning Talk Show were hoping to have Collin and yourself appear on our television program. They will fly you two and anyone else you would like to New York. You will have a hotel suite for the week all expenses paid in exchange for an exclusive interview." He cleared his throat. "I told them I knew you and that you would be more receptive to the idea if I presented it. Would you please call me at your earliest convenience? They are anxious to meet you. Thank you. Have a great day!"

Tim rattled off his telephone number. Sharon scribbled it on a piece of paper. She picked up the receiver and dialed his number. After their conversation, a wave of regret overwhelmed her. She started to redial his number when Collin walked into the room.

"Ready to go to the bank?" He winked.

A little distracted, she finally answered, "Um...in just a bit. I have to make a phone call." She brought the phone to her ear and frowned as she heard the operator.

"You must first dial a one when...." Sharon groaned and hung up.

"Who ya calling, Mom?"

"Tim Lorie," she responded automatically too focused on the telephone number.

"Tim Lorie!" Collin exclaimed. "What does he want?"

She put the phone to her ear. "He wants us to go to New York for a TV talk show. At first, I said yes, but now I'm rethinking it." The receptionist answered. "Tim Lorie, please." Sharon listened. "It's Sharon Sims."

Collin jumped up and down. "Hang up! Hang up, Mom! Let's go! C'mon let's go to New York!"

Bill stood in the doorway listening to the conversation. He interjected as he sipped on his morning coffee. "Hang up, Sharon. It'll be fun."

"But...."

"Nope, hang up. I'll go with you. I've been to New York several times."

She hung up the phone before Tim answered. He did not return her call.

33

New York was wonderful, everything Collin, Sharon, and Bill imagined and much more. The television producer hired a driver for their week-long stay and the trio enjoyed viewing the city from the back seat of a limousine.

"I could get used to this," Collin teased.

"You may have to," Bill added, laughing.

Sharon did not find the comments amusing. Often she wondered how she could shelter her son in the midst of this popularity. It disturbed her sleep.

At the week's end, they boarded their Cleveland bound plane. Everyone was exhausted. The television interview proved to be the most relaxing. After viewing the program for years, Sharon was surprised at the studio set. It was much smaller, more intimate, than she imagined. The hosts were genuine in their interest of Collin's tale. Their eyes danced *with excitement when they held one of the antiquat- ed coins.*

Sharon felt uncomfortable sharing the family's hardships on national television, but the hosts in- sisted. She spoke of her husband's illness and ear- ly death, the inability to pay their mortgage, how the bank showed little mercy and compassion, and how the situation brought her closer to one of her high school friends. No one mentioned the 'Branding Gang' or Jesse's death. Only Collin understood their intimate connection.

Sharon shared in detail the day she went into the bank to satisfy the mortgage. "After an expert au- thenticated and valued the treasure," she explained, "we paid the balance with the appropriate amount of gold coins."

"Yeah, and they should've given us ten bucks back," Collin laughed. "But they were too mad about the coins to even realize it. It was hilarious!" The studio audience joined in the chorus aided by the prompter begging for applause.

After the show aired, many people stopped to chat about Collin's luck. A few asked the total dol- lar value contained in the box, but Sharon declined to reveal the amount to the studio hosts as well as any outsider that asked. Only five people knew of its worth – the appraiser, her attorney, Bill, Collin, and Sharon.

Within a few months, Sharon grew weary of the pressure. Soon, people littered her lawn begging for handouts. At first, she gave some money away, but when a homeless man begging for money for his next meal ridiculed her for her stinginess when she gave him one-hundred dollars, she realized that it would never be enough.

She decided to look for a home outside of her immediate area. She chose a modest home on Union Street in Alliance, Ohio. Their home, situated a few miles south of the city limits, allowed for a gate and a security system to be constructed without suspicion. The real estate agent handled the cash sale discretely, which allowed Sharon to keep a caretaker at the old farm in Minerva hoping to return someday when the treasure notoriety settled.

Collin welcomed the move without a problem. He grew tired of the questions and strangers lingering around their property as much as his mother did. He anxiously waited for the covert move, which occurred in the middle of the night. By morning, they collapsed inside their new home on new furniture.

Sharon gently sat on Collin's bed and caressed his hair. She admired her son for the strength and courage he displayed over the past several months. She stared at him smiling until Collin opened his eyes.

"Well, good afternoon, sleepyhead."

He rubbed his tired eyes. "What time is it?"

"Time to get up!" Sharon teased. "We have a wedding ceremony in an hour, remember?"

Collin threw off his covers and jumped out of bed. He rummaged through the boxes in his room until he located his clothes. He put on a pair of dress pants and a t-shirt, wet his comb, which helped to groom his disheveled pillow perm, and walked down the open staircase to join his mother in the kitchen.

Sharon giggled, "Oh, no you don't." She pointed to his chosen attire. "That will not do. Today you wear a suit."

"But I don't have one."

"Yes you do. I bought you a new one. Just for this special occasion. It's hanging in your closet, with a shirt and tie, all pressed and ready to wear." Collin groaned. "No guff today, Mister. This is my day, remember?"

"Yes, Mom. Whatever you want," he joked.

"Go get dressed. We don't want to keep Bill waiting."

Collin raced up the staircase, taking two at a time. He opened his closet door surprised to find his clothes hanging in place. A multitude of clothing hung beside the suit, many with price tags attached. He looked carefully at every new shirt, pant, jean, and short selecting a few as his favorites and crinkling his nose at some ugly ones. He hung the less desirable pieces at the end of his closet rod.

He found his suit, shirt and tie covered in clear plastic. He noticed a note written by his mother - To my #1 man - pinned to the lapel. He smiled as he dressed and closed his bedroom door to check his reflection in the full-length mirror that hung on its back. He looked handsome.

He glanced out his bedroom window and saw Bill walking through the back yard with the pastor. He thought of the differences between his father and Bill. He wiped the falling tears from his cheeks and spun when he heard a noise behind him. It was Sharon. Embarrassed that she found him crying, he turned from her.

"I'm sorry."

She wrapped her arms around him. "I miss him too, Collin. I loved your father. I still love him. He will always be a part of our lives." She used her fingers to comb his damp hair. "Bill will never replace your dad."

"I know." He melted in Sharon's arms. "I just miss him."

"We all do." She pulled his face to meet hers. "Someday, we will see him again." She hesitated, "And we will go fishing."

"And catch big fish!"

"Heavenly fish," she quickly added.

"Fish that will magically clean themselves," he grimaced.

"And cook themselves." She pinched her nose.

"And we will eat them." He smirked. "And they will be good." Collin rubbed his empty stomach as it growled.

Sharon marveled at the grace of her child, grateful she was chosen to be his mother. "I love you."

Collin's verbal reply, "I love you more," occurred simultaneously.

Sharon looked toward the window facing her new back yard. "Are you ready to do this?"

His feet hit the floor with a loud thud. "I'm ready! Let's go get you married, Mom."

They walked down the staircase, arm in arm, Collin dressed in his grey suit and Sharon wearing a mid-length ivory lace dress. Just as their feet left the bottom stair, the front gate alarm sounded. Sharon walked to the intercom.

"Yes?"

"*Delivery for Sharon Williams,*" *the driver of the van stated.*

Sharon made a funny face at the sound of her new name. Collin squeezed her hand. They watched the vehicle pass through the front gate and continue up the drive. The logo – Catering to Your Needs – covered the side of the van. A young man and woman rushed to the front door with chaffing dishes and a box filled with burners. The fragrance of the food arriving with them wafted from their uniforms.

"*I didn't call for,*" *Sharon began, but the young man cut her off.*

"*You're soon to be husband, Bill, called us.*" *He winked. "We will be ready for you in a jiffy.*"

The couple hurried around the kitchen organizing their wedding meal. Sharon and Collin walked toward the back door as they placed a small stack of plates at the beginning of the service line. Sharon giggled like a young girl. Bill's surprise was quite a treat. She opened the back door.

"*Wait!*" *the young man ordered. He offered Sharon a bouquet of Casablanca lilies, White Orlaya, and Ranunculus tied together with a wide ribbon and several trailers of English Ivy. "He wants you to carry this.*"

Her face flushed at Bill's romantic gesture. She smiled and accepted the bouquet.

"*Ready?*" *Collin asked.*

"*Ready!*" *Sharon nodded.*

The ceremony lasted for barely ten minutes. There were no guests, music, or processional, only four attendees - the bride, groom, pastor, and Collin, who doubled as the bride's escort and the best man. Sharon looked radiant and Bill's smile seemed permanently etched on his clean-shaven face. Collin felt honored to be a big part of the ceremony.

After the service, all joined the caterer in the dining room for a feast fit for royalty. They celebrated with a toast of champagne and a slice of Burnt Almond Torte.

"I could get used to this." Sharon poked Bill's ribs.

"You may have to."

"Thank you. Everything was perfect."

"You are the best thing that ever happened to me." He kissed her hand. "I just wanted to do something special and unexpected."

"Well, that you did."

Collin watched the intimate exchange. It made him uncomfortable. He pulled at his collar begging for a bit more room. He fidgeted in his chair, tapped his foot on the bottom chair rung, and drummed his fingers on the table — all without conscious thought.

He lifted his eyes to both Sharon and Bill's smirk.

"What?" he questioned, realizing his actions.

Bill laughed aloud. "You can go, buddy. Get out of that monkey suit."

Collin jumped off his chair and raced up the stairs. He stripped off his suit and pulled on his favorite t-shirt and shorts.

"Ah, that feels better."

As he bounced down the stairs, he felt the pressure of the day melt away. By the time he walked into the dining room, he became a normal twelve-year-old.

"Yuk!" he shouted when he saw Bill and Sharon kiss. "That's gross!"

284

"I'll remember that," Bill laughed. *"In a few years from now."*

"I am so happy to find you!" Belle jumped up and down while clapping her hands.

Collin jumped at the sound of her voice halting his reminiscences. He did not see her approach their bench. "Geez, you scared me half to death!" he scolded.

"I have some wonderful news to share. We have a new Headmaster and he is wonderful! He is so kind, soft spoken, although a bit portly." She covered her mouth as if ashamed of her comment.

"Portly?" Collin questioned.

"Yes, you know, chubby." She covered her mouth a second time. "He has a wife too. She's very nice, but a bit stern."

"What happened to the mean guy?"

"He's gone."

"What happened?" He watched Belle shrug. Her reaction made him uncomfortable. Quickly he added, "I guess that's okay and all since he was mean, huh?"

"Yes, I guess." Belle lowered her eyes.

"Tell me more about the new guy."

"Well, he has grey hair, glasses, and laughs a lot. He likes to have story time in the inspection hall. He brought some of his own furniture to make the empty room feel cozy and added several rugs so we all have a soft place to sit while he reads. Sometimes he tells make-believe stories about princesses, fairies, and dragons. He looked at our rules and made a new number one rule–Rules are good, but kindness is better." Her shoulders relaxed. "I like him a lot." Her eyes filled with tears.

"Then what's wrong, Belle? Why are you sad?"

"I can't find Henry. I haven't seen him for a long time."

"Do you think he ran away?"

"Without taking me? Without saying goodbye?"

"You're right. He wouldn't go away and leave you there." Collin stiffened at his thought, "Perhaps he is finding a safe place for you both and he's going to come back for you?"

Belle clapped her hands at Collin's idea. "Yes, that must be it! He wouldn't leave me there, even with the new nice Headmaster." Suddenly, she jumped off the bench and shouted, "Did I tell you that the Headmaster knows Santa Claus?"

"Huh?" Collin reeled at the conversation and attitude swing.

"Yes, he knows him well. He said Santa is coming to visit us this Christmas, and he will ask us what we want."

Collin laughed at her innocence. "What do you think you will ask for, Belle?"

"Maybe a dolly or a new dress. No wait! I think I would like a friend instead."

"You don't need to ask Santa for a friend. You have me!"

Both laughed and enjoyed the next hour basking in the hot, drying summer sun. By the time Belle decided to head for the Home, Collin's clothes were dry, his hair tousled by the wind, and the bridge of his nose sun-kissed.

Collin rode beside Belle as she ran. When they came to the place where she turned to cut across the fields toward the property, she waved and promised to return the next day.

"As long as I can sneak away," she giggled and disappeared into the thicket.

Collin watched her long blonde curls float on the breeze as she ran toward the Children's Home. His heart felt light. She seemed happier, more content, even without her brother. He wondered where Henry was and why he left.

34

Collin did not see Belle for nearly a week. He rode to the park every day looking for her, even in the rain, but she did not come. He asked several people if they saw her, but everyone's answer was the same — no.

On the seventh day, he took his time riding to the park. When he crested the last knoll in the road, he saw Belle seated on their park bench. He peddled as fast as he could to meet her. Out of breath, he leapt off his seat, and tossed the bike on the ground.

"Where in the world have you been?"

"I'm so sorry. It has been very busy. Since we grow our own food, it's a lot of work come the harvest."

"I've missed you," Collin admitted.

"I have missed you too. I may not be able to come every day with all the extra work required right now, but I will try to come as often as I can."

"I understand," Collin whispered, dejected.

"I decided on the way over here today that I am going to ask the Headmaster if I could bring you back with me someday." She held her hands in prayer fashion. "Do you think your Mom will let you come? It could be a quick visit. I just want to show you around. We have a big barn, fields, hog pen, chicken, horses, and lots of places to play." She kept her hands in the same position and waited.

"I would love it!" Collin replied. "Since we moved, you're the only person I've met. I'm sure I will meet lots of kids when school starts, but since its summer break, I only come here."

"We go to school on the property until tenth grade," Belle announced proudly.

"Really? How does that work?"

"It's independent study mostly. We have one teacher, but she is usually busy with the older children. I find myself more interested in third grade work than my own." She pointed to her brain, "Mom, always said that Henry and I were extremely intelligent. In fact, Henry skipped two grades when we arrived and I started first grade one year early."

"That's great!" Collin kicked a few stones at his feet. "I wish I had your enthusiasm for school. Sometimes I think it's a colossal waste of time."

"Oh, please, don't say that! Your studies are important. It is like a hand-written ticket toward your better self and only you can be the author." She stared into the distant tree line. "My mom used to say that."

"Sounds like a wise woman," Collin concurred.

"Well," Belle slapped her legs. "I best be on my way. Those cucumbers aren't going to pickle themselves."

"See you later."

"I will come as soon as I can." Belle started to skip away from him and suddenly stopped and turned around. "Don't forget to ask your Mom if you can come to the Home."

"I'll ask as soon as I get home," he promised.

Collin slammed the back door as an announcement of his arrival. He felt winded from a quick ride home. Summer sweat drifted down his back and dotted the floor as he walked through the house.

"Mom?" He heard a muffled reply. "Where are you?"

"I'm upstairs in the spare bedroom."

"What are you doing up there?"

"Painting."

Collin walked into the bedroom. The bright yellow paint reflected the sunlight illuminating it like a floodlight. "Holy cow is that bright!"

"Too much?" Sharon grimaced. "I thought it looked cheery on the little card."

"Cheery?" Collin teased. "It's screaming loud!"

"I'll probably have to re-paint it at some point," she defended. "Right now, I'm finished and it will stay this way."

"It's bright, but it is pretty."

"Thanks, Collin. You always have my back."

They walked down the stairs together in silence. Sharon thought about the paint color while Collin thought about the Home.

"Mom, do you know where the Children's Home is?"

"Fairmount?"

"Yes."

"Yes, it's just down the road from here about a mile. Why do you ask?"

"I met a little girl who lives there." Collin stammered, "At the park."

"Oh, it can't be Fairmount. It closed in the 70's."

"I thought that's what she said, but maybe I heard her wrong. Anyway, she asked me if I wanted to come see it sometime." He pleaded with his eyes. "Can I?"

"Sure. Just call me before you go, so I know." He started to walk away. Sharon called after him, "Just be sure you come back here."

"Oh, no problem. From all of the stories she's told me I wouldn't want to stay."

"Stories?"

"Yeah, lots of them." He scratched his head. "But it sounds like it is getting better since they got a new Headmaster."

Collin lay on his bed that evening staring at the ceiling. He wondered when he would see Belle next. He could not help but feel excited to see the Home.

35

The summer slowly slid to a memory and Collin dreaded the idea of attending a new school. The past few months felt like a dream — the treasure, the notoriety, the move, the marriage, and especially meeting Belle. Nearly two weeks had passed without any contact with her, although he rode to the park every day.

He sat on the bench as he had for the past few weeks disappointed. He was about to leave when he spied her approach from the distance. She skipped toward him, her hair blowing gracefully around her face.

"I have a funny story to tell you," she began. "But first, do you have permission to come?"

"Yes, I do."

"Great! Let's go. I will tell you the funny story on the way."

Collin jumped from the bench, eager to follow her. "Wait!" he stopped. "What should I do with my bike?"

"Put it over there against that tree. We can come back this way after I've shown you around."

He agreed and leaned his bicycle against the large maple that shaded their bench from the morning sun. In his haste, he forgot to call his mother.

"Our new Headmaster's wife had a bit of a problem yesterday." She looked at Collin to be sure he was listening. "You remember me telling you about the large family of children that came the day Henry and I left the infirmary?"

"Yes. There were like thirteen kids?"

"Fourteen, to be exact. Anyway, the Headmaster and Mr. Davis took the high school boys on an overnight camping trip. While they were midnight raccoon hunting, his wife had a problem with one of that big family's older girls. She slapped the Headmaster's wife and knocked her glasses onto the floor. As if she had not caused enough trouble for herself, she picked up her foot and ground her heel into the glasses. The lenses minced like powder and the frames were bent beyond repair."

"Ouch! I bet she got beaten."

"Actually, no because this was the new Headmaster's wife, and although she remained calm, her stern voice left no doubt that Helen was in deep trouble. She called a nunnery in West Virginia to come pick her up. They arrived a few hours later. Helen left kicking and screaming. The Headmaster's wife warned all of us standing near that our fate would be the same if we disobeyed. She made it very clear that type of disrespectful behavior would not be tolerated."

"Well at least she didn't get a big whipping."

"When the Headmaster returned, he called a meeting of the entire Home. He explained that he did not believe in excessive force, but he was not opposed to appropriate punishment for bad behavior. When he finished his lecture, everyone understood him clearly. Despite his jovial personality, he was not a push over. If we were bad, we would be punished."

"I guess I would rather go to a nunnery than be beaten to death," Collin added quietly. Belle did not respond.

She talked non-stop as they walked through the backfields toward the Home. Finally, Collin caught a glimpse of the roofline. He gasped at the size.

"Wow! It's huge!"

"Yes, the main house is quite large. Wait until you see my staircase. It is spotless!" She only walked a few steps in silence, and then quickly began a new story.

"Did I tell you about the elderly couple?"

"Umm...I'm not sure. Which one?"

"Agnes and Orvey Dowling. They pick up a few of the high school girls on Sundays and take them to church. After the service, the girls go to the Dowling's home in Alliance. They go out to dinner and play with the neighbor's children." Belle stopped for a few minutes. "Sometimes I wish I was a high school girl and could travel with the Dowlings to their home. They are a bit too old to adopt any children now, but Agnes said they are blessed to have a relationship with so many of the Home's girls." Belle began to walk. "I just hope I am chosen when I am old enough. I would love to see their home. I hear it is beautiful! They have crystal chandeliers and fluffy pillows. I am told the beds are so soft and comfortable you feel as if you are floating on a cloud." Belle paused, conjuring the vision. She sighed, "But it's the Dowlings themselves that are so priceless. They are kind and generous. At Christmas, they bring several gifts for children of all ages, expensive special gifts."

"Like what?" Collin asked.

"Well, one year they bought every child a bathrobe. Another year, they bought dolls for the girls and baseball gloves for the boys. Another holiday, they bought enough turkey for three Christmas dinners and all the trimmings that went with it, even cranberries!"

Collin wrinkled his nose. "Do you like cranberries?"

"I don't know. I have never tasted them."

"But I thought you said the old couple...."

Belle cut him off, "That was before I lived there. I'm just telling you what I heard."

"Oh, I'm sorry."

"It's okay. They have been a big financial supporter for the Home for years. I guess since they did not have any children of their own, they decided to help all of us instead."

"Wow! I bet that gets expensive." Collin stared at the Home as they walked closer. "How many kids live here now?"

"I think there are about 200 of us. I am not certain of the exact count. With new ones coming, adoptions, children running away, and indentured...."

"Indentured? What's that?"

"It's like adoption except those children never assume the new last name. They just live with them as family members until they are old enough to be on their own, college, or the armed services."

"Oh, so it's like Foster Care?"

"I'm not sure. I've never heard of that before."

"It sounds like the same thing. It's just my words aren't as fancy as yours," he laughed.

Belle lifted her eyes to look at the Home. It was as if she was looking at it for the first time. "You'll have to forgive the disrepair. Much of the woodwork needs a new coat of paint. Some of the tin ceiling inside suffers the same fate and a few sections are missing all together." She put her hands on top of her head. "I had one section in the bathroom fall and hit me on the head. The nurse said I was knocked out for three days." She rubbed her head, "Boy did I have a bump!"

"Did they fix it?"

"Nope."

"Why?"

"No money. The old Headmaster called it 'proper funding.' He said the repair money needed to be used to buy things that were necessary, like food and clothing. That never made any sense to me, because we ate stewed tomatoes three meals a day more often than I could count." She shivered. "I hate stewed tomatoes."

"What about clothes?" Collin asked certain of her response since her outfit never changed. Belle always wore her faded cotton dress, no matter the weather.

"Clothes? We don't have much." She looked down at her feet. "See my shoes?"

"Yeah?" he replied.

"Until that tin ceiling fell on my head I wore a pair of boy's shoes. They were the only ones that sort-of fit me, yet they were too large. Their constant rub blistered my heels. After the tin ceiling accident, I noticed the heel of a girl's shoe peeking out of the hole in the ceiling. I stacked several boxes on top of one another until I could see into the space." She lifted her hands as if she held her finds as she spoke. "I found two pair of girl's shoes – these and another pair the next size bigger. I hid them in the bottom of my locker for safe keeping until they fit me." She sighed. "I also found a doll." She cradled her arms and rocked them across her stomach, "But she was missing an eye." She shrugged. "It's okay. I still love her."

Collin felt as if someone punched him in the stomach. He knew what it was like to go without, but to hear Belle's stories of want vs. need repeatedly, he felt ashamed of his abundance. He decided to buy her a new doll and give it to her the next time he saw her.

When they came to the front door, it stood ajar. Dry leaves blew through the entrance and gathered in the corners, covering hickory nut casings and spent acorns. Collin opened his mouth to say something, but the pride in Belle's voice stole his words.

"Here's my beautiful staircase!" She stood on the third step with her hands outstretched.

"Wow!" was all Collin could manage.

"Isn't it beautiful?"

"Sure," he lied. "Looks more like a train wreck," he thought.

"Come on," she motioned. "Follow me." Her feet pattered up the staircase but made no sound.

Collin felt the wood crack and groan under each forward step. Suddenly, a tread broke beneath his weight, forcing his foot to slide through the hole. He reached for the railing, but it was not there. Pieces of what once was littered the floor beneath him.

He listened to the beckoning of Belle's voice two floors above him. When he lifted his eyes to find her, a chill coursed through his body leaving his extremities chilled as ice. Belle stood on what should have been the top step, yet none remained. Collin gulped the frozen air around him. He tried to speak but could not.

"Come with me, Collin," she begged. Her voice sounded hollow, distant and surrounded by echoes.

Finally, he managed to squeak out, "I can't." He watched Belle's motion as if she walked down the staircase. Many treads and risers were missing as well as the banister and a multitude of spindles. When she knelt beside him, she appeared normal.

Her innocent eyes were flooded with concern. "Are you hurt?"

"No, I just fell through this rotten board."

"Rotten? Where?"

"Right here," he pointed to his feet. "I fell in that hole."

Belle looked at the stair tread and began to laugh. "Silly Collin. Always playing games. There is no hole. My staircase is beautiful." She ran her hands through the open air and floated up the vanished staircase. "I just dusted it this morning. Look at it shine."

Collin, immobilized by his fear, immediately thought of the princess. He drew in a deep breath and crept back down the first three stairs. When he stood on the floor, he called up to her.

"Why don't you show me your cottage instead?"

Belle bounced up and down at the suggestion. "Sounds great!"

She brushed past him and walked out the opened front door. "Follow me," she begged repeatedly.

Collin walked down the front porch stairs taking great care to not misstep. The grand building surrounding him that once teemed with hundreds of voices at play, now fell to ruin from years of neglect. He followed Belle to a vacant parcel of ground that she referred to as cottage #5.

He listened closely as she explained how it looked, smelled, and functioned. He chuckled to himself as she hid behind non-existent chairs to avoid a confrontation with her Matron. He told her to pretend that he was blind and could not share her vision so she would have to describe every detail. Collin listened for nearly an hour as she led him around the property.

At times, Collin felt the presence of another. Belle would stop and share a laugh or a quick conversation with the child. Often, she asked of her brother and became more withdrawn at their negative reply. He watched her actions ebb and flow with the various buildings. She giggled in the barn as she petted her show pony, Star.

"Want to pet her?"

"Nope," Collin lied, "I'm afraid of horses."

"Let's go pick her a few apples!" Belle coaxed. "She loves them."

He followed her to the orchard, overgrown and choked with weeds. A few withered apples dangled near the top of the tree. He jumped in the air pretending to pick a few. He handed the imaginary apple to Belle.

She took a big bite, "Yummy! This tree is my favorite."

Of all the buildings they pretended to tour, only one cottage, part of the main building and the tunnel system remained. The barn, slaughterhouse, hog pen, and chicken coop had long disappeared. Even the silo lay in rubble, yet Belle did not see it that way. To her, it was beautiful, perfect, scary, and Home.

They sat together under a large oak tree. Belle recalled a memory.

"Henry planted this tree last fall. He dug it up from the edge of the woods over there," she pointed to the tree line that remained beyond the cornfield. "That is where we made parched corn." She picked at her teeth. "That stuff was sticky and black." She looked at Henry's sapling as Collin inspected the sprawling pin oak trunk towering twenty feet above them.

"Belle," Collin whispered as he looked at the treetop. "What year is it?"

She placed her hands over her abdomen and began to laugh deeper and fuller than ever before. "Silly, Collin. Everyone knows what year it is. It's 1945."

1945

The Conclusion

Henry ran back down the stairs unaware of his speed as he zeroed in on Belle's cry for help. He called her name repeatedly. No reply came. When he entered the room, Enoch stepped off Belle's body. He untied his bound hands and lifted the noose from his neck. As he began to kneel to the floor, he saw Henry. His eyes filled with fear and he ran in the opposite direction.

Henry whispered to his sister. Her still body lay in a heap, used as a step stool to save Enoch from suffocation. Henry lifted Belle's limp body and cradled her in his arms. He sobbed uncontrollably.

"Belle! Belle...I'm sorry. I love you. Belle. Wake up, please. Belle! Belle...."

They buried Belle two days later beside her baby brother, Willy. Henry refused to speak. Rage consumed him.

Enoch hid in his office and paced the floor. He feared for his life. Henry was out of control. If Enoch could catch him, he vowed to use whatever tools necessary to suppress Henry's hostility. His eyes moved toward the shock therapy equipment. He whispered, "Whatever is necessary."

Enoch took inventory of the equipment and realized the main cord was missing. He remembered last seeing it in the dark room. He opened his office door.

"Miss Twill. I need to check on something of utmost importance. If I do not return within the hour, send someone to look for me."

Janet reeled at the odd comment, but did not question his order. She shook her head to confirm and watched Enoch as he walked down the hall.

Henry stormed into the schoolhouse. He grabbed a piece of paper from the teacher's desk, scribbled a few words, and walked out of the room. He ignored the threats and demands to sit. No one could control him.

He stomped his feet as he walked up the main house circular staircase. He walked past Miss Twill without a word and pounded on the Headmaster's door.

"He's not in!" Miss Twill screamed for the third time.

Henry turned the doorknob and walked in. He slammed the paper onto Enoch's desk and stormed out of the room, ignoring Miss Twill's comments.

Henry ran down the stairs and out the door toward the slaughterhouse. He rummaged through the shelves until he found the cleaver. He slid the tool into his pants and walked back toward the main house. He hid in the bushes and waited for nearly an hour before a police car pulled into the driveway. He crouched deeper for cover. When the car doors opened, two uniformed officers stood and walked to the front door. Henry dared not move, certain they came for him.

A Matron answered the door. "May I help you?"

"We are looking for Enoch Rumsted." He flashed his badge. "Is he here?"

"Yes. He is in his office, I believe." She hesitated, "I'll go get him."

"No ma'am. We will go to his office."

She did not question their intent. She meekly responded, "Follow me."

Miss Twill's eyes flew open wide at the sight of the police officers. She explained that Enoch had just stepped out, but would return shortly.

"We will wait in here," the officer demanded.

"I'll see if I can find him," Janet stuttered and rushed out the door.

One officer walked to the window while the second sat in Enoch's cushioned chair. Without a spoken exchange, he lifted the note that Henry had placed on his desk. It read:

You are a dead man.

"Look at this," the officer held the paper up for the standing officer to read.

He chuckled and responded, "That's the truth."

Enoch entered his office minutes later with Miss Twill on his heels. The men wasted no time.

"Mr. Rumsted?"

"Yes," Enoch answered hesitantly.

"Mr. Enoch Rumsted?"

"Yes. What's this about, officers?"

"Mr. Rumsted you are under arrest for embezzlement and excessive cruelty to a minor."

Henry watched as the uniformed men escorted Enoch to the waiting car. The police officers recited his rights as they handcuffed him and forced him onto the backseat.

Enoch watched Henry slip out from behind the bushes. He held the butcher's cleaver in his hand.

Henry left the Home that day. He never returned. With his pumpkin money in his pocket, he hid in the back of the farm truck as it traveled to the Bucker property. He found Mae preparing to close the house for the winter.

When she saw Henry, she ran to him and threw her arms around him. He told her of the recent events. She never once interrupted him. They cried together and talked until the morning. They left Bucker together.

"Where are we going?" Henry asked. "I can't go back there."

"There, there, dear." She patted Henry's hand. "Of course you can't go back there." She shook her head. "Enoch is a bad man. His greed got the best of him." She did not mention Belle.

"So..." Henry begged. "Where are you taking me?"

"Someplace special."

"Oh? And where is that?"

"My house, Henry. I'm taking you to my house." She wrapped her arms around him and lifted his tear-stained face. "No one is ever going to hurt you again. I promise."

Henry sat in the passenger side as Mae drove toward her home. They drove in the opposite direction of his former life, bad memories, and the Home. It felt as if Henry could breathe freely for the first time in a long while. They rode in silence for many miles.

Mae looked at Henry and patted his knee. "Once Enoch is in prison for all his wrong doings, we will visit Belle as often as you wish."

"And Willy."

"Yes, of course," she added, "and Willy.

Karen Biery

Karen Biery has spent the majority of her adult life living within the creative realm. She began her career in retail management with a major corporation until she designed, created, and accomplished her dream of opening her own retail environment — Olde English Garden Company — in Salem, Ohio. At a young age, she studied the art of watercolors under the instruction of Tom McNickle and later attended Kent State University for creative writing. At that moment, Karen realized that the two — painting and writing — were two halves that performed best together, creating the whole picture. She spends her time satisfying that dream.

Karen lives in northeast Ohio with her husband Jeff, when they are not enjoying their home in Florida. She is a step-mom and a proud grandma of two.

Other works by Karen Biery

Chattels, River Road Press 2012
believe, River Road Press, 2010
speakeasy, Red Engine Press, 2014
pieces, River Road Press 2011
(used as an anchor for *of Home* – 2016)

CPSIA information can be obtained
at www.ICGtesting.com
Printed in the USA
BVOW11s0017240916

463133BV00004B/17/P

9 781943 267187